DRAGON RIDERS OF AVRIA

DRAGON WINGS

N.A. DAVENPORT

To the kid who stays up late reading with a flashlight under the covers; this book is for you.

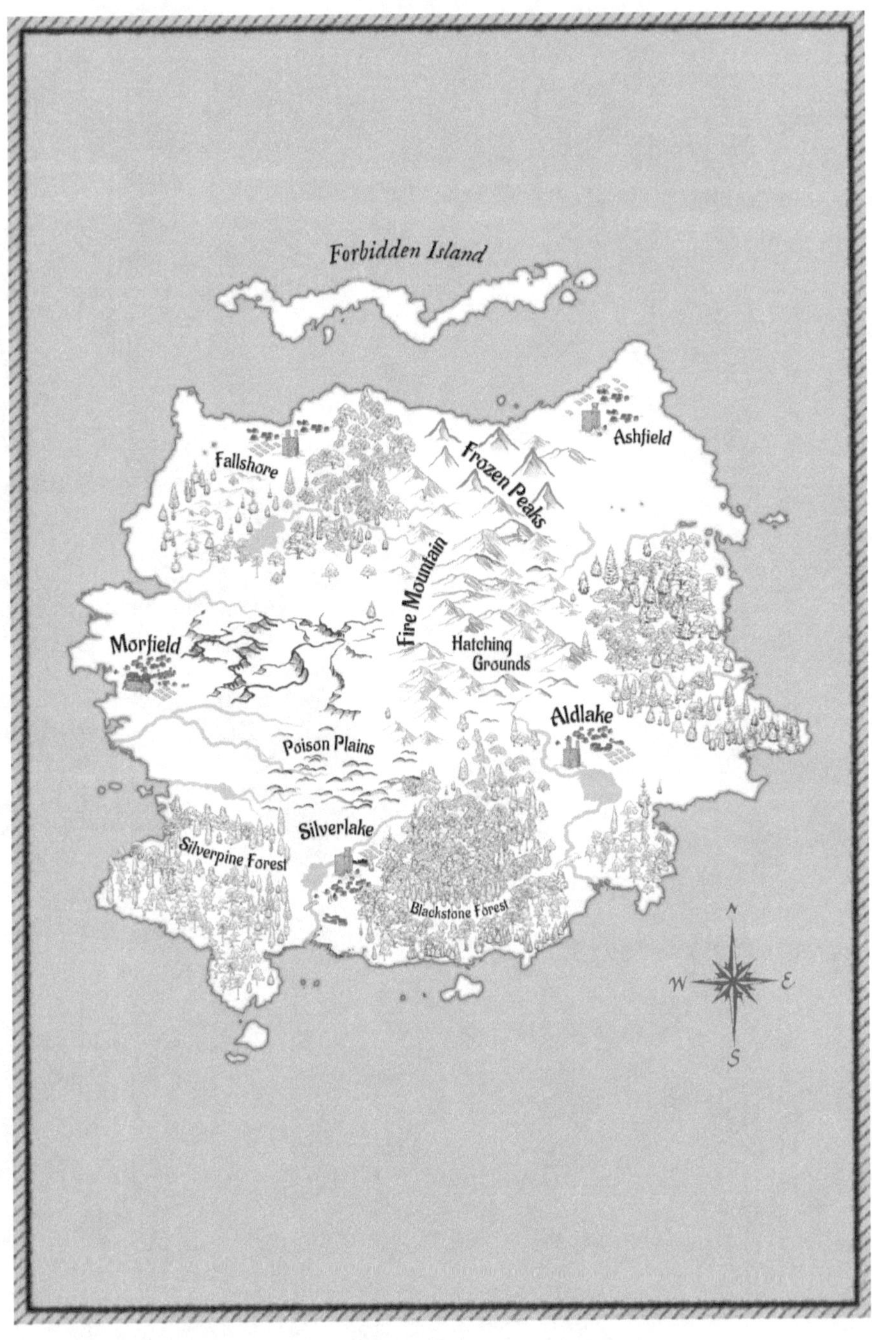

Forbidden Island
Fallshore
Frozen Peaks
Ashfield
Fire Mountain
Morfield
Hatching Grounds
Poison Plains
Aldlake
Silverlake
Silverpine Forest
Blackstone Forest
N
W
E
S

Contents

Chapter One

Will's body ached as he tossed restlessly in his bed. The shufflo-wool mattress under him grew warmer with each passing moment. The downy pillow cradled his head but did little to ease the aching in his jaw and neck from when Tavin had punched him. His ribs hurt from crashing into a tree while falling down the mountainside. The deep cut on his foot, which had never properly healed, twinged whenever he moved. His back and head hurt too, and he didn't even know why. But the longer he lay there, trying to sleep despite the discomfort, the more a pain in his stomach grew to drown out all the others.

I'm hungry. . .

Will groaned and shifted. Pain stabbed through his rib cage, but it didn't distract him from the hollow emptiness of his stomach.

I'm hungry! the thought came, pitiful and piercing.

It was the middle of the night. He'd get breakfast in the morning. Fire Mountain Dragonhold offered the best breakfasts he'd ever tasted—seared meat, crusty bread, mugs of lightly sweet cider, spicy flame-grilled vegetables . . .With the way his stomach felt, he wasn't sure he could make it to morning. Especially if he kept thinking about all the delicious food.

I want to eat now. Please, I'm HUNGRY!

The thought was so loud that Will's eyes snapped open. He jerked upright, causing his throbbing head to swim and a sharp pain to flare in his ribs. "Huh? Wha—?"

Twin leathery white sails flapped in his face, and pinprick claws dug into his chest and neck, making him hiss with fresh pain.

Vortex squawked in alarm, releasing his hold on Will's pajamas, and fell end over end onto the bed.

"Vortex!" Will scooped up the tiny white dragon, set him on his feet, and helped him fold his wings flat. "I'm sorry, pal. I shouldn't have startled you like that."

Vortex gave a sad croon and looked at Will with glistening eyes, shuffling his wings against his back. *I hurt you!*

"No! It was my fault. I shouldn't have sat up so fast." He stroked the little dragon's head reassuringly.

Another pang of hunger pierced his belly. Now that he was awake, he could tell that the hunger wasn't his own.

He was feeling the hunger of his dragon through the mysterious mental connection they shared.

"Oh, you need to eat!" Will blinked and tried to sweep the cobwebs out of his brain. "Yeah . . . That's right." He peered down at Vortex, who was watching him hopefully. "I bet they have food around here somewhere."

He and Vortex had been staying in the flapling barracks at Fire Mountain Dragonhold for a few days. So far, the new hatchlings hadn't been eating much at all. The older dragon riders assured them this was normal. For the first several days after hatching, their dragons could survive off an internal store of food. Soon enough, they would take regular meals and put on weight. Will just hadn't expected Vortex's need for food to happen in the middle of the night.

He swung his legs out of his bed, a bunk carved out of the stone wall of the barracks, and stood, stretching his aching back and wincing when his sore ribs twinged.

When he'd shown up at the Hatching Ground with his strange golden egg, broken ribs, swollen jaw, and sweaty clothes, the dragon rides of Fire Mountain hadn't known what to make of him. The healers had done their best to tend to his injuries, administering salve, wrapping his ribs, bandaging his cuts, and welcoming him as a new dragon rider, even though he was an off-lander and Vortex didn't fit in with any of the usual dragon colors.

Will held out his arm and allowed Vortex to climb up

his white linen sleeve and perch on his shoulder. The tiny dragon spread his pale wings to keep his balance and sniffed the air.

I can smell food! he said, wrapping his tail around Will's neck. A surge of hunger and anticipation accompanied the thought.

"All right, let's go." Will smiled sleepily at the little white dragon.

He limped quietly through the room and out into the darkened courtyard. His sore foot protested with every step he took.

The flapling barracks, like the bunks within, were a row of wide-mouthed caves that were carved directly out of the smooth rock of the mountain wall. Each cave contained two or three bunks and was furnished with heavy chest for storing belongings. The barracks were situated a little ways from the main dragonhold. Although red riders and their dragons preferred the blistering heat from the volcano, visitors, herd animals, and riders of other colors didn't appreciate it.

The dining hall was a short walk from the barracks, along the courtyard where the rocks were warm. Across the open space, a herd of shufflos huddled in the moonlight behind a wooden fence.

With Vortex perched on his shoulder, Will limped sleepily to the entrance of the dining hall. Orange firelight flickered through the windows. Will wondered if anyone else was in there, and whether they would also be wearing pajamas. Maybe he should have gotten dressed first. Oh well. He wasn't about to turn back now.

Warm air enveloped them as they entered. The dining hall was a large room with long stone tables standing in a row. Several other kids, all blinking groggily and wearing the same white linen nightgowns as Will, sat around the tables, bearing plates of bloody meat to feed their hatchlings.

The serving station held a raw shufflo haunch and a stack of ceramic dishes, too shallow to be called bowls and too rounded to be called plates. He frowned at the sharp knife, which was as long as his forearm, projecting from the meat. He'd have to be careful, or he'd end up slicing his own hand off.

The other kids in the dining hall were grouped by dragon color. Yellow dragons at one table, reds at another, greens at another, none of them mixing. He scanned their faces, hoping to spot his friends, Anri and Rin. Even though Anri had bonded with a green and Rin with a red, he was sure they'd welcome him at their tables. But his friends weren't there.

Will scratched his head and cleared his throat. His mind flitted back to memories of trying to join a dining table at a new school and being turned away by every group of kids he'd approached.

Vortex sniffed the air and gave a soft whine, begging for food. *It's right there! What are we waiting for?*

Will set his jaw and marched inside. It didn't matter if he felt awkward. He had to feed his dragon. He grabbed a dish and sliced off a few chunks of meat for Vortex, then turned and joined the closest table.

Three green hatchlings perched on the tabletop, eagerly scarfing the meat their riders offered them. Vortex scrambled down Will's arm and hopped on the table near the green hatchlings, his claws scrabbling on the stone. The green riders shot him slanted glances and shifted away.

Will rolled his eyes and grabbed a chunk of warm meat in his fingers, holding it out to Vortex. His dragon snapped it up and swallowed it whole, trilling his happiness and hopping up with his forelegs, eager for more.

The kid next to Will made an annoyed face. His green hatchling blinked curious orange eyes at Vortex, then squawked impatiently at his rider.

Will fed Vortex the entire dish of meat, wondering where the little dragon was putting it all. He didn't think Vortex's stomach could be big enough to fit another bite, but when the meat was gone, his dragon licked up the remaining juices and chirped at him, asking for more.

Will chuckled and rubbed a bleary eye with his fist. "Are you sure you won't pop out of your skin if you stuff more meat down your throat?"

The boy sitting next to him grumbled, "Why don't you

fill your dish and take him to one of the other tables? He obviously isn't a green. He doesn't belong here, and he's confusing Snakebite."

Will wrinkled his brow, blinking between the strange boy and his little green dragon. "You really named your dragon Snakebite?" He stifled a laugh.

"Just get away from our table! Your dragon isn't a green. Go sit somewhere else!"

Will frowned at the anger in the boy's tone. Vortex crooned in worry, sensing Will's displeasure.

"You shouldn't be so rude, Albin," a girl at the table behind them spoke up. "The little white dragon could be a green for all we know. Or even a blue. I heard the dragonlords talking about him after the hatching."

Will scooped up Vortex and grabbed his dish, returning to the carving station.

"I heard the same," the boy seated next to the girl said. He absently rubbed his blue hatchling's horn buds. "Sometimes dragons hatch a lighter color than usual. His dragon may just be a more extreme case of that phenomenon."

"I heard them say that too." Will nodded to them and added a few more pieces of meat to his dish. "They want me to figure out what kind of dragon Vortex really is before we all go to our separate dragonholds."

"Well, he isn't a green," Albin said. "Dragonlord Lamar said so, and he would know."

Will was too tired to care about the conversation

anymore. So he just mumbled "whatever" and made his way to the back of the room. A lone figure sat in the dark corner with his head resting on the table. The strange kid weakly offered bits of food to a little yellow dragon.

"Mind if I sit here?" Will asked.

The boy shrugged one shoulder, not lifting his head from the table. "If you want to."

Will recognized the voice and looked closer. "Oh, it's you, Corin. I didn't recognize you back here in the dark. And with your face buried in your arm like that."

Corin was his roommate in the barracks and was also the first kid who'd bonded with a dragon on Hatching Day. His little dragon, Leika, was the color of butter.

"Swarms, I'm so tired!" Corin moaned. "She keeps wanting to eat. And just when I think we can get some sleep, she needs to use the dirt lot. Then she wants to eat again."

Will grimaced and looked uncertainly at Vortex. The little white dragon opened his mouth for a chunk of meat, and Will obligingly popped a piece in.

"The um . . . dirt lot?"

"It's over by the shufflo pen." Corin waved a hand vaguely out the door. "Our dragons are eating now. What goes in one end has to come out the other, if you know what I mean. They can't do it in the barracks, of course, so we have to take them out to leave it with the shufflo manure."

Will wrinkled his nose, finally understanding.

"My mother used to tell me I'd wake her up every two hours when I was a baby," Corin went on, offering another piece of meat to Leika. "I never really appreciated that until now."

Will chuckled and rubbed his forearm across his eyes. "Yeah. I guess it's like we have new babies now, isn't it?"

When Vortex finished most of his second serving, he was satisfied and ready to go back to bed. Corin showed Will a trough of clean water, where they washed the blood from their hatchlings' heads, necks, and forelimbs. Then they massaged some dragonbalm—a soft mixture of oil and beeswax—into their hatchlings' skins to keep them from drying out.

Finally ready to go back to bed, Will perched Vortex on his shoulder and limped across the courtyard to the barracks. Crawling gingerly into his bunk, he buried his head in his pillow, trying to find a position that wouldn't aggravate any of his still healing injuries.

Vortex curled up against his neck with a deep, luxurious sigh, folding his wings against his body and wrapping his tail around his legs, drifting to sleep almost instantly.

Will sighed, too, listening to the relaxing sound of his dragon's gentle snores.

After Corin had mentioned his parents, Will couldn't help thinking about his own mother and father working on Elder Madoc's estate.

When Will had found Vortex's egg, he'd been able to escape that place. But his parents were still trapped, working for the greedy, hardhanded man. Their jobs were much harder than his had been. Who knew if they could ever pay off their debt? Especially since Elder Madoc kept adding more to what they owed him.

Will wondered how they were doing. Did they know he'd made it to the Hatching Ground with his egg? Did they know he'd bonded with a dragon? Had they heard about Vortex?

He wished he could see them again to let them know he was okay. He wished he could tell them that the dragon riders had searched for Uncle John. Since he'd already been missing for months, it did not surprise Will that they hadn't found him, but it was nice of them to have tried.

When Vortex grew big enough to carry Will instead of the other way around, he'd be able to fly all over Avria. He'd be able to visit his parents every day and search for signs of his lost uncle as much as he wanted to.

But for now he couldn't do anything except shift on his mattress, stare at the dark stone ceiling, and wonder what his mom and dad were doing and whether his uncle was still alive.

With a soft warm breeze washing through the barracks, Will's thoughts drifted into uneasy dreams.

Moments later, a cool snout poked his cheek and Vortex squawked imploringly.

"W-wha?" Will cracked one eye open and yawned. "What's the matter, buddy?"

The tiny dragon, ghostly white in the dark, made a tiny uncomfortable growling sound and curled his tail in.

"Oh? Ooh!" Will took a deep breath and let it out in a resigned sigh. "I guess it's time for us to visit the dirt lot."

Chapter Two

Will couldn't help but feel like a mindless zombie as he went about the daily tasks of caring for his hatchling. The new riders were entirely focused on feeding, bathing, and applying dragonbalm to their new winged companions.

They spent the days in a hazy, dreamlike existence. They slept when they could, day or night, and ate with little awareness of what was going on around them. Sometimes Will met Anri and Rin in the dining hall, but even then, the friends were never awake enough to make conversation.

By the end of the first week, Vortex had only put on a couple of pounds, and Will could still carry the little dragon in one outstretched hand. But then, like a switch flicking on overnight, he started growing at an astounding pace, eating alarming amounts of meat and never staying full for more than an hour or two at a time.

After two weeks in the flapling barracks, Vortex had doubled his size. His wings, which at first seemed so delicate and transparent, were thicker and leathery now; it wasn't long before he started flapping them on occasion, too, even though he still tripped over them a lot.

So far, the only structure to their schooling was occasional assistance from Tumi, the dark-skinned dragon rider in charge of flapling school. He would saunter into the dining hall or in the barracks periodically, making his rounds and asking the children whether they had any questions or concerns. They always did.

"Should Ember be eating so much?"

"Why doesn't my dragon ever stay asleep?"

"Is there something wrong with Tundra's wings? He's always getting his claws caught in them!"

"Strawberry sneezed last night. Is she sick?"

Tumi was quick to assure them all that their dragons were maturing normally, and helped them immediately whenever any actual problems arose.

Ruby, Tumi's enormous red dragon, stayed at a respectful distance from the new riders and their hatchlings, but she often shared comforting thoughts with the little dragons, assuring them they were all growing properly and would someday be as big and strong as she was.

Will was as concerned as the others about Vortex

eating, sleeping, and waking so frequently in the night. But from Tumi's responses to the other kids, he could tell this phase of their growth would pass soon enough. What he was more worried about, but afraid to bring up, was his dragon's unusual color.

When Vortex had hatched from his strange shining egg, it shocked everyone to see his pale, creamy hide. But nobody dared suggest that he was actually a white dragon, like the legendary White Dragon of old, the savior of Avria whom people spoke of in tones of reverence.

The dragonlords speculated about what might be the actual cause of Vortex's unusual coloration. In the end, they all seemed to agree that he was either a regular color and very pale, or there was something wrong with him.

That was the part that worried Will the most. The part that kept him up at night, even in the brief hours when Vortex was sleeping. What if something was wrong with his dragon? What if he was sick? What if his strange condition caused other, more serious problems?

He didn't bring up his concerns with Tumi, though. If there was something wrong with Vortex, Tumi wouldn't know any more about it than the dragonlords. And expressing his worry in front of the others would only expose Vortex to more harassment from kids like Albin, who insisted that he was a freak, hardly a dragon at all.

As the weeks passed, the hatchlings ate more and more meat at each sitting and were satisfied that much longer between meals. They slept a little bit longer every night, and with the added sleep, Will felt more awake during the day, like coming out of a long, restless dream.

One morning, when he entered the dining hall with Vortex clinging heavily to his shoulder, the room was already filled with most of the other young riders. Their little dragons perched on the tables eating meat from clay dishes, or lounged on their sides with bulging bellies, licking their claws and snouts clean.

Will filled a dish for Vortex and sat at the blue table like he usually did. The three blue riders, Liza, Jayda, and Beck, never complained when he sat with them. And their table was next to the greens, where Anri sat feeding Jade.

Will knew that Anri would be happy to let him sit with her and would fiercely defend him and Vortex if the other green riders picked on them, but Will preferred to avoid the confrontation altogether, especially so early in the morning.

"Good morning, Anri." He set Vortex's dish on the table. His dragon hopped off his shoulder, carefully keeping his claws out of Will's skin, and landed on the tabletop, tucking into his breakfast next to the blue hatchlings.

"Hello, Will." Anri turned to him with a yawn. "I see Vortex let you sleep in this morning."

Anri's furry kisnit, Trouble, stretched in her lap, extending her claws and curling her fluffy, striped tail.

Will chuckled and reached across to scratch behind Trouble's huge, fuzzy ears. "He's been sleeping better. I still feel like I'm half zombie, though."

Anri's brow wrinkled, and she cocked her head. "A zombie? Is that some kind of off-lander monster I've never heard of?"

"What? Oh, zombies aren't real. They're just pretend. They're . . . dead bodies that can walk around somehow."

She nodded and pushed a dark strand of hair behind her ear. "Oh. We have stories about monsters like that in Avria too. Here they're called draugar."

"I understand how you feel," Jayda said, resting her head in her hand as she watched her little blue dragon eat. "Like a draug that can barely pull itself out of the burial mound. Our dragons seem to have plenty of energy, though. Don't you, Tundra?"

Tundra lifted his messy snout and chirped at her, fanning his wings.

"The hatchlings seem to function well on a short sleep-wake cycle," Beck said. His dragon, Icicle, stretched out on the tabletop, snoozing next to an unfinished plate of meat. His little belly was so full it bulged, but a content smile stretched along his snout.

"Well, I'm not made to wake up every two hours," Anri said. "It's no wonder we all feel half dead most of the time. I'm glad Jade is finally sleeping longer now."

Anri's brilliant green hatchling cocked her head sideways and twitched an ear, then began grooming her claws primly with her pink tongue.

"Yes, I know you need to eat when you're hungry and sleep when you're tired," Anri said with a crooked smile, answering her dragon's thoughts. "I'm just glad you're a little more tired and a little less hungry now."

The other children murmured in groggy agreement.

I'm still hungry, Vortex said, licking the last of the meaty drippings from his empty dish. *Can I have more food?*

Will grabbed the dish and pushed away from the table, but as he stood, Beck held up a hand to stop him. "Is Vortex asking for more? Icicle won't finish this." He waved a hand at the dish full of meat next to the sleeping blue. "It was his fourth serving. He's stuffed himself so much he probably won't be able to walk for a while. Vortex can eat it if he wants."

"Oh, thanks!" Will sat back down, and Beck pushed the dish of unfinished meat across the table to Vortex, who started gobbling it up.

"I wonder when we'll learn things other than how to stuff our dragons full of meat," Jayda said, stroking Tundra's wings. "We've been here for weeks and all we do is feed them and take them to the dirt lot." Her dragon crooned, and she added, "Of course I don't mind at all. You're worth it."

"I'm glad they haven't been trying to teach us anything

else," Will said. "Imagine going to classes after being up all night with a hungry hatchling!"

"But we have so much more to learn!" Jayda said.

"I wonder when our dragons will learn to use their powers!" Corin called from the yellow dragons' table. He grinned in eagerness, even though the circles under his eyes showed how tired he was. "That's going to be so much fun!"

The other yellow riders and the kids around the red table chattered in agreement. A few of the hatchlings chirped and flapped their wings in excitement.

I want to learn how to use my powers, Vortex said, lifting his head and blinking his amber eyes. *What powers will I have?*

"Um . . . that's a good question," Will said, rubbing the back of his neck and giving a half shrug. "I'm not exactly—"

"So, you're ready to start your lessons, are you?" a man's familiar voice boomed from the doorway.

The kids turned to see Tumi standing there, tall and broad, dressed in leather riding gear, and silhouetted by the morning sun. He flashed them a brilliant grin. "Since your dragons have eaten, why don't you follow me out to the courtyard? Training begins today!"

The children sat speechless as Tumi turned, swinging his long braids, and marched out of the room.

Will turned around to look at Anri, who was still

staring at the empty doorway. "Did you hear that?" he asked.

"We're going to start our training! Finally!" Beck jumped up, waking his blue hatchling with a startled squawk. He picked up the little dragon. "Come on, Icicle! We're going to start training."

Chapter Three

Ruby, Tumi's massive red dragon, waited in the courtyard while her rider marched up to her.

As the kids approached, she spread her wings in greeting, catching the sunlight and casting long shadows over the sandy ground. The colors of the leathery membranes shifted from deep red to fiery orange in the morning light.

"Listen up, everyone!" Tumi said. "I want you to group up according to dragon color. Reds to my left, greens to my right, yellows and blues somewhere in the middle." He gestured to where the four groups should gather as he spoke. "Oh, and Will, you and Vortex pick whichever group you'd like to be a part of for now."

Will watched as the other kids sorted themselves into groups, which he called "wings," according to their dragon's color.

Anri looked at him with Jade on one shoulder and

Trouble perched on the other. She looked like she wanted to invite him to join their wing, but all the other green riders avoided eye contact with him. All except Albin, of course, who watched him as though daring him to take a step in their direction.

"It doesn't matter which wing you choose," Tumi said, noticing Will's hesitation. "We're just going to be learning the basics at first."

Will met Anri's eyes for a moment. It looked like she was on the verge of calling him over. But Albin's scowl reminded him of how the other boy had treated Vortex when they'd tried to join the green table in the dining hall. He didn't want to put his dragon in that kind of situation again.

"Will!" It was Rin's voice that called out from the group of red riders. "Come over here. You can join our wing!"

The rest of the red riders joined in, waving him over with welcoming smiles.

"Yes, join us!"

"Come on, you and Vortex can be with us!"

Will smiled and shrugged. "Yeah, okay." And he walked over to join the red wing.

The kids in the red wing clapped him on the back and bumped fists with him.

Vortex chirped a greeting to Ember, Rin's dragon, and the two stretched out their necks to touch noses.

"Ember is glad that Vortex is going to be with us," Rin said, beaming at her dragon.

When Will looked over at Anri again, he saw her brow furrow a moment before she turned away.

"Perfect!" Tumi said. "Now you're all grouped up. I hope you've already been getting to know the kids standing around you because this is your flapling wing. You'll be learning together, practicing together, and building friendships that will last your whole life."

"Um, excuse me?" Will raised his hand, and everyone turned to look at him. "Maybe it's because I'm an off-lander. But I don't know what a flapling is. I keep hearing that word. What does that even mean?"

Tumi tucked his thumbs under his leather belt and nodded. "A flapling is what your hatchlings are quickly becoming. Dragons that are too small to carry their riders, but big enough to learn how to fly. I suppose you've all noticed that your hatchlings' wings are growing thicker? They've started stretching them and fanning them in the air?"

The kids nodded and murmured in agreement. Corin lifted one of Leika's wings to examine the delicate membrane stretched between the bones.

"They are beginning the long, exciting journey to becoming full-sailed dragons. We don't want them trying out their wings just yet, though. An injury to flight muscles, or even worse to the bones and cartilage in their wings, could leave them crippled for life. So, to begin with, we'll be teaching you more about how to care for them as they continue growing bigger."

"You mean there's more?" Corin blurted, releasing his dragon's wing with a start.

Tumi raised a quizzical eyebrow in his direction.

Some of the other kids laughed.

"I just mean . . . we feed them and wash them and take them to the dirt lot, but . . . well, what else do they need? Shouldn't we already be doing those things if there's more?" He hugged Leika a little tighter to his chest, as though worried he'd been neglecting the little yellow dragon.

"Don't worry, lad." Tumi squeezed Corin's shoulder. "Your dragons have had everything they need up to this point. But now that they're a few weeks old, their needs are going to grow. They'll be able to handle more activity. They'll want to stay awake more in the day and sleep more at night. Their appetites will only continue to grow as well. Soon the dining hall won't be able to feed them, and you'll need to take them to the stock field where the adult dragons will help feed them with fresh kills until they're big enough to hunt for themselves."

He chuckled and shook his head. "But I'm getting ahead of myself. Today you're learning simpler tasks. Blue wing and red wing, you'll head to the lower cavern for your first lesson in proper dragon care." He waved an arm down the hill to a broad-mouthed cavern in the mountain wall which Will had thought was just used by red dragons for taking naps in. "Yellow wing and green wing, you will join Nader to turn the dirt lot, sweep out the barracks, and assist the cooks with preparing the evening meal." Tumi flashed a smug smile toward a red dragon rider who was leaning against the wall at the edge of the courtyard.

The kids in the yellow and green wings groaned and whined in dismay.

"What?" Albin demanded.

"You're joking, right?" Corin asked.

"Why do we get stuck doing chores?" Jayda demanded. Her green hatchling squawked indignantly. "Why don't they have to work too?" She pointed an accusatory finger at the red and blue groups.

"Don't worry." Tumi said. "Tomorrow the roles will reverse, and the red and blue wings will have the honor of doing chores while the rest of you attend lessons."

"I don't suppose our roles will reverse tomorrow as well?" Nader called, still leaning against the wall.

Tumi laughed and shook his head. "Ruby and I won that race, and you know it!"

"But why do we have to do chores at all?" Albin whined. "We're dragon riders!"

"That's right. Part of being a dragon rider is helping to keep your dragonhold working smoothly. If the work doesn't get done, nobody has clean beds to sleep in, food to eat, riding gear or clothes to wear. Everyone will take turns turning the dirt lot, cleaning the barracks, helping to prepare meals, mucking the shufflo pens, and doing everything else needed to keep the dragonhold a comfortable place to live."

With only a bit more grumbling from the green and yellow wings, they all moved their separate ways. The yellow and green wings shuffled across the courtyard to meet with Nader while Ruby and Tumi led the blue and red wings into the ground-level training cavern.

Will's feet sank into the warm brown sand covering the floor of the cavern. Heat radiated up from the floor, as though the sand was a protective layer keeping them from walking on a hot stovetop. The air smelled of smoke and hot minerals.

As the kids filed in, Ruby paced across the sand ahead of them to where a large metal chest sat by the wall. She lowered herself into the sand next to it with a low rumble, folding her wings against her back.

Tumi approached his dragon and gave her nose an affectionate pat. "Come closer, everyone! Come on, don't worry. Your little ones should be used to Ruby by now."

As they crowded around, Tumi lifted the lid on the chest and withdrew a long metal bar with sharp ridges carved down the length of one side. It looked like a larger version of the tool Will had once used to file cormant talons when he worked on Elder Madoc's farm.

"We're going to learn how to file your dragon's claws," Tumi announced with a grin. "Of course, you won't be using one of these." He held up the metal bar; it was as long as his forearm. "But the practice is the same no matter the size of your dragon, so I'll demonstrate on Ruby. Filing claws is important. If your dragon's claws get too long, they might end up chipping or splitting. And overlong claws can cause pain when your dragon walks. I'll show you the proper technique, then I'll give each of you a small file to try it for yourselves."

They spent a good hour in the cavern while Tumi showed them the proper angle to hold their files, how to hold their dragon's toes steady, and how to know when they were done.

"Be careful not to make them too short either," Tumi said. "Your dragons need their claws for gripping ledges and hunting, and if you shorten them too much, you might grind into the quick and make them bleed."

After this warning, a few kids refused to file their dragons' claws at all, horrified that they might hurt their little winged friends. But with coaxing and encouragement from Tumi, they all managed to learn the proper technique and were filing away at their dragons' tiny talons by lunchtime.

The following day, it was time for the red and blue wings to take their turn doing chores. The first couple hours after breakfast, Will washed dishes and scrubbed linens while they waited for the older riders to herd the shufflos out of their pen. Then it was time to clear out the smelly piles of muck the shufflos had left behind. By the end of the day, Will's arms and back ached, and he was ready to collapse in his bed.

The next morning it was school time again, and Tumi sat them down to learn about the proper feeding of their dragons. Explaining that while their dragons were thriving on a diet of fresh shufflo and cormant meat, they would naturally want to expand their menu as they grew older.

"They might snap at insects or lizards or rodents that wander too close. Don't worry when that happens. Those are all healthy parts of a growing dragon's diet. But I will warn you, there are some creatures in Avria you must never allow your dragon to eat." He held up a finger and gave a stern expression, making sure he had their attention before turning to the charred black wall behind him with a piece of chalk.

"Pine-spur grubs have needle-sharp barbs that can get lodged in your dragon's throat." He scratched the image of a striped caterpillar with spiky hairs growing along its back. "The spurs are devilishly hard to remove. But even worse, than those," he continued, starting on a new drawing, "unless you're a green rider, never let your dragon eat a ringed bluefish. These fish thrive off the western coast. Dragons rarely try to eat them, since they taste bad. But when they do, only green dragons ever survive the meal. They're deadly poisonous, and the death is horrible at that." The second drawing took the shape of a fat fish with low-lying fins, an ugly broad mouth, and little circles marking its whole body.

"Ew, an ugly fish that tastes bad? Why would anyone want to eat that, anyway?" Will muttered, wrinkling his nose.

Next to him, Rin and Timmin nodded in agreement, but they still paid close attention to Tumi's presentation as though pine-spur grubs and ringed bluefish wandered through the barracks all the time.

Will glanced down at Vortex, thinking that he'd get his dragon's opinion on the matter, but Vortex had fallen asleep with his head in Will's lap. Will sighed and let his gaze wander out to the sunny courtyard.

Leaning against the side of the cavern's entrance, Nader stood picking at his teeth while he waited for the green and yellow wings to finish whatever chore they were doing.

Nader was a pleasant young man who hardly looked out of his teens. The only reason he escorted them to their menial work was because he'd bet Tumi that his dragon, Scorch, could beat Ruby in a race through the magma caverns. He'd lost.

Even now, Scorch looked miffed whenever he was near Ruby, and Ruby often regarded the younger red dragon with a smug arch in her neck.

Nader noticed Will and nodded to him. Will nodded

back and turned to Tumi in a renewed attempt to listen to the lesson.

It wasn't easy, though. With the soft sand under them, the warm air around them, and the lack of sleep, his eyes drooped.

It all seemed pointless. Why would Vortex ever try eating fuzzy, striped grubs? When they left Fire Mountain, their dragons would be too big to bother with little prey like that. And when would his dragon ever be tempted to eat a gross, spotted blue fish? Tumi said they tasted bad, anyway.

If Will was more like his dad, he'd love learning about this stuff. Biology and exotic animals always fascinated his dad. When he talked, he could make even the most boring subjects sound interesting. His dad had an extensive knowledge of animals and loved to learn about different species and how they all lived together in harmony.

But right now, Will's dad was stuck working in the hot, blistering sun, picking grapes on Elder Madoc's farm in Aldlake or shoveling cormant droppings as likely as not.

Will looked out the cavernous entryway again, across the concourse and beyond, to the mountain peaks that separated them from the rest of Avria. Was there no way he could get in touch with his parents? He'd at least like to find out how they were doing.

"Is everything all right, Will?" Tumi asked, snapping Will out of his thoughts.

"Huh?" Will blinked and turned back to their instructor. "Oh. Sorry. Yeah, I'm just tired."

Tumi nodded in understanding. "I see. But what I'm teaching now may save the life of your dragon one day. Perhaps we should take a quick break so everyone can stretch their legs and drink some water."

Everyone lumbered to their feet, brushing warm sand from their breeches. Some kids made their way to the water barrels while others grouped up and began chatting amongst themselves.

Will lifted Vortex's head in his hand and rubbed the soft hide over his dragon's nose and horn nubs. "Hey, buddy, are you thirsty?"

The little dragon blinked his eyes and yawned, showing his pearly white teeth. *Not thirsty. Sleepy.*

"Yeah, me too. I need to walk around or I'm going to pass out right here. How about I carry you for a bit?"

Vortex only yawned again and clung to Will's neck as he lifted the little dragon into his arms, careful not to squeeze his delicate wings.

He carried Vortex out into the warm sunshine and arched his back, stretching as well as he could with a sleeping baby dragon in his arms. Vortex wasn't as little as he used to be. It was like trying to stretch while carrying a Christmas ham.

"Are the others giving you a hard time?" A young man's voice caught his attention.

Will turned and saw Nader push off the wall and walk toward him.

"Well, not too bad. The kids in the red wing have been pretty nice so far." Will shrugged and shifted Vortex's weight. "Why do you ask?"

"You seem distracted is all. New riders rarely daydream when learning about things that could save their dragon's life." Nader's voice was neutral, but his eyes narrowed as he spoke, and Will sensed the reproach in his words.

He grimaced. "I'm sorry. I guess I'm just worried about my parents."

Nader's expression shifted to surprise. "Your parents? Did something happen to them?"

"That's the problem. I don't know. I haven't seen them since I left for the Hatching Ground. They work at Elder Madoc's farm in Aldlake. Or at least that's where they were when I left them. My mom kind of made the elder mad before I left. I don't know if he kicked them out or punished them somehow. That guy sucks."

Nader frowned in thought. "I see. I've never met Elder Madoc, but I've known others like him. Disturbing the lives of men like that is something of a pastime for me." He flashed a crooked grin. "Aldlake you say? How would you like to pay a visit to your parents after lunch today?"

Chapter Four

"I can visit my parents?" Will shifted Vortex in his arms and stared disbelieving at Nader. "But how? I have Vortex to look after and—"

"Scorch and I will take you. Make sure Vortex gets a good meal before we go, and he should sleep the whole time. We won't be gone more than a few hours."

Will's mind reeled. It had taken him a whole week to get to the Hatching Ground from Elder Madoc's estate. And Nader could travel there in a few hours!

"Wow! I-I don't know. I mean, I want to. Would Vortex be safe flying with us?"

Nader smiled and clapped Will on the shoulder. "Perfectly safe, I promise. I'll tell you what. Scorch and I will be ready to go after lunch. If you decide you still want to visit your parents, just come find us."

"Yeah. Yeah, okay. Sure." Will nodded and glanced

"

back at Scorch, who was lounging on the warm, sandy courtyard. He blinked his shining green eyes at Will.

For the rest of the day, Will kept debating with himself whether to take Nader up on his offer. Would it really be safe to ride a flying dragon with Vortex? Dragon riders always clipped belt straps to their dragon's saddles to secure them to their necks. Without those straps, Vortex might end up falling off, and he couldn't fly yet. Will shuddered at the mental picture of Vortex plummeting to the ground, flapping his wings uselessly.

But surely Nader and Scorch wouldn't do anything to put a hatchling in danger. And if they took Nader up on his offer, Will would get to see his parents again. They would get to meet Vortex! Was it possible that they already know about his dragon? After the hatching, everyone who'd stayed for the naming ceremony had seen Vortex, and word of the little white dragon surely had spread to all corners of Avria by now. It was possible that his parents had heard the news.

And Tavin! The bully had tried to steal Vortex's egg while Will was carrying it to the hatching ground. The last time Will had seen Tavin, the boy was fleeing down the mountain after losing the egg over the side of a cliff. Will didn't like the idea of meeting Tavin again, even though some smug part of him enjoyed the thought of showing the bully that there really was a living dragon in the shining egg and that he was a dragon rider now.

By the time Tumi finished telling them how to deal with dragon indigestion, bloat, and tooth care, Will had decided. He couldn't miss an opportunity to see his parents again.

They all made their way to the dining hall for lunch. Will and Vortex sat at the table with the red wing next to Rin and Ember.

The young dragons were too large to crowd onto the tabletops anymore, so the children set bowls of meat on the floor for them.

"That was a lot to learn in one class," Rin said once Ember was gobbling up her lunch. "I don't know how I'm going to remember it all!"

"I don't think we will have to remember it all," Will said. "The stuff about using lemonwort for indigestion and chicory bark to brush teeth is useful. But do we need to know how to treat nickleweed stings? Why would our dragons try to roll in nickleweed in the first place? It seems a lot like 'stop, drop and roll' to me." He shrugged.

"What does that mean?" Rin asked. "Are you talking about more off-lander stuff?"

Some of the kids at the other tables turned to listen.

"I guess so." Will shrugged. "Where I'm from, kids learn that if we ever catch on fire, we should stop, drop, and roll to put the flames out. Only I've never heard of any kids who actually caught fire."

"It probably happens here all the time," Corin said

from the yellow wing's table. "Especially when red dragons are learning to use their powers." The rest of the kids laughed, and Will joined in with a chuckle.

"Yeah, I bet. But back in Florida, kids almost never spontaneously combust."

"Is that why you were talking with Nader? You thought the lessons weren't important?" Anri asked.

"That's not what I mean," Will said. "I never said they're not important. I just don't think we'll need to remember everything we learn. And, no, it's not what I was talking to Nader about. He was just offering to take me and Vortex to visit my parents."

"He did?" Rin said with a bright smile. "That's a great idea! I know you've been worried about them."

"You're so lucky, Will!" Corin turned all the way around to face the red wing's table, leaned in, and rested his elbows on his knees. "You and Vortex get to ride Scorch all the way to Aldlake and back. I wish I could get one of the adult dragons to give me a ride somewhere."

"You only get special treatment if you're an off-lander with a *white dragon*!" Albin sneered.

Will's face heated, and he clenched his jaw.

"Oh, shut your face, Albin!" Anri snapped.

"Why? Because you're sweet on the off-lander boy?" Albin snorted and tossed a little piece of his meat pie to Snakebite, who snapped it out of the air.

Anri's face went rigid. She glared at Albin for a second, then grabbed her dish.

Will thought for a second that she was going to throw her food at the other green rider, but she hefted Jade under her arm and stormed out of the dining hall without another word. Most of the green wing laughed.

Will almost got up to follow her, but Rin put a hand on his arm. "Not now, Will," she said under her breath. "You'll only make it worse."

Will hesitated, then settled back onto the bench with a frown. He'd be sure to talk to Anri later. It wasn't like her to let jerks like Albin get on her nerves.

After lunch, Will found Nader outside the training cavern with Tumi.

"Will! Vortex!" Tumi greeted them with a wave. "Nader tells me he and Scorch are taking you two to visit your parents. You should have told me you were worried about them."

"I didn't know it was possible to visit them," Will said with a shrug. "We've been so busy with our hatchlings."

"But that's what dragon riders are good for," Nader laughed, "flying places!"

"First we have to get you some riding gear and make sure Vortex is protected on the flight." Tumi rested his fists on his hips. "I think an extra-large riding jacket will do the trick."

"You want to stuff Vortex inside his jacket?" Nader wrinkled his brow.

"His skin is still too delicate for the stiff wind of high flying. It seems the best way to keep him warm and secure too." Tumi started across the courtyard and waved a hand for them to follow. "I've got just the thing."

When they reached the far end, Tumi led them into a passageway next to the shufflo pen that Will hadn't noticed before. The tunnel led on a downward slope to a dark and surprisingly cool room.

Tumi lit a lantern, revealing walls lined with stone shelves and huge crates stuffed with huge metal discs, cracked clay pots, long metal poles, thick cords of rope, massive cauldrons, folded reams of wool, and chests stuffed with leather riding gear, preserved in layers of waxed burlap.

It didn't take long to find sturdy riding boots, leather britches, a thick riding belt, a wool undershirt, and a cap with flaps that covered his ears. Only the belt fit properly. The boots were too big and his feet wiggled around in them when he walked. The wool shirt was bulky and itchy, but it worked. Finally, Tumi found an extra-large riding jacket that, when Will put it on, had enough room for Vortex to crawl inside with him.

With Vortex buttoned up inside the heavy riding jacket, Will followed Nader out to the courtyard. He was sure he looked ridiculous, with a dragon-shaped bulge over his belly and too-big boots making him stumble, but he didn't care. He was just excited that he was going to visit his mom and dad and see that they were okay.

When they made it to the open area, Scorch dropped off a high ledge, gliding to the ground in a steep dive, and landed in front of them with powerful beats of his red wings. The wind kicked up dust in twin swirls and made Will's heart beat faster in excitement.

"Are you ready to ride?" Nader grinned, as though he knew what Will was feeling.

"Yeah!"

Scorch offered a foreleg, and Will scrambled up to his neck. The dragon's skin felt hot to the touch, like a park bench that had been sitting in the summer sun all day.

Once he was astride the dragon's great neck, Will found the loose riding straps and clipped them to his belt.

"It looks like you already know how to clip in!" Nader said approvingly, vaulting up into the saddle behind him.

"Yeah, I got to ride Boreas once. Just for a little while," Will said.

"Dragonlord Perrin let you ride Boreas?" Nader asked, surprise in his tone. "That's a bit out of character for a blue rider. Especially for a dragonlord!"

"He was friendly to me," Will said a little defensively. Perrin had been one of his first friends in Avria.

"Oh, don't get me wrong. He's a decent man. I've heard nothing bad about him. It's just that blue riders tend to keep their own company. And their dragons are fickle. They rarely agree to carry anyone other than their own riders."

"Oh, I didn't know that."

Nader patted his dragon's red neck. "Scorch, on the other hand, loves meeting people and giving rides to friends. Don't you, pal?"

Scorch arched his neck and gave a happy rumble that vibrated through his chest.

Vortex poked his face out of the neck of Will's jacket and chirped up at the red dragon in greeting, then swiveled his head around to look at Will.

I wish I was big enough to fly you places, he said.

"Don't worry." Will scratched under his dragon's chin. "You're eating so much and growing so fast you'll probably be able to fly off with an entire herd of shufflos by the end of the week!"

Vortex tilted his head in confusion and twitched his ears while Nader laughed and Scorch cocked a shining green eye at him.

"Besides," Will shifted Vortex's weight, "what happens when you're too big for me to carry around anymore? You'll have to walk everywhere with your own legs, then."

Vortex made a tiny disgruntled noise and pulled his head back into Will's jacket, making himself as small as he could, as though that would make him lighter.

None of the hatchlings enjoyed walking much. They

were all still so gangly and uncoordinated that they kept tripping over their own claws and getting their wings caught under their feet.

Nader patted Scorch's shoulder and the dragon stood, unfurled his wings, and gave himself a little shake to loosen his muscles. Then the he reared back on his haunches and sprang into the air.

Will clutched a thick riding strap in one hand while holding tight to Vortex with his other arm, clenching his muscles and gritting his teeth against the surge of power that hurtled them upward.

Scorch beat the air with his wings, sending violent eddies of dust swirling as the courtyard dropped away below them.

A few moments later, they slipped over the nearest mountain peak. An updraft caught them, carrying them high above the outer hills and beyond the border of the dragonhold.

"Hey, that's the road I took to get to the Hatching Ground!" Will yelled, noticing a brown rocky path winding along the mountainside.

With the wind rushing past his ear flaps, Will could barely hear his own voice. Nader didn't hear him at all. But Vortex poked his face out to look down. *It is?*

"When you were just an egg, I was so afraid I wouldn't make it in time." He stared at the road, remembering the wild race to make it to the hot, sandy cavern in time for the hatching, an event that took place in Avria only once every four years.

Had it only been a few weeks since then? His still aching ribs and fading purple bruises said so, but it seemed like a lifetime ago.

Scorch followed a winding valley between the southern mountain peaks, carrying them high over the dense forest. Now and then, herds of graceful horned animals sprang to get under cover as the dragon's shadow flashed over them.

Icy wind whipped against their faces, and Will's lips chapped in the dry, frigid air. Tucking his chin, Will crouched low against Scorch's neck to shield himself from the chill. He was glad that Vortex was protected within the thick leather of his oversized riding jacket.

It seemed only minutes passed before they were sailing over foothills dotted with occasional towns. Then they were passing over open plains filled with farms, crops, and herds of grazing shufflos.

Scorch started circling and Will leaned over to see colorful flocks of cormants, a vast vineyard, and a large stone-walled manor below them.

A small crowd of people was gathering on the gravel road outside the manor, shading their eyes as they stared up at the circling red dragon.

"This is the place, right?" Nader shouted over the roaring wind.

"I think so!" Will shouted back. "I've never seen it from above!"

Scorch tucked his wings and dropped into a smooth dive, aiming right for the gravel road.

Flocks of cormants squawked and fled as the dragon descended into view. The watching people shouted in fear and scattered, leaving the road clear.

Will's ears popped with the change in pressure as they dropped. At the last moment, Scorch flapped his wings, bringing his rear legs forward to touch down on the ground.

As the dust settled and Scorch folded his massive red sails against his back, Will looked around, recognizing the place better now that he was seeing it from ground level. There was the path leading to the dormant stables. And by the kitchen door of the manor stood a massive oak tree that had often shaded him while he ate.

"Yeah, this is the right place!" he told Nader. "I used to work in the cormant stalls over there." It was still hard to believe it had only been a few weeks since Will had been wrapping cormant legs and mucking out stalls.

The scattered crowd was slowly gathering again now that Scorch had landed. Will recognized some of the well-dressed house staff and Elder Madoc's carriage driver among them.

He peeked into his jacket and saw that Vortex was curled up against his chest, fast asleep.

"All right," Nader said, "you run off and find your parents. Scorch and I'll wait here for you." He eyed the manor with a slightly mischievous grin as he gave Will a hand down.

More people poured out of the manor doors, staring in disbelief at the huge red dragon on the road. From the barn by the fields, Will saw Stablemaster Gellan emerge, brushing dust from his cap and squinting as he peered at them.

"Non-riders," Nader muttered, shaking his head at the wary crowd of onlookers. "They always think dragons are going to eat them."

Will hefted Vortex a little higher in his arms. "Well, Scorch does have pretty big teeth. He probably could eat them if he wanted to."

Scorch gave a disgusted snort and lifted his nose.

Nader laughed. "He says he thinks people would be stringy and taste bad."

Will grinned up at Nader. Then he pulled the cap off his head to let his sweaty hair dry out and started making his way toward the manor.

The gathered people chattered nervously, and a few of the braver souls crept forward to see what was going on.

"It's Will!" someone said.

"Hi everyone!" Will shifted Vortex's weight and waved at them with a crooked smile.

"Will came back!"

"He's back from the Hatching Ground!"

"I never believed those rumors."

"Someone should tell Mike and Kim!"

"Will! Is that you, my boy?"

Will paused at the sound of the familiar voice. Stablemaster Gellan approached him, walking closer to the enormous dragon than any of the others dared as he squinted at Will.

"It is you!" He took off his cap and rubbed his sleeve over his sweaty brow before trotting over to him. "I hoped I'd be seeing you again soon! So this dragon rider brought you back home? That's kind of him. I suppose the egg didn't hatch, then?"

"Stablemaster Gellan, no, it's just—"

"Never mind that. Never mind." Gellan patted Will's back. "There was nothing you could do. An egg left out in the cold for so long . . . it wasn't your fault. Perhaps it's for the best. I'm still in need of an apprentice, and you're the most promising candidate I've ever met!"

"Please, sir, you don't understand!" Will shifted his grip on the heavy dragon-shaped lump under his jacket.

Vortex wiggled and gave a tiny, sleepy growl.

"What's that?" Gellan's eyes flashed from Will's face to the baggy, lumpy jacket he wore.

"You see, sir. The egg did hatch. And I did bond with a hatchling. I have him right here. He's just asleep."

Gellan removed his hand from Will's shoulder, blinking, and gulped. He opened his mouth, as though on the verge of asking if he could see Vortex—maybe to make sure Will was telling the truth—then he shook his head, as though dismissing the idea.

"I came to see my parents," Will explained, glancing around at the crowd. His mom and dad weren't among them.

"What is the meaning of this!" A deep voice boomed from the front door.

Everyone turned to see Elder Madoc stomping down the steps in bright yellow and blue silk clothes, his beard blowing in the wind and sweat glistening on his reddened brow. "I demand to know why a dragon rider is harassing my farm! Dragons are nothing but a nuisance. We should banish them from farmlands altogether!"

A few of the others grumbled in quiet agreement.

"Ah, Elder Madoc, I presume," Nader greeted him with an elegant bow. "If the swarmers should ever return, we just might oblige you. It would mean less work for us."

Some in the crowd gasped and murmured at Nader's words.

Swarmers—horse-sized flying scorpions as far as Will could tell from pictures he'd seen in tapestries—hadn't terrorized Avria for hundreds of years. But the horror of these monsters had never died from the stories and legends of their attacks. Will had only heard a few of the stories and songs about the old days when the swarmers used to attack, and it was enough to make him shudder.

"The swarmers will never return!" Elder Madoc spat at him. "They've been gone for generations. You dragon riders are a menace to Avrian society. If you want to be welcomed, then you should learn to do useful work!"

Elder Madoc didn't even seem to notice Will standing there as he stomped through the crowd to rant at Nader.

The older dragon rider took the abuse with a tight-lipped smile and fire in his eyes.

With everyone engrossed in the heated argument between their employer and a man with a fire-breathing dragon behind him, Will started backing slowly toward the manor.

Gellan placed a hand on his shoulder and he stopped.

"I see you can't be my apprentice after all," the stable-master said with a resigned smile. "In any case, I'm glad to see you again, Will. I wish you well with you dragon."

Will smiled at the kind old man. "Thank you, Stable-master Gellan. I'm glad I got to work with you while I was here."

Gellan pressed his lips together and nodded, giving Will's shoulder a squeeze. "You'll find your parents in the servants' quarters."

"In their quarters? But it's the middle of the day! Won't they be working somewhere?"

Gellan sighed and brushed his knuckles through his

mustache. "You'll see when you get there. Go on, then, before Elder Madoc notices you."

Brow wrinkled in confusion, Will wove his way through the crowd and into the nearest servant's door of the manor.

Chapter Five

Will made his way through the servants' dining hall to the narrow corridors that ran behind the walls of the estate. The laundry room billowed with fragrant steam just as it always had. The wooden floorboards bore a smooth path, worn down from thousands of servants pacing over them as they went about their business. Murky light filtered through dirty windows set high in the walls let. Dirty because Elder Madoc's staff was far too busy working to bother with cleaning the servants' areas.

It was unusual for staff to be in their quarters during working hours. Those rooms were the places where they slept and bathed and dressed when they were done with their daily duties.

Everyone who worked for Elder Madoc rose early in the morning and didn't return to their quarters until late at night. For his parents to be there in the middle of the day was strange. Will bit his lip and hurried forward, stumbling as his feet caught on loose floorboards.

When he reached the family quarters, Will scrambled up the rickety stairs to the loft room and found his parents there. His father was lying on the bed, wincing as his mother wrapped strips of fabric around a brace on his leg.

"Mom? Dad?"

They both looked up at the sound of his voice, and their expressions shifted from curious to shocked.

"Will!" His mom ran to him and threw her arms around his shoulders, planting a kiss on his forehead. Then she pulled him across the room to sit next to his dad on the bed. "You came back. We haven't heard anything in so long, I almost thought the worst!"

"Now, Kim, we know Will's a smart and resourceful boy," his dad said with a proud smile and relief in his voice. "He's good at taking care of himself."

"Of course he is. But I'm his mother, so I worry."

Will couldn't help smiling at the exchange between them. But seeing his father in bed with a leg brace quickly wiped the smile from his face. "I came to see how you guys were doing. How did you get hurt, Dad? Is it bad? What happened?"

"Oh, I'll be fine." His dad scooted back to lean against the wall and winced as the motion jostled his leg.

Will's mom shot his dad a look. "He fell off the harvesting wagon and broke his leg."

Will furrowed his brow in confusion and looked between his parents. "Elder Madoc is just letting you stay here to heal? And you're allowed to stop working to take care of him?" That sounded nothing like the Elder Madoc Will remembered.

His mother sighed and shook her head, laying a hand on his dad's knee. "He's not exactly letting us. He's charging us for room, board, bandages, medicine, and everything else he can think of." She gave a mirthless laugh and a crooked grin. "But it doesn't matter so much. It's not like it makes a difference anymore. You shouldn't be worried about us."

"At least we have food to eat and a warm bed to sleep in," his dad said with a nod of agreement. "What about you? You went off with that egg all by yourself to find the Hatching Ground. How did that work out?"

"And what is that you're hiding in your jacket?" His mom pointed at the wiggling lump Vortex made under the leather.

"Well, about that . . ." Will shifted Vortex's weight to one arm and started unbuttoning the riding jacket. "I made it to the Hatching Ground. And that egg I found hatched . . . into him." He pulled the jacket open to reveal Vortex's sleeping head and the clawed tips of his folded wings.

His mom's eyes popped wide.

His dad leaned forward, ignoring how the motion jostled his injured leg. "Is that . . . a dragon? But he's white! I thought . . ."

"The dragonlords think he's a pale shade of a normal color," Will said. "We're waiting to find out which color he really is. I was wondering if he might be an albino."

His mom leaned in to get a better look while his dad rubbed his chin in thought. "Your dragon doesn't look like an albino," he said. "For one thing, his skin isn't pink. You see, it's dark around his eyes and nose, and tan in other places. What color are his eyes?"

"They're golden," Will said, staring at Vortex. His dad was right. The little dragon had darker skin around his eyes and nostrils, and even inside his ears.

"That's pretty definitive, then. If he were albino, he'd have blue or pink eyes. Whatever makes him white, I'm sure it's not that genetic mutation."

"So you think the dragonlords are right and he's one of the normal colors?"

"I can't say for sure." His dad shrugged. "I'd have to learn a lot more about dragon genetics. Even then, I'm no geneticist. But whatever kind of melanin dragons have, he's got some. It just looks gray or cream colored, that's all."

"Will," his mom rested a hand on his arm, "while you were out there with the dragon riders, did any of them mention finding evidence of your Uncle John?"

He blinked at her. "Oh, that's right! Some dragon

riders did go out and look for him. Dragonlord Perrin, the blue dragonlord, took a group of riders all around the coast of Avria . . . only they didn't find anything."

His mom's face fell.

"But they can keep looking, you know. Just because they didn't find anything, doesn't mean he isn't out there somewhere."

She lowered her gaze to the woven wool comforter on the bed, twisted a few threads between her fingers, and nodded.

Will noticed how tired and thin she looked. Shadows haunted her eyes, and her face held a pained expression that never vanished completely, even when she smiled.

Life on Elder Madoc's estate also seemed to be ageing his father. His face was rougher and more weathered than Will remembered. His hair, which used to be brown and smooth, was now sun-bleached, dry and rough. His formerly sparkling eyes were red and tired. It wasn't fair that Will should live in a dragonhold with nightly feasting, a luxurious bath whenever he needed it, great friends, and a wonderful dragon while his parents sweated day after day for Elder Madoc.

I have to get them out of here, he thought.

Vortex stirred and stretched his forelegs, then lifted his head on a slightly wobbly neck and blinked his bleary golden eyes at Will's parents.

"Well, would you look at that." His dad leaned forward

and reached out a hand as though he were coaxing a skittish dog to come closer.

His mother lifted her eyes and released the stray threads she'd been twisting between her fingers, watching Vortex.

Will held his breath and clutched the corner of the comforter in his fist. Would his parents like Vortex? Or would they think he was a mutant, like everyone else seemed to?

These people do like me. Are they your parents? Vortex asked, swiveling his head around to gaze up at Will.

"This is my mom and my dad," Will said.

Vortex turned his head back around and flicked his ears as he studied their faces. After a moment he said, *You care about them a lot.*

At the same time, Will's mom asked, "He can understand you?"

"Yes," Will answered them both. "He chose me on the Hatching Ground, and our minds linked somehow. He can understand my thoughts and feelings even if I don't speak out loud. And I can understand him."

Do I have parents too? Vortex asked.

"I'm pretty sure you have to have parents," Will said. "I don't know who they are, but some dragon had to lay that egg you were in."

"I can hardly believe it," Will's mom murmured, a slow smile forming on her lips.

"This is so fascinating!" his dad said. "Can he come out? I'd love to get a good look at him."

"What do you say?" Will asked, dropping his chin to look at Vortex. "Can they look at you?"

Vortex immediately started wiggling his way out of the opening in Will's riding jacket. Will unfastened the last few buttons to let his dragon crawl free, and Vortex stepped out onto the foot of the bed.

"Wow," Will's mom breathed, bending closer.

"He's simply amazing!" his dad said.

Will chuckled nervously and rubbed the back of his neck with his hand, grinning. "He is, isn't he?"

Vortex lifted his wings, half furled, and walked in a neat circle around the bed, holding his head high. His eyes were half-closed in a modest expression that didn't quite disguise how pleased he was with being admired.

"Look at his chest! He's got a keel, like a bird!"

"A what?" Will asked.

"A keel. The bony structure that supports flight muscles and allows them to breathe without a diaphragm. But his wings are leathery with finger bones, like a bat's. I wonder whether Avrian dragons are related to pterosaurs."

"He doesn't look like a pterodactyl to me," Will said, wrinkling his brow. "They didn't have tails, did they?" He ran his fingers along Vortex's long, smooth tail.

"The early ones did. They even had tail vanes." His dad pointed a finger at the spade-shaped tip of Vortex's tail. "What throws me off is the fact that they have four legs and grow to such a large size. I haven't seen an adult up close yet, but from a distance, they look positively huge."

"They are huge. When they're full grown, they're about the size of a school bus. But I thought breathing fire would be more of a difference than having four legs. Unless dinosaurs breathed fire too."

Both his parents froze for a moment, speechless.

His mom glanced warily at Vortex, then back at Will. "Hold on a minute . . . Did you say they can breathe fire?"

Will chuckled and gave half a shrug. "Yeah, they can."

Chapter Six

Will's parents stared at him, blinking slowly. "Are you sure they actually breathe fire?" his dad asked in a breathless voice.

At the foot of the bed, Vortex paused in his prancing and sat down, grooming a foreclaw with his pink tongue.

"I've only seen it a few times." Will shrugged. "Red dragons don't just go around breathing fire everywhere. And the other colors do different things. Yellow dragons make electricity, like lightning. Blue dragons can make ice breath. Green dragons are poisonous."

"We've heard people talk about dragon abilities." Will's dad watched Vortex in amazement. "The idea that fire-breathing dragons exist in the world . . . It's almost beyond belief. It would be too much to believe if I didn't have a dragon sitting in front of me right now."

"We're both so proud of you, Will." His mom squeezed

his elbow with a smile. "I admit I was worried when you left. The journey to the hatching ground sounded so dangerous, but I'm glad you've found a place where you can fit in here."

Will's gaze traveled down to his mom's hand, the skin cracked and bleeding from hours of scrubbing pans with harsh soap and scouring pads.

He rested a hand over hers and turned to his dad, who lay helpless on the bed with his broken leg. His heart ached and moisture blurred his vision. "You guys will never be able to leave here, will you? With your broken leg and Mom taking care of you, you'll never be able to pay off your debt."

Vortex looked up at him and tilted his head.

A small shadow flashed over his dad's face for a moment before he wiped it away with a wry smile. "Never is a long time, son. Who knows what will happen?" He ran his hand through the stubble on his chin and took a deep breath. "With any luck, I'll be able to work as a house servant when my leg heals. The pay is a lot better, and it's not nearly as dangerous."

"Yeah, that would be great." Will raked his fingers through his hair. He had a hard time believing that Elder Madoc would move his dad to a house servant position. Not when he was an off-lander who didn't know all the customs and traditions of Avrian society.

Vortex walked across the bed and scrambled into his lap, making worried little chirps.

You feel sad and scared, the little dragon said, nuzzling Will's chin with his head. *Why? What's wrong?*

This place is bad for my parents, but they can't leave. I wish I could help them, but I don't know how.

Vortex looked around the room, a sense of confusion whirling in his mind. *There's a door. Can't they go through the door?*

Will chuckled and scratched behind Vortex's horn buds. *It's more complicated than that,* he thought. *The man who owns this place makes them stay so they'll work for him. He says they can leave when they've worked enough, but he keeps adding more and more work.*

As he was speaking to Vortex, he pictured Elder Madoc, wearing his disgustingly fancy silk clothes with his pompous vast belly, his garish gold and silver rings, and his self-important bushy beard and mustache. Every part of the mental image dripped with pent-up loathing.

Vortex gave a fierce little growl. Or, at least, it would have been fierce if he was a hundred times bigger. Since he was only about the size of a small beagle, it sounded more adorable than scary.

Will smiled indulgently and tried not to laugh.

I'll tell Scorch to scare that man. It's not right that he won't let your parents go.

"What?" Will asked.

Scorch says men like him have no respect for others and always take more than they deserve.

"Are you talking to your dragon?" his mom asked, both she and his dad watching Vortex with fascinated smiles.

Will shrugged and chuckled. "Vortex was talking with Scorch, the red dragon who brought us here. It sounds like Scorch doesn't like Elder Madoc very much."

"Can't say as I blame him," Will's dad grumbled under his breath.

A sudden violent roar shook the air, followed by terrified screams from outside.

Will jumped and clasped Vortex tight to his chest.

His parents flinched at the sound, their eyes widening, and his dad winced, clutching his broken leg with a pained groan.

"That sounds like it might be your red dragon friend," his mom said.

"I'd better go see what's going on!"

His mom leaned in and gave him a quick hug. "Thank you for coming back to visit us. I know you'll be a great dragon rider."

He hugged her back. "I should have come sooner, it's just— "

"We know," his dad said, reaching out an arm to give Will a side hug. "You have a lot on your plate right now. Take care of yourself, and Vortex too." He held out a tentative hand and patted Vortex's head.

Vortex wiggled his ears and chirped happily at him.

"I will, Dad. I promise."

Will bundled Vortex back into the oversized riding jacket, then hurried back downstairs.

Every step he took felt like tearing out a piece of his heart.

He was leaving his parents in a horrible situation. It wasn't right. They were suffering here on Elder Madoc's estate, and he had no idea when he'd ever be able to see them again. He felt like he should stay, help them somehow. But what could he do?

When he made it back outside, the crowd of people gathered on the white gravel road had grown. It seemed like every servant, house staff and field hand alike, had gathered to see what was going on.

Most were standing well away from Scorch and Nader, huddling near the walls or crowding behind the sparse shelter of the decorative cedars lining the manor.

Scorch glared at Elder Madoc as thin smoke streamed from his nostrils. A low growl rumbled in his chest, barely audible, but shaking the ground like an oncoming train.

Elder Madoc was putting on an impressive show of not caring about the huge red dragon. He stood a few steps away from Nader, his thumbs tucked into his belt and his chest puffed out as he stared down at the dragon rider. Only the sweat glistening on his brow hinted at any sort of fear.

"If you don't get that beast under control immediately . . ." Madoc roared.

"Swarms, man! I'm telling you, I don't know what got into him!" Nader protested, looking half irritated and half worried. He turned to Scorch and patted his foreleg. "Calm down, will you? These people aren't going to hurt us!"

Scorch bared his sharp teeth at Elder Madoc, wisps of smoke flowing from between his teeth.

"I know that," Nader answered his dragon's thoughts. "But that doesn't mean you need to terrify everyone here, okay?"

"Your dragon is a danger to us all!" one woman called.

"All dragons are like this," a boy shouted from the edge of the crowd. "They have to be fierce so they can fight swarmers!"

"Arik, what are you doing out here?" the woman snapped. "Someone gather up the children. Make sure they're all inside!"

"What swarmers?" someone else asked. "The White Dragon banished all the swarmers centuries ago!"

"Haven't you heard? Fishermen have been finding them out at sea. From what I hear, they keep getting closer every spring."

"Fishermen's tales!" Elder Madoc scoffed. "Fishermen will say anything to make themselves feel important. If you believe their tales, you're a bigger fool than they are."

Frowning at Elder Madoc's declaration, Will nudged his way through the crowd. Most of the people didn't seem to notice him, too caught up in the drama unfolding in front of them.

Nader saw him coming, though, and flashed a relieved smile.

"My uncle is a fisherman," a young, haughty voice piped up.

Will paused at the familiar sound. A shiver of distaste ran up his spine and he turned to see his old nemesis, Tavin, pushing his way to the front of the crowd.

"He lives in Fallshore, and he's seen loads of swarmers. He's even killed one before."

Will smirked in disbelief.

The crowd erupted in amused laughter.

"It's true!" Tavin shouted, face reddening as he scowled at everyone.

Nader laughed loudly and wiped a hand over his eyes. "Now that's one I've never heard before. Please tell me more, lad. I'd love to share the harrowing tale of the brave swarmer-slaying fisherman in our dining hall tonight."

Tavin aimed his glare up at the dragon rider, clenching his fists until they trembled. "We don't need dragon riders anymore. Even if swarmers do come back, they aren't that dangerous. If my uncle could kill one, why can't the rest of us? We can fight them off without dragons!"

Will couldn't stand by and let him get away with that.

He stepped in front of Tavin, staring the other boy down with a narrowed gaze. "If that's true, then why did you want to be a dragon rider so much?"

Tavin stumbled back with a gasp, but quickly recovered and lifted his chin.

"Only a few weeks ago, you stole my dragon egg just for the chance to be on the Hatching Ground!" Will said.

Murmurs of surprise rolled through the crowd. Some frowned at Tavin and shook their heads in disapproval.

"What?" Nader asked, looking hard at Tavin.

Tavin flushed so deeply his face went purple. He set his jaw and lifted his chin even higher.

"You only think dragons are useless because you never made it there to bond with one," Will said, aiming a finger at the other boy's chest. "Not that any hatchling with half a brain would choose you!"

Tavin's eyes darted to the people watching them as sweat beaded on his forehead. His lip curled in a sneer. "And you think a hatchling would choose a stupid off-lander? It's a good thing that rotten egg got smashed at the bottom of the cliff. It was never going to hatch, anyway!"

Will remembered watching the last glint of Vortex's shell before it dropped over the edge of the ravine and how callously Tavin had dismissed it. He'd never cared about the baby dragon inside the egg. To Tavin, Vortex's egg had only been a ticket to becoming a dragon rider.

Without thinking, Will's fingers clenched into a fist,

preparing to smash the smug look off the other boy's face. But before he could throw a punch, the lump in his jacket shifted and a little white snout poked out of the opening.

It's loud out there, and you're very angry, Vortex said, blinking his amber eyes in the sunlight. He wiggled farther out, gripping the jacket opening with his front legs and swiveling his ears as he peered at the people standing all around.

The entire crowd gave a collective gasp. Some backed up a step or two. Others came forward, bending in to get a better look. Elder Madoc's eyes bulged. Gellan mopped his glistening brow with a hand. Tavin's mouth fell open in a gape that could have been disbelief or horror, maybe both.

Why is everyone looking at me? Vortex asked, swiveling his head around to look up at Will.

Will shifted his weight and glanced around, licking his lips. Nader, already sitting on Scorch's neck, only watched quietly.

"By the White Dragon!" someone exclaimed. "It's a new White Dragon!"

"A new White Dragon," others echoed.

"The rumors were true," one farmhand said. "It's a sign. The swarmers really are returning."

"Wait. Hold on." Will protested. "Vortex is just a hatchling. He looks different from the others, but he's not a sign or a god or anything like that."

He took in everyone's shocked and awed faces. He

couldn't tell if they were ready to fall at his feet and make him their king or run him out of town with pitchforks and torches. Either way, his heart pounded behind his ribs and his knees shook.

He licked his lips and gulped.

Tavin still stared at him with a sickened expression like he'd swallowed a toad.

"He's really a White—" someone started.

"Listen!" Will interrupted. "Don't get carried away. The dragonlords say he's a normal color, just very pale. His actual color might come in later. And when he learns how to use his powers, we'll know for sure what kind of dragon he is."

Those surrounding him muttered uncertainly. He could still hear people murmuring "White Dragon" under their breaths. But he wasn't sure whether they were swearing by the White Dragon, as Avrian's often did, or insisting that Vortex was a white dragon.

Elder Madoc stepped closer and bent down to study Vortex with a critical eye. Will shrank back, instinctively wanting to protect his hatchling.

"Hmm, I see." Madoc straightened and scrubbed his knuckles across his nose. "It's an aberration. A mutation. Probably sickly and won't live long. If it was a cormant, I'd have had it culled the moment it hatched."

Will choked on his breath, staring at the rotund man as stunned disbelief gave way to white hot rage. The idea that anyone would kill a baby dragon just because it was born different made the blood rush hot in his ears and his face burn.

"You take that back!" he screamed, hugging Vortex to his chest.

Elder Madoc's back stiffened. He stared at Will with cold, bulging eyes.

From the corner of his vision, Will saw Nader drop to the ground and step forward, face set and grim. "Hold your tongue, Elder. We do not speak of dragons so. We do not cull dragons any more than you would cull a baby. They are not common beasts, as you seem to think."

Tavin snorted and shook his head with a mocking grin. "I'm glad I didn't go to the Hatching Ground if it meant I'd get stuck with an ugly freak like that."

So blinded by rage at what Elder Madoc had said about killing Vortex, Will didn't notice Tavin reaching out a hand to snatch one of Vortex's wing joints.

Vortex shrieked in pain.

"Ha! Look at this. Its wing is so thin I could tear it apart just by breathing too hard."

Will's arm flew out, knuckles colliding with Tavin's nose. Tavin staggered to the ground, blood gushing from his nostrils.

"Don't you dare touch my dragon again!" Will roared.

In an instant, Tavin sprang to his feet, charging at Will.

Will braced himself, preparing to knock the other boy

down again if he got the chance. Blood pounded in his ears. Adrenaline surged through his body.

But before Tavin could reach him, the adults closed in, grabbing them both and holding them apart.

"Tavin!" Jerrol the footman said, hauling the boy back by his shoulders. "Stinging swarms, boy, mind yourself!"

"Easy now, lad," Gellan said in Will's ear. "If you throw fists with Tavin now, your dragon might get hurt."

His words were like a bucket of ice water thrown down Will's back. In an instant, his temper disappeared, replaced with horror at what he'd been prepared to do. Brawling with Tavin while Vortex was nestled in his jacket? What had he been thinking?

Elder Madoc pushed his way forward and gripped Tavin's shoulder in a firm hand, but he aimed his stern glare at Nader. "I'd say it's time you were off my property, dragon rider. If I never see another dragon again, it will be too soon."

Chapter Seven

As Scorch took off, leaving the manor and fields far behind, Will's anger cooled and his thoughts turned to his parents.

He had a nice home in Fire Mountain Dragonhold, friends, and a wonderful life with Vortex, but his parents were still suffering on Elder Madoc's estate. Working there wasn't good for them, and they didn't seem to have any way out of it.

Was there something he could do to help them? If Vortex was bigger, maybe they could fly away from Avria altogether. What would it be like to return to "the off-lands" with a fully grown dragon? Will snorted in amusement. Surely the Coast Guard or the Air Force would be called in if an enormous dragon started flying toward the coast. People would panic.

But maybe there was some other way he could help his parents. There had to be something he could do.

Scorch tipped his wings and curved his tail, and they began a descending spiral over the flapling barracks. Moments later, they landed in a flurry of wind and sand.

Will unclipped his belt from the saddle and slid down Scorch's shoulder, landing with a clack of riding boots on the stone courtyard.

As he turned to thank Nader, the older dragon rider gripped his shoulder and looked him in the eye with a solemn expression. "There's something I need to say to you, Will."

Will paused and regarded Nader warily, wondering if he was in trouble for some reason.

Nader took a breath and let it out with a sigh. "I know that other boy got under your skin—I daresay he deserved to be knocked down—but as a dragon rider, you must learn to control your temper."

Will frowned, remembering the horrible things Tavin had said. What he'd done. "But I couldn't just let him get away with—"

Nader held out his hands. "I'm not saying what you should or shouldn't do. I'm letting you know that acting rashly in anger has consequences. Not only for you but also for Vortex. For your dragonhold as well, when you join one. And should the swarmers ever return, as some think they will, your actions will have consequences for all of Avria."

Will frowned as he took in Nader's words. His brow furrowed in thought."What am I supposed to do? Just smile and take it when Tavin hurts my dragon?"

Nader leaned back, raking both hands through his hair as he let out a heavy breath. "No, of course not. But maybe you should think about how far you were prepared to go. Were you protecting your dragon, or were you out for revenge?" He gave a crooked half smile. "I'm not sure I would have done much better if I'd been in your place. But the point remains."

Scorch lowered his head and pressed his red snout against his rider's side. Nader patted his nose affectionately. "Common folk don't appreciate dragons the way they did in the old days. So we can all look forward to more of the same treatment you saw today. If our dragons weren't so big and intimidating, most farmers would probably refuse to even give us the dregs from their herds."

Will hugged Vortex a little tighter. "Does everyone really hate dragons so much? I thought it was just Elder Madoc. If people hate them, why do so many kids want to be dragon riders?"

"Oh, they don't hate dragons." Nader clapped him on the back as they walked toward the dragonhold. "Shufflo herders don't appreciate how big their appetites can be. And dragons have lost most of the respect people used to have for them. But I'd say many people downright love them when it comes time for the Dragon Games!" He laughed. "Everyone loves a good show and a chance to place bets. You'll see. This summer, people will travel from all over Avria to pack into the Cliffs of Charramor. All for the chance to watch dragons showing off their skills for prize money."

"Dragon riders earn money at the Dragon Games?" Will's mind raced as they entered the storage room and Nader lit the lantern on the wall.

How much money would it take to pay off his parents' debt? Was it possible that he and Vortex could win enough? Was Vortex even big enough to enter?

Nader lifted the lid on the storage chest so Will could return his riding gear. "Of course they do." He gave Will a knowing smile. "But I'm afraid it will be a few years before Vortex is big enough to enter any competitions."

Will frowned. He removed his heavy riding boots, tossed them into the chest, then put Vortex down to unbutton and return the jacket. The little dragon grumbled in annoyance. He'd enjoyed being carried around inside a warm leather hammock.

As they made their way outside again, Vortex yawned and looked up at Will. *Is there food? I'm hungry.*

Will smiled and rubbed his dragon's horn buds. "I'm sure we can find something in the dining hall. Let's see what's there."

He continued puzzling through the problem of helping his parents as he led Vortex to the dining hall. He wasn't sure what, if anything, he could do for them. With no money and no way to contact the outside world for help, the best he could do was keep his eyes and ears open for any opportunities that came his way.

As for right now, he had a baby dragon to take care of.

DAY BY DAY, the hatchling grew. It seemed that one day Vortex's wings were paper thin and translucent, and the next they were sturdy and leathery.

When he was a hatchling, the baby dragon had gazed about with an oversized head on a wobbling neck. But almost before Will noticed what was happening, his neck thickened with muscle and his body grew to match his head.

A few more weeks and he stopped waking to feed in the night. He was more alert during the day, too, watching, listening, learning about the world.

Will remembered lifting Vortex in a single outstretched hand when he was tiny. But now, after a month of growing, he was so heavy Will struggled to pick up his dragon at all.

Vortex was highly miffed at this new development and

grumbled between his teeth as he trudged around the grounds on his own four feet.

"Well, look at it this way," Will rubbed his dragon's head, which now reached up to his waist, "you're getting enough exercise to work off all those shufflos you keep eating!"

Vortex sniffed irritably and flapped his wings. *Dragons are meant for flying, not for walking!*

Will grinned and put his hands on his hips. "If that's your argument, dragons aren't meant to be carried around like giant babies either."

Vortex gave an affronted squawk. *I thought you liked carrying me.*

Will chuckled. "I did. But you're getting so big, pretty soon it'll be your turn to carry me around. You could probably carry me on your back now while you're walking. Want to try it?"

Vortex squawked an emphatic *no*, fluttering his wings in alarm. An image of himself getting squished under Will's weight flashed between their minds.

Will chuckled and elbowed his dragon's neck. "I was only teasing, ya big goofball! And I'm not *that* heavy. I bet I really could ride on your back if we tried."

Vortex huffed and butted his head into Will's arm at the joke.

"Hey, look at that!" Corin came up alongside them with Leika following. He pointed to the training field.

Three unfamiliar dragons perched on mountain ledges around the training field, a yellow, a green, and a blue.

In the middle of the field, Tumi was waiting for them with three other dragon riders, each wearing distinctive riding gear based on their dragon's color.

"Who are they?" Will wondered.

"I've never seen them before," Corin said.

As the rest of the kids emerged from the barracks to join them for the day's training, more started pointing to the newcomers and chattering in excitement.

"What do you think it means?" Rin asked. She and Anri joined Will and Corin.

Rin's red dragon, Ember, looked about as happy to be walking on his own feet as Vortex was. But Jade marched forward proudly, as though determined to prove she didn't need to be carried anymore.

"I don't know," Corin answered. "Do you think they're here to take us to our separate dragonholds?"

"Don't be ridiculous," Anri said. But when her eyes flashed to the green dragon on the ledge, her face paled a little.

As he passed by, Beck turned to them with a confident smile. "That's impossible. Our dragons aren't big enough to fly with us. We have to stay here until then." At his side, Icicle flapped his wings as though eager for that day to come.

They continued musing among themselves as they

made their way across the open space. As they approached the middle of the field where Tumi and the newcomers waited, they split off into their separate wings. Will stayed with the red wing as usual.

"Good morning, young riders," Tumi greeted them. "Your dragons are all looking healthy and well-fed. I hope you're encouraging them to flap their wings daily to build their flight muscles?"

They all nodded in agreement. Not that any of them had to encourage the young dragons to exercise their wings. The hatchlings were flapping their wings almost constantly. It seemed an irresistible impulse at times.

"I'm sure you're all wondering who our visitors are." Tumi gestured toward the other three dragon riders, two slender women and one large, bearded man. "This week you will begin training your dragons in elemental powers. Since my Ruby is a red, we won't be much use teaching your blue dragons to breathe ice or your yellow dragons to make electricity. And, of course, you green riders have very specialized training, as well."

Some kids chuckled nervously, but most murmured in excited surprise. Their dragons were going to start using their powers!

Will grinned and gazed down at Vortex. "This is it, pal. We're going to find out what power you have!"

Vortex shuffled his wings and swished his tail, giving a happy chirp.

"This is Aleri, rider of Cobalt," Tumi said, resting a friendly hand on the shoulder of the tall woman in blue-trimmed riding gear. "She's come from Frozen Peaks Dragonhold to help your blues learn to breathe ice."

Aleri smiled mildly and gave a slight bow of her head.

"And here we have Gwin, rider of Freefall," Tumi announced, moving on to the friendly looking short-haired woman. "She's here to help you yellows learn to use electricity."

Gwin flashed a smile at the yellow riders and winked, sending them all nudging each other and whispering together.

"And finally—" Tumi slapped the broad shoulder of the man in green-trimmed riding gear.

"I am Joric," the bearded man announced, stepping forward and gazing down at the green riders, "rider of Vinna, and I will not be teaching you to use elemental powers. Using poison isn't what makes green dragons and riders the best. We're the best because we're the strongest, the most agile, the most determined. I am here to teach your dragons," his intense gaze swept over the thunderstruck kids, "to fly!"

All the kids erupted into shouts of surprise and exclamations of jealousy and indignation. The green riders cheered and jumped. The red, yellow, and blue riders gasped and shouted their displeasure at the unfairness of it all.

"Why do they get to learn how to fly?"

"Leika can fly as good as any green!"

"Fireball wants to learn to fly too!"

"It's not fair!"

Tumi stepped in front of Joric, raising his hands to settle them all down. His mouth pulled into a grimace that showed he'd been expecting this reaction.

"Now, everyone. Quiet down. Listen. Here on the training grounds, we don't let most dragons learn to fly until their muscles and bones have grown strong. Pushing your dragons too hard, too fast, can lead to serious injuries that could leave them grounded for life. One careless landing and your dragon could end up with a broken wing that never heals properly."

"Then why do their dragons get to learn to fly?" Corin jabbed an accusing finger at the smugly grinning green riders.

Vortex eyed the green dragons with a wordless fog of jealousy clouding his thoughts. *I want to fly too!*

"I know you do, buddy. You will. Someday." But Will didn't go so far as to join Corin in complaining. The thought of Vortex breaking a wing and never being able to fly was enough to keep him from begging along with the others.

"Green riders have their own traditions and training regimen," Tumi answered Corin.

"Our drekhems are on the ground," Joric added. He

shot a hard look at all of them. "Green dragons don't have the luxury of taking off from mountain ledges or cliffsides all the time. They need powerful flight muscles to get in the air every day. In a year's time, your greens must be strong enough to lift off from the ground bearing riders and gear, and still have strength to fly when they reach the Poison Plains. If they can't, they aren't fit to be part of our dragonhold."

Will frowned and exchanged a glance with Rin. It sounded like Joric was saying that any green dragon who wasn't strong enough would be banished from the Poison Plains. That couldn't be right, could it?

He glanced over at Anri and saw that she was frowning in thought as well.

Tumi clapped his hands and rubbed them together. "Let's get started with your training!"

Chapter Eight

The three new flapling instructors broke off into separate areas and the kids joined them according to their colors. But before Will could walk off with Rin and the rest of the red riders, Tumi drew him aside.

"So far, you and Vortex have been with the red wing," he said in a low voice. "But the two of you are free to join whichever training you like. You can always switch classes until we find out what works best for Vortex."

Will nodded. "Thanks, Tumi. Which group do you think we should join?"

His teacher flashed a brilliant smile and chuckled. "If you ask me, I'll always say the reds. You can't trust a red dragon rider to be objective."

Will grinned at Tumi and glanced at the groups of young riders forming around their instructors. He really wanted to know what ability Vortex would end up having. According to the dragonlords, this was what would determine his dragon's true color.

Would Vortex be a red dragon, able to breathe fire? Would he be a yellow with electric powers? Maybe he'd be a blue, with the ability to freeze things solid in a single breath.

But suddenly, the idea of letting Vortex learn to fly with the green dragons seemed really appealing. Tumi said they could join whatever wing they wanted.

I do want to fly! It would be so much fun. I also want to know what powers I have.

He smiled at his dragon, then glanced over at Anri. Would she want them to join her in the green wing? She stood amongst the other green riders, Trouble scurrying across her shoulders. The kisnit chittered at the other kids, tail bushy and ears flat. Anri was trying to grab the little critter to calm her down while Jade sat at her feet, watching anxiously.

"Why do you even keep that thing around?" Albin asked, laughing at her predicament.

"Swarms, Anri. It's nothing but a nuisance!" Dal rolled his eyes and shook his head.

Trouble scurried up to the top of Anri's head and chattered angrily at the boy.

"I know she's a nuisance. But she's my nuisance! And I couldn't get rid of her if I wanted to. She always comes back." Anri continued awkwardly trying to grab Trouble by the scruff of the neck and follow the green wing to a nearby trailhead.

She never even turned to look at Will.

"Hey, Will!"

Will turned to see Rin waving him over to the red wing gathering around Tumi. At her side, Ember crooned a greeting to them.

"Come on! We're gathering in the red training cavern. I heard there will be snacks." Rin grinned and waggled her eyebrows.

Will sighed with a smile and patted Vortex's head. "What do you think, buddy? Want to try breathing fire?"

Vortex glanced back at the greens, then back at Rin and Ember.

Flying sounds like fun. But I do like snacks!

Will snorted and shook his head. "It's probably safer this way anyhow. I wouldn't want you to get hurt because you tried to fly too soon."

Vortex grumbled in begrudging agreement, and they joined Rin and the rest of the red wing following Tumi to the main dragonhold.

Tumi wasn't taking them to the usual sandy cavern where the young dragons and riders had been taking their daily lessons. Instead, he led them to the head of the courtyard, past the Hatching Grounds and the massive double doors of the main hall, to a downward sloping alley between red stone mountain walls.

The air grew hotter with each step they took, but the others didn't seem to notice. Tumi led the way as the other kids chattered about how great it would be once their dragons could breathe fire.

Will licked his lips and wiped beads of sweat from his brow. Full-grown red dragons lounged in the sunlight on the surrounding cliffs. Their bright eyes glinted as they gazed down at the young riders.

Will was constantly amazed at how much bigger the adult dragons were. Their horns long and gleaming. Their claws sharp and strong. Wing muscles bulging. Even though he'd complained about how heavy Vortex was getting the last few times he'd carried his dragon, he was sad that those days were over. The last time he'd held Vortex in his arms, he hadn't even realized it would be the last time ever. If he'd known, he might have held on a little longer, complained a little less.

Will wiped some more sweat from his forehead with his sleeve and fanned out his shirt. "Don't you guys think it's hot here?"

Rin cocked her head. "It's kind of warm, I guess. But it feels nice to me."

"It's kind of cozy," Dilin said with a shrug.

"I think it's a little warm," Timmin chimed in, looking

around as though to see whether anyone agreed with him. "But I like the cold."

"You're handling the heat rather well for a non-red rider," Tumi said, nodding to Will and Vortex. "It's usually only green riders who ever try to come this far into our dragonhold. And they usually give up by now. Vortex might be a red dragon after all!" He winked at Vortex and grinned at Will.

They followed the road to a long tunnel that led to a deep, open cavern with blackened walls. A thick mixture of sand and ash covered the floor, and the air sizzled with the smell of charred rock.

"Now!" Tumi clapped his hands together, turning to address the group. "The important thing to remember today is that we're here to explore what our dragons can do. It isn't supposed to be stressful. Your dragon doesn't need to perform perfectly the first time, or ever! Every dragon learns at their own pace."

Dilin and Rin smiled and nudged each other with their elbows. Timmin nodded and flashed a friendly smile to Will.

"I've asked the kitchen to provide casks of water and baskets of steam buns to refresh ourselves with. And there's a trough of fresh meat for your dragons. If you ever feel overwhelmed with the lesson, feel free to take a break. Have a snack and chat with your friends if you want to. If there's anything that makes breathing fire difficult for red dragons, it's feeling pressured. So stay relaxed, keep it casual. No matter what happens today, make sure your dragon doesn't feel like they're letting you down."

Everyone nodded in solemn agreement.

"We're going to space ourselves out facing the far wall. No targets for our first few lessons. We're just going to focus on making fire, not aiming it. With that in mind, every dragon must be facing away from Will and Vortex while practicing."

"Why?" Rin paused in her walk across the cavern. When the others shot her confused looks, she added, "I mean, why only them? I don't think any of us want to get burned."

"Because Vortex might not be a red dragon," Tumi said. "If Ember flames another red, or even one of you riders, the worst that would happen is singed clothing or an annoyed dragon. Being a red rider means you and your dragon are as fireproof as steel. If Vortex or Will get flamed, they could get serious burns."

"Oh, I see," Rin murmured, eyes wide.

"So, until we see Vortex breathe fire," Tumi addressed the whole cavern, "keep your dragon's snouts pointed away. Understand?"

The other kids nodded in agreement, shooting slightly worried looks at Will and Vortex.

"Until we see you breathe fire, huh?" Will muttered as he and Vortex made their way to the far side of the cavern.

"I guess everyone's going to be watching us. No pressure, right?"

Vortex gulped and tucked his wings extra close to his body. *I don't want us to get burned. What if I can't make fire?*

"Don't worry, buddy," Will said, patting his head. "Nobody's going to aim their fire at us. Just do your best, and if it doesn't work out, we'll try something else."

When everyone was well spaced and facing the charred rock walls, Tumi stood in the middle of the cavern, where everyone could hear him. With his fists planted on his hips, he called out, "Is everyone ready?"

"Yes!" Will cheered along with everyone else.

"Good! Now, have your dragons think about their fire sacs. It's like a second stomach low in their belly, right under their lungs."

There was a moment of silence while, all around the room, the young dragons cocked their heads, closed their eyes, and gave soft growls of concentration.

"Can you feel it?" Will asked. "Is there a fire sac in your belly?"

Vortex tipped his head and flicked an ear. *I feel . . . something. It doesn't feel like fire. But I think there's something in there.*

"Once your dragons can feel their fire sac, ask them to squeeze the surrounding muscles. Not too much. Just enough to get a feel for it. They should taste the fire in the backs of their mouths when they do this."

One by one, all the red flaplings clenched their bellies.

Timmin's dragon, Strawberry, coughed and choked.

Dilin's dragon, Fireball, wheezed a thin stream of black smoke between his teeth.

Ember actually produced a slight flash of flame that flickered up his snout. He jumped back, snapping his jaws shut and flapping his wings in surprise.

A few others didn't seem to have any success at all.

"Doesn't look too hard, does it? Give it a try, Vortex," Will said.

Vortex faced the wall, lashed his tail, and clenched his belly.

Nothing happened.

"Do you taste anything?" Will asked, bending forward and running his hand along Vortex's neck. "Tumi said it should taste like fire, whatever that means."

Vortex ran his tongue along his teeth and swallowed. *It tastes like water.*

"Like water?" Will didn't bother pointing out that water didn't taste like anything. He sighed. "Okay, maybe try again. A little harder this time."

Vortex did as he was told, bracing his legs and aiming his snout at the wall. To Will's amazement, pale smoke streamed out from between his teeth.

"Hey, that's something!" Will said, knuckling Vortex's head. "You did it! Something happened!"

Vortex trilled and fluttered his wings in excitement.

"Very good!" Tumi called, smiling in their direction as he walked from dragon to dragon around the cavern. "Once your dragons have a feel for it, let them try harder. Tell them to open their mouths wide to let the flames out, or they'll end up with a nasty taste in their mouths." He chuckled and patted Timmin's back.

Strawberry was still smacking his tongue against his teeth after choking on his own smoke.

"Don't worry if that happens, though. It's nothing a good mouthful of meat won't fix. And if all your dragon produces today is a few sparks and hot air, that's nothing to be ashamed of. There's still plenty of time to learn."

Tumi continued walking around the cavern, giving individual instruction to each dragon and rider pair. Some of the reds coughed up clouds of black smoke. Some sent out thin showers of sparks. Ember and Fireball actually produced plumes of flame, causing everyone to erupt in cheers.

"Want to try again?" Will turned to Vortex after watching the other dragons' fire show.

Yes! I think I can do it!

"Okay, pal. Let's see what you've got!"

Vortex braced his legs, flapped his wings once, and faced the wall in a determined stance. He sucked in a breath of air, opened his mouth wide, and spewed a small cloud of pale mist.

Will blinked. "Um . . . "

Vortex cocked his head, then dropped his wings and looked up at Will. *That isn't what I meant to do.* He smacked his tongue and teeth together. *It still tastes like water.*

Will frowned thoughtfully. "That's really weird."

Tumi strode up to them and grabbed Will's shoulder with a friendly shake. "How are you two coming along? Has Vortex made any sparks yet?"

"Well, he's trying. But . . ."

"No? Let's have him try again, then. Let me see how it goes. Sometimes a change of stance is all it takes."

Vortex braced himself again.

Tumi had the little dragon lower his head and straighten his neck. He kneeled down and pressed his fingers gently against Vortex's belly. "Your fire sac should be right here, Vortex. Feel for the heat that comes from this spot."

Vortex took a breath and a thick cloud of steam shot out of his mouth, evaporating almost instantly in the hot air. The moisture turned the dry, smoky cavern humid, feeling ten times hotter and making Will's clothes stick to his skin.

Tumi raised his eyebrows, somehow looking impressed and confused at the same time. "That is strange. I've never seen anything like it!" He stood, rubbing a hand against his chin. "It's very impressive actually. That was quite a large amount of smoke. Maybe with a little practice, that smoke cloud will turn into flame. Well done, Vortex! Keep practicing and we'll see what comes of it." Tumi patted Will's back and turned back to the other flaplings.

Vortex looked up at Will.

Will shrugged. "I guess we'll keep practicing, then."

For the rest of the day, Vortex tried again and again to produce flame, or even a few sparks, with no luck at all. The group took breaks for food and water and to let the young dragons take a quick nap on the warm sand.

By the end of the lesson, all the red dragons had produced fire in one form or another. Vortex had only made damp vapor, varying from clean white steam to muddy brown smoke.

While they waited for dinner, the red flaplings and their riders gathered in the courtyard, enjoying the cool evening air as the sun set below the mountains.

"Maybe Vortex just isn't doing it right," Dilin suggested, scratching under his dragon's chin. "Fireball only made smoke at first too. Then Tumi told him to open his throat more, and it worked."

"Vortex was opening his throat, Dilin." Rin narrowed her eyes at the boy. "Ember and I were next to him. I saw him doing it right."

Dilin dropped his hand and frowned at her. "I'm only

trying to be helpful. They shouldn't give up, that's all I'm saying."

"Well, what if Vortex isn't a red?" Bree chimed in, stroking her sleeping dragon's wings. "He could be a blue or a yellow. If he isn't a red, no matter how hard he tries, he won't be able to make a flame."

"Does it matter?" Timmin asked. "The elemental attacks are for fighting swarmers. But the swarmers are gone."

"They're for the dragon games too." Dilin shrugged, then looked at Will and Vortex. "But Vortex is fine the way he is, even if he can't make fire."

Rin scowled at Dilin. But before either could say anything else, Will excused himself and stood. He and Vortex made their way across the courtyard toward the dining hall.

"Now look what you did!" he heard Rin say as they walked away.

"What? What did I do?" Dilin protested.

Will didn't feel like being a part of that conversation anymore; not because he was angry at Dilin—he wasn't— But he didn't know how he felt about what happened in the training cavern.

He'd known the odds were against Vortex being a red dragon, but part of him had hoped that training with the red dragons would answer all their questions. He'd hoped that Vortex would produce at least a little flame. Or if he didn't produce flame, at least he'd do something to show what ability he had. Then they would know where they fit in among the dragon riders.

But after their lesson, it seemed like they had come away with more questions than answers.

Chapter Nine

When Will and Vortex wandered into the dining hall well before dinnertime, Will wasn't expecting anyone else to be there. Even though meat was always available for the dragons and light snacks for the riders, everyone usually waited until mealtimes to show up.

To his surprise, Anri was already sitting at the green table with Jade eating meat from a bucket at her feet.

Trouble scurried around Jade, twitching her fuzzy striped tail and snatching up any bits of meat that scattered to the floor.

Will grabbed a bucket of meat for Vortex and a steam bun for himself and joined her.

"Hello, Will," Anri greeted him. "How was your day?"

Will set his bucket on the floor, and Vortex immediately began gobbling up the meat. "I don't know." He sighed and ran a hand through his hair. "It didn't go how I expected, that's for sure."

"Really?" She cocked her head and a raised eyebrow.

"I thought I'd have some answers once Vortex started learning to use his powers. But now I only have more questions! If he's a red dragon, then why can't he breathe fire? If he's not a red, then why can he make smoke?"

Vortex paused to look up at Will with a blood-stained muzzle. *I really tried to make fire.*

"I know you did, pal. You did great. It just doesn't make sense what happened when you tried." He turned back to Anri and shrugged. "I don't want to give up, but I also don't want to make him keep trying to breathe fire if he isn't a red dragon."

"You shufflo-brained dope. Of course, he isn't a red dragon. Just look at him!"

Will blinked at the sharpness of her words and his mouth fell open.

"I don't know why you ever believed that nonsense about Vortex being a regular dragon. He obviously isn't. Don't you remember how different his egg was?" She gestured to Vortex and glared at Will.

"Are . . . Are you mad at me?"

She rolled her eyes and heaved a sigh. "You shouldn't try to make Vortex into something he isn't, that's all. He's not a red dragon."

"Well, at least the red dragon riders are friendly!" he

said, crossing his arms. "If you wanted us to go with you and the greens, maybe you should have invited us!"

Anri scoffed. "Now you think you belong with the greens?"

"Why not? Vortex is every bit as smart and strong as the green dragons."

"Most of the green riders are complete jerks! And the rest are at least half horrible. You don't know what it's like training with the greens!"

"So, what were you doing all day? Flapping wings and practicing takeoffs? It can't be that hard." Will knew he was baiting her, but he couldn't help it. He was sure that Vortex could learn to fly just as well as any green dragon. And he was also pretty sure Anri was trying to make it sound harder than it was.

Anri blew a dark strand of hair out of her face and turned back to her food with an irritated snort. "For the dragons, that's about right. Jade can stay in the air for a few wingbeats now." She nodded at her dragon. "But Joric is teaching the riders how to fight. We're starting with staves and spears. We'll be learning bows and arrows soon too."

Will's eyes widened. "Fight? He never said anything about that on the training ground!"

She lifted one shoulder in a half shrug. "Green riders use spears and bows in the dragon games. They . . . *We* used to fight swarmers with long weapons and shoot poison-tipped arrows at them. It's traditional for green riders to be skilled fighters. Even with swords. Joric says we have to learn early if we want to be any good.

"That . . . sounds really cool," Will said.

Anri rolled her eyes and rubbed her ribs with her hand, as though massaging a bruise. "If you say so."

The clacking of riding boots striking the stone made them turn. Aleri, the blue instructor, strode into the dining hall, aiming right for their table.

"Ah, I've found you," she said, walking up to Will. "Tumi told me what happened during training today." Her expression was almost neutral except for the slight lift of her brow and quirk of her mouth. "I'm very intrigued. Making steam in the heart of Fire Mountain. That sounds like what would happen if a blue dragon tried to make ice in there." Her gaze shifted to Vortex, who was licking the last meaty drippings from his bucket.

"I believe it's possible that your dragon was trying to breathe frost. In the hot air of the training cavern, weak frost breath could easily have melted into vapor."

"Really?" Will's heart leaped, and he jumped to his feet.

Vortex flapped his wings in surprise.

"Do you think Vortex could be a blue? No wonder he couldn't breathe fire! That's like the opposite of making ice!"

"We won't know until we try," Aleri said, "but I believe

there's a chance he's a blue. Would you consider joining us for ice training tomorrow?"

"Yes! That'd be awesome!" Will rubbed Vortex's head. "Hear that, buddy? You might be able to make frost breath!"

Vortex gave a happy chirp and hopped on his front legs. *I would like that!*

"In that case, we'll see you on the training spire bright and early tomorrow morning," Aleri said with a satisfied nod.

Will sat back down next to Anri as Aleri marched out of the dining hall, boots echoing on the hard floor.

"Wow, isn't that great news? Vortex might have been making frost breath the whole time!"

Anri shrugged and took a silent bite of her steam bun.

"If he's a blue, it's no wonder he couldn't make ice in the Fire Mountain training cavern. It was just too hot in there!" Will laughed weakly. It made perfect sense! Of course a blue dragon would have trouble making ice in the heat of Fire Mountain. Vortex would be able to fit in after all!

Anri shook her head.

"What? What is it?"

"You just don't get it," Anri muttered.

THE NEXT MORNING, Will and Vortex woke early to join the blue wing on their way to training. They weren't as outgoing as the kids in the red wing, but they were interested in learning about Vortex and hearing what had happened in his attempt to breathe fire. As they walked along the winding trail up the rocky spire, Jayda and Beck plied him with questions the entire time. Did Vortex make steam or smoke? Did the mist feel cold or hot? How did the mist smell? Had he shown signs of other abilities? And a hundred more questions, some of which Will couldn't even answer.

When they reached the top of the spire, an entirely new world greeted them. A brisk wind blew right through their hair and clothes and made Will shiver. His nose, ears, and cheeks were quickly chilled, but in a way, it felt exhilarating. Especially after spending the previous day in the red dragon training cavern, where the temperature was scorching hot.

From their high vantage point, they had a panoramic view of snow-capped mountains all around. The hot valley of the dragonhold, hazy and small, nestled in the distance below them.

A sudden gust of wind whipped over the ground as they gathered on the peak. Vortex stretched out his wings instinctively, and the wind snapped them open, nearly knocking him over.

"Careful, pal!" Will grabbed his dragon and pushed his wings flat. "You don't want to get blown away, do you?"

I like the wind. It makes me want to fly.

"Okay, so maybe you do want the wind to blow you away. But it's a long way down from here, isn't it?" He glanced down the side of the mountain.

"We come up here because it's cold," Beck said, patting down his own dragon's wings. Icicle also kept lifting them to catch the wind. Apparently, Vortex wasn't the only one who wanted to fly. "Aleri says the cold air helps our dragons make frost easier. See?" He gestured to the ground where dozens of icy patches dotted the dirt.

The sight of ice on the ground surprised Will. Was it that cold? It felt chilly, but not cold enough for the ground to be frozen. He wasn't even wearing a coat.

"It's nice to be out of the heat," Jayda said, "but I wish we didn't have to climb up this mountain every day."

The others nodded in agreement as they arranged themselves on the level ground at the top of the spire. There was more than enough space for them all to fit comfortably while being nowhere near the edge.

Once they'd all taken their positions, a gigantic figure soared over their heads, blocking out the sun in a silent flash. A moment later, a massive blue dragon landed in a flurry of swirling, chilly wind. It was Aleri's dragon, Cobalt.

"Good morning, students." Aleri slid down Cobalt's

shoulder and tugged off her riding gloves. "Will, I'm glad to see that you and Vortex joined us today." She dipped her head in his direction.

"Yeah, thanks for inviting us," Will said. "If there's any chance Vortex is a blue dragon, I want to know."

"Of course." She nodded and turned to the blue riders. "Since the rest of your dragons have already learned the basics, I'll have you spend some time practicing frost breath. I want your dragons to work on making frost with every attempt. And Will, Cobalt and I will be working with you and Vortex."

Will pushed back his shoulders and nodded. He knew Vortex would try his hardest. They wouldn't waste this opportunity.

While the young blue dragons spaced themselves out on the peak and started breathing small clouds of frost, Aleri guided Will and Vortex to a little outcrop overlooking the northern peaks.

"This will do just fine," she said as Vortex perched on the raised stone. "Now, I don't know what Tumi taught you about fire breathing, but from my understanding, the mechanics are similar for frost breath. Tell me what you've learned so far and we'll work from there."

"Okay." Will rubbed his neck, trying to remember. "Tumi told the dragons to clench the muscles around their fire sacs. He said they should be able to taste the fire, but Vortex only tasted water."

Aleri pursed her lips and nodded. "I see. Why don't you have him show me?"

Will turned to his dragon. "Vortex, show Aleri what happens when you try to breathe fire."

Vortex lifted is head and swallowed. Then he braced himself, aimed his snout over the edge of the drop off, sucked in a breath, and opened his mouth wide.

Chapter Ten

A cloud of vapor sprang from between Vortex's teeth. The cold mist swirled and drifted away in the wind, then the dragon looked back at Will and Cobalt expectantly.

"That was a good try, buddy," Will said, stifling his disappointment, then turned to Aleri. "Could that be frost breath?"

The blue rider frowned, rubbing her chin. "I'm not sure. It may be, with some focus and practice."

"What do you mean?" Will clenched his fists in frustration. Her answer was much too close to how Tumi had reacted to the smoky mist in the red training cavern. Couldn't anyone give him a straight answer? "Is Vortex a blue dragon or not?"

"I don't know. We'll need more information. From

what I've seen, it seems possible that your dragon has an ice lung, as all blue dragons do."

"An ice lung?"

"It's an organ that stores water and a chemical mixture that super-cools for attack. Vortex appears to have the water needed for ice attacks. If he's a blue, he should be able to chill that water so it freezes on contact with his targets."

"So the mist is a good sign." Will chuckled weakly and ran his fingers through his hair. "You hear that, Vortex? You might be a blue after all."

Vortex chirped and swished his tail.

"Try again," Aleri said. "This time, try to feel for your ice lung. Make the mist as cold as you can before you breathe frost."

Vortex braced himself, took a breath, and spewed out another cloud of mist.

Aleri pursed her lips and tapped a finger against her chin.

Cobalt stretched out his neck and sniffed the air over the dissipating cloud.

Aleri turned to her dragon and nodded. "I agree. It smells a bit smoky."

"Try again, Vortex." Will clenched his fists. This had to work. "Try really hard to make it cold!"

Vortex ran his tongue along his teeth and took a deep

breath before trying a third time. Then a fourth. Then a fifth.

Each time he attempted to breathe frost, a stream of smoky mist spewed from his mouth, dissipating in the wind.

Will glanced around at the other blue dragons. When they breathed frost, sharp white streams of ice spewed from their mouths, scattering flurries of snow that encased the rocks before them in layers of hard ice.

"Can he feel his ice lung?" Aleri asked. "It should feel like a cold lump behind his stomach."

Will turned a hopeful gaze to his dragon. "Do you feel anything like that?"

Vortex's nose dipped. *No. I don't feel anything cold inside me at all.*

Will sighed and shook his head, folding his arms across his chest. "He says no."

"I think it's impressive, though," Beck called from where he and his dragon were practicing a short walk away. "I asked Icicle if he could make steam the way Vortex does, and he says he can't get his frost breath warm enough."

"That is interesting," Aleri said, pursing her lips and nodding. Then she turned to her dragon. "What about you, Cobalt? Can you make steam like Vortex?"

Everyone stopped to watch as Cobalt tilted his head and flicked an ear. Then the massive dragon turned away from them, opened his mouth, and blasted a flurry of damp, freezing wind. The swirling moisture struck the ground and froze solid, leaving a slick patch of hard ice.

The blue dragon sniffed the ground and tapped the ice with a claw, giving a disgruntled rumble.

A few of the other kids chuckled and grinned at one another.

Aleri smiled and gave the dragon's leg a gentle pat. "Don't worry. It was only an experiment."

This was all very interesting to the blue riders, but Will felt like they were getting off the point. Was his dragon nothing but an interesting puzzle for them to figure out?

Will rubbed his hands over his face. "So, does this mean Vortex isn't a blue dragon?"

"We haven't learned anything definitive yet," Aleri assured him. "All this means is that producing mist, the way Vortex does, isn't something all blue dragons can do. But we already knew that Vortex is unique. He may be unique in more ways than we thought."

"What if he's a new kind of dragon?" Jayda asked. "He could be a steam dragon!"

"I don't think so," Liza said. "I agree with the dragonlords. It's more likely that he's a regular color but with some kind of defect."

"But any dragon color could look like a defect if there's only one of that kind of dragon," Jayda countered.

"That is true," Aleri agreed. "But the fact that he is the only one of his kind is evidence for his having a genetic mutation. Even so, he could teach us a great deal about all dragons."

The others went on discussing the evidence for Vortex being a unique dragon versus being some sort of mutant. To Will, it felt like they were going through some sort of intellectual exercise. Everyone said whatever they were thinking without caring how their opinions might affect him or Vortex. They weren't trying to be insulting, but that didn't stop Will from feeling insulted.

For the rest of the day, Vortex practiced making frost breath with the blue wing, only managing to make clouds of white or smoky steam.

The sun was setting as they made their way back to the barracks. After being out in the freezing wind all day, Will's cheeks were red and his lips chapped, and the dry warmth of Fire Mountain Dragonhold felt more intense And after hiking all the way up and down the mountain spire, he and Vortex were both exhausted.

"Hi, Will! Hi, Vortex!" Corin greeted them when they entered the barracks.

Will tossed his jacket onto his trunk and flopped down on his cot. "Hi Corin. Boy, am I beat."

Vortex dropped to the ground next to him with a weary sigh.

Corin jumped off his cot and bounded across the room to them, Leika bouncing along at his heels.

"You two went to the blue dragon training today, didn't you?"

"Yeah," Will said, struggling to tug off his sweaty tunic without having to sit up. "I thought Vortex would be able to make frost breath. It didn't work out." He reached out to scratch behind his dragon's ears.

"Well . . ." Corin sat on the edge of Will's cot and grinned. "Since you tried the red wing, and you tried the blue wing, why don't you come with Leika and me to yellow training tomorrow?"

Will paused and raised an eyebrow at the other boy. "To the yellow training? You think Vortex is a yellow?"

Corin laughed. "How should I know? But I bet you'll like it."

Leika chirped, eyes sparkling at Vortex.

Leika says yellow training is a lot of fun, Vortex said.

Will sat up and tossed the tunic into his pile of dirty laundry. "But . . . what if he can't make electricity?"

"So what? It'll still be fun. You know, when we found out the greens were going to learn how to fly, I thought we were getting the short end of the stick. But wow, was I wrong. We all were." He gave Will a friendly punch on the arm. "Come on. You have to at least try. You and Vortex will love it, I promise."

Will rubbed his hands over his face before grabbing a

bar of soap and tossing his towel over his shoulder. "What do you all do that's so much fun?" he asked.

Corin grinned and shook his head, wagging a finger at him. "That would spoil the surprise."

Will snorted and grinned back. "You jerk! You won't tell me because you think I'll come just to find out what it is."

Corin laughed. "All right. You got me. But it's working, isn't it?"

Will stood and stretched his back. "Ugh, all right, I guess. We might as well try. It won't do any good to keep going to the red and blue lessons, anyway."

"That's the spirit!" Corin said, smacking Will's back. Noticing the sweat on his palm, he wiped his hand on his trouser leg with a mildly grossed-out expression.

"I'm going to take Vortex and get a bath in before bed. Did you know the blues have to climb a whole freaking mountain to do their training? All the way to the top where there's snow on the ground."

"Swarms! No wonder you're beat. I'm glad Leika's not a blue!"

The bathing spring was tucked away at the end of a long tunnel that ran under the barracks. The air in the corridor smelled of smoky incense, and the passage was wide enough for adult dragons to walk through. Flaming sconces lined the walls on either side, shining with flickering orange light that gave it a mysterious and medieval look, even on the sunniest days.

When they reached the bottom, the tunnel opened to deep frothing water just right for bathing a dragon. Vortex jumped into the warm pool, his wings billowing as he flip-flopped underwater. He came up for air and looked around excitedly before diving down again to enjoy himself in the steaming bath.

Chuckling, Will jumped into the deep end with a splash and came up sputtering. "I've got enough soap for both of us. Do you need me to scrub your hide for you?"

Vortex surfaced and sprayed water from his nose disdainfully. *I am not dirty.*

"Are you sure about that?" Will smirked. "I thought I saw some dirt behind your ears."

Vortex shook his head like a dog, spraying water droplets around the pool, and swiveled his neck around in a fruitless attempt to see the back of his own head. *I don't see any dirt. Where?*

"Right . . . THERE!" Will jumped on his dragon, attacking him with the sudsy bar of soap and scrubbing the back of his head before he could squirm away.

Vortex squealed a dragon-laugh, sputtering and flailing as he tried to escape the soapy attack.

Will hooked his arm around Vortex's neck, avoiding his dragon's delicate wing membranes, and scrubbed all the hard-to-reach areas as quick as he could. Vortex grumbled and bucked and splashed halfheartedly the whole time.

"Well, isn't this a heartwarming sight?" a sneering voice echoed through the bathing chamber.

Will released his dragon, and they both looked up to see Albin and Snakebite standing at the edge of the pool with a few other green riders and their dragons.

Will stood up, water streaming from his hair and dripping from his nose and ears. "What are you doing here?" The moment the words were out of his mouth, he realized how stupid the question was. All the other boys were wearing only their undershorts and carrying towels, bathrobes, and soap. Of course, they were here to bathe, just like he was.

"What does it look like we're doing, shoveling dragon apples?" Albin asked, laughing. The other kids laughed with him.

Will's face grew hot with embarrassment and Vortex nudged his arm encouragingly.

"Learning to fly is dusty work, isn't it?" Albin patted Snakebite's head. "But you wouldn't know anything about that, would you, off-lander?" He said the word off-lander as though it was a nasty subject no civilized person would want to talk about.

"Vortex will learn to fly," Will said firmly, wishing he were strong enough to just ignore these jerks.

The rest of the green riders walked around the room,

draping their towels and bathrobes over the stone benches as they prepared to enter the pool.

"That little freak?" Albin asked with a disgusted snort. "That'll be all he ever learns. And he'll never be as good at flying as a green."

Will clenched his fists under the water, jaw tight as he fought the urge to climb out of the pool and teach Albin a lesson he wouldn't forget.

The other boy reached out and stroked Snakebite's horn nubs. "But there is something I wanted to talk to you about."

"Yeah? What's that?" Will asked, grinding his teeth.

"I heard that you've been joining all the different dragon wings. You've been in the red wing, the blue today, and tomorrow you're joining the yellow wing for their lesson."

"So? What about it?"

Albin patted Snakebite on the head one more time, then gestured to the water. The young green dragon leaped into the air, flapping his wings. He soared over Will and Vortex's heads and splashed into the water at the deep end of the pool.

As if on cue, all the other greens followed his example, jumping into the air, flapping their wings as they soared over Will and Vortex, sending down gusts of wind before diving into the water all around them.

Vortex squawked and lifted his wings, not quite fast

enough to shield himself from the onslaught of splashing water.

Albin crouched down at the edge of the pool to look Will in the eyes. "Your dragon will never be as good as a green. Stay out of our wing if you know what's good for you. Nobody wants you there."

Will glared back, jaw still tight with anger. "Believe it or not, Albin, you don't get to tell me and Vortex what classes we can take. But don't worry, if we join the green wing, it won't be because I think you want us there. Come on, Vortex. I think we're done with our bath now."

He marched out of the pool, threw his towel around himself, and made his way back up the passage, Vortex following behind him.

"You're a fool if you do!" Albin called, his voice echoing in the cavernous tunnel. "I'll make sure you regret it!"

Chapter Eleven

Will marched onward through the firelit tunnel, not looking back. Uncertainty and concern flowed through Vortex's mind like a wave; it was clear that his dragon did not understand what was wrong, but he could tell that Will was upset.

When they reached the courtyard, he turned to Vortex, lifting his dragon's chin with one hand. "Listen. You are as good as any green in this place. The only reason they can fly at all is because they've been practicing."

I don't care about that, Vortex said. His thoughts were meek and hesitant. *I just want you to be happy.*

Will took a steadying breath. "I know, it's just . . ." He stopped and gritted his teeth, frustrated that his thoughts weren't forming into words the way he wanted them to. "I wish everyone could see how amazing you are, the way I do."

Vortex butted his head against Will's chest, and Will wrapped his arms around his dragon's warm neck and rubbed his soft ears and budding horns.

"All right." Will cleared his throat. "We should get some sleep. We've got a big day learning with the yellow wing tomorrow."

Vortex trilled and followed Will back to the barracks.

WILL and Vortex joined the yellow wing for breakfast. There were five yellows in the hatching, and after Corin's introductions, Will did his best to keep their riders' names straight.

Sipping mugs of hot creamy kaffa, they chattered about the coming day's lesson. But to Will's frustration, they refused to give him any details about what they actually did in their classes, talking vaguely and side-eyeing him and Vortex with mysterious grins whenever he asked for details.

"I bet Goldwing and I will make the fastest run today!" a boy named Tato boasted. "I've got a plan that'll cut our time in—"

"That's what you said yesterday!" Corin laughed. "Leika and I still beat you every time!"

"Okay, but this time we're going to—"

Will leaned in to listen, holding his breath in anticipation. Finally, he'd figure out the yellow wing's secret.

But a girl swatted the other boy before he could finish his boast and hissed, "Hush! Don't give it away!"

Will rolled his eyes and groaned in disappointment.

The girl's yellow flapling, bright enough almost to be called orange, lifted her nose with half-closed eyelids in a smug expression.

The girl, Will thought her name was Vala, gave him an apologetic smile. "Tato just gets excited, you know. He doesn't mean to spoil the surprise."

Will shrugged and gave her a wry grin. "I don't mind. Vortex and I are curious about what the lessons are like. Leika says you have a lot of fun. We're excited to try it, right, buddy?" He glanced back at Vortex, who was still stuffing his mouth with gobs of meat.

The little dragon lifted his head with a sharp-toothed grin. *Yes. Whatever they do, it must be fun. Leika is excited to go back.*

"You will have fun. I know that much." Vala grinned, then turned back to the rest of the yellow wing as they continued chatting about the day's lesson.

Will sat back and took a long drink from his mug of kaffa, savoring the sweet creamy flavor as he listened to their chatter. If he and Vortex ever made it back to Florida, he'd have to bring kaffa seeds with him. Aside from his dragon, kaffa was one thing he wouldn't want to leave Avria without.

After breakfast, the group headed through the courtyard and around the mountain to a hidden trail that Will had never noticed before. The downhill trek wound on a wide gravelly path between rocky hills, past trees with thin prickly needles, and boulders left behind by ancient mudslides. Finally reaching the end of the trail, they came upon a rolling hillside with thick, dry grass covering the ground. The golden, grassy landscape was only interrupted by the occasional pine tree and fallen log.

Slick trails ran down the length of the hillside where something had pressed into the grass, sliding down to where the ground leveled out far below.

As they approached the hilltop, a large, yellow dragon soared overhead. Circling around, the dragon landed and folded its wings, revealing a rider perched on its neck. It was Gwin and Freefall.

"Good morning, young riders!" Gwin called. "I hope nobody filled their stomachs too much at breakfast. We don't want a repeat of what happened the first day!"

Most of the kids laughed.

Corin's face went beet red. "You guys will never let me forget that, will you?" Then he joined in the laughter and rubbed his hands through his blonde hair.

"What's she talking about?" Will asked under his breath.

Corin's eyes shifted around, face still flaming red. "Well, I ate a big breakfast that first day, you know? With all the bouncing and everything, I just couldn't keep it down."

Will raised his eyebrows and pursed his lips, trying hard not to laugh at his friend.

"It doesn't matter," Corin said, wrapping an arm around Leika's neck. "It was still a blast and a half. You'll see. I can't wait to go again!"

"I trust nobody's spoiled the surprise for Will and Vortex." Gwin slid down from her perch on Freefall's neck with a bundle of brown cloth under one arm.

"No!" the kids cheered, nudging each other and grinning at Will. Even their dragons looked excited.

"Excellent!" Gwin stepped up to Will and gripped his shoulder in a friendly shake. "In that case, Will and Vortex will be first today."

Will choked out a startled laugh, looking wildly around for help.

All the other kids just grinned at him.

"W-what? Us? I don't even know what we're doing!"

"That's the whole point," Gwin said with an amused smile. "Come on. Nobody's going to hurt you." She led the way to where the grassy hill sloped into one of the slick paths.

Biting his lip, Will stepped up to the edge with Vortex at his heels.

Gwin unrolled the cloth, which looked like burlap, and spread it over the flattened grass like a blanket.

"Vortex, please lay flat on this cloth, if you will."

Vortex did as he was told, crouching on the thick fabric with his legs tucked under his body.

"Now, Will, climb onto your dragon's shoulders. Right behind his neck, as though you're preparing to fly together. Be careful of his wings."

Will stretched one leg over Vortex's neck and rested his weight on his dragon's shoulders. "I'm not too heavy, am I?"

No. You're not too heavy, Vortex said, giving a little shrug.

"Of course not," Gwin said, smiling at him. "He can't fly with you yet, of course, but this won't be too much for him. Now, do you see the trails in the grass?" She waved a hand down the hill.

Will licked his lips and nodded. "Yeah."

"This sheet will slide down the grass like a hot blade through butter. Your dragon rides the sheet, and you ride your dragon. Make it to the bottom as fast as you can." The corner of her mouth pulled up and her eyes twinkled. "Then zap the copper wire strung over the finish line."

"Z-zap? With electricity? How does he do that?"

"I can't tell you that." Gwin shrugged nonchalantly. "Nobody can tell a yellow dragon how to make electricity.

It's just something they know how to do, especially when they're having fun."

"Okay, but—"

"No more talking. Now go!" Gwin placed her hands on Vortex's rump and gave him a quick shove.

They plunged down the hill. Will yelped in surprise and clung to Vortex's neck as the crackling dry grass whooshed past them. The sudden drop made him feel like his stomach had launched into his throat.

Vortex squealed and tightened his wings against his sides. All the muscles in his body tensed.

"It's okay, buddy. We're going to be fine," Will panted, trying to comfort his dragon while his own heart pounded in his chest.

The ground zipped under them at blinding speed. Mounds of earth rushed forward like waves on a stormy sea.

Will tried to get his bearings. Tried to see where the slick grassy trail was taking them.

This isn't scary. This is fun! Vortex said, letting out a jubilant bugle.

Just like that, everything shifted in Will's mind.

This wasn't a death-defying plummet down a mountainside. This was mountain biking!

Back when Will and his family lived in the off-lands, he used to enjoy taking his Trailcraft bike out to the biking trails every chance he got, hurtling down hills and jumping over obstacles, zipping back and forth between trees mere inches from splatting against their trunks in utter annihilation.

Even though biking had landed him in the ER a few times, it had been worth it to feel the sensation of flying downhill with the wind in his ears, riding his own personal rollercoaster.

This hill was no different. The trail stretched out before them, twisting here and there. It split off at the turn of a hill, ran through a gap jump, and merged again later on.

You're right. It is fun! Will thought, laughing. *Try this. Lean to the right at the turn!*

Vortex shifted his weight as they rounded the bend, and they broke off onto the alternate path.

The trail dropped sharply, and they flew over the ground toward a distant grove of scraggly trees.

"Woo hoo!" Will whooped as they hurtled over the jump.

Vortex squawked midair and gripped the sheet in his claws to keep it under him.

They landed farther down the slope, twisting around smaller hills as they entered the grove. Trees flashed past, blurring into vague brown and green smudges at the edge of Will's vision.

The trail narrowed, and the grass thinned, but they were still going fast. Too fast. The turns were now too sharp to rely on momentum to carry them where they were supposed to go.

Lean left! Will thought. *Now right! Right again!*

Vortex did his best to follow Will's directions. They rushed past obstacles, narrowly missing sharp rocks and roots. An overgrown branch lashed against Will's cheek, stinging like a whip.

Will didn't have time to wonder why the trail was getting so deadly. Gwin didn't seem like the kind of teacher who would try to kill one of her students. And Corin never said anything about training being dangerous before. For now, all he could do was watch the trail ahead and hope he had time to tell Vortex what to do before they splattered against a tree.

As they careened around another turn, Will noticed a tree had fallen over the trail. One broken branch jutted out right at them like a spear. If they didn't do something fast, the branch would skewer Vortex for sure. But if they jumped off the trail, they'd land on a jagged hillside covered in sharp rocks and spiky trees.

Seeing the broken branch at the same time as Will, Vortex reared his head back in alarm.

We have to jump for it! Will said.

Jump!? Vortex thought back, panic laced through the word.

You have to! Vortex, jump now!

Vortex made a half-strangled cry of terror just as they

reached the branch and kicked off the ground as hard as he could.

As they sailed over the fallen tree, time seemed to slow down. Vortex's talons skimmed the dead branches. His white tail barely cleared the splintered wood.

Then Vortex spread his wings, and the creamy white sails stretched wide, catching shafts of warm sunlight.

Will's breath caught in his throat. His eyes widened in alarm. Before he could say anything, Vortex beat the air once . . . twice . . . three times, slowing their descent.

They hit the ground on the far side of the tree, tumbled and crashed to a stop among a clump of thorny bushes.

"Ow!" Will groaned. His head was spinning, and thorns dug into the skin of his arms and face. He blinked and realized that he couldn't see his dragon anywhere. "Wait, Vortex? Vortex! Are you okay? Talk to me!" He scrambled to his feet, yanking thorny branches off his arms and giving himself deep bleeding scratches in the process. He couldn't even feel them past the adrenaline surging through his veins.

The bushes in a nearby thicket rustled along with the sound of a frustrated and grumpy dragon growl. *There are thorns in my tail.*

Will crawled through the thick bushes, earning more scratches on his arms and neck, until he found Vortex, who was struggling to remove the thorny vines clinging to his tail and hind legs.

"Hold on, pal. I got you. Just hold still or you'll make it worse."

You're bleeding! Vortex said, twisting his neck around to watch as Will untangled the thorns from his rear end.

"I'll be fine. They're just scratches." Will grimaced as he unwound a thorny branch from his dragon's foot.

The scratches on his cheeks were starting to throb and burn like they'd been branded into his skin with hot irons.

A sudden gust of wind flattened the grass and bushes on the lower slope. The next moment, the huge yellow form of Freefall touched down on the hillside, clutching the earth with his talons and fluttering his unfurled wings.

Gwin launched herself off her dragon's shoulders and scrambled through the bushes to meet them, face pale and eyes wide. "Will! Vortex! Are you okay? Stinging swarms, you're hurt!" She unbuttoned her belt bag and pulled out a jar of salve and a roll of bandages.

"I'll be fine. They're just scratches," Will said, pulling the last thorny vine free from Vortex's tail. "And thank goodness Vortex didn't get hurt too bad, just tangled up." Then something occurred to him, and he turned to face Gwin with a fierce scowl. "If the trail was so dangerous, why'd you send us down it at all? We could've been killed!"

Gwin paused with her hand in the salve jar, eyes widening even more. "That wasn't supposed to happen!"

He frowned at her and eyed the thin scratches on

Vortex's legs and tail. Pale blood oozed onto his dragon's creamy white skin. "We could've been skewered on that broken tree branch." He waved an arm up the trail. "Now my dragon is bleeding, and all you can say is it wasn't supposed to happen?"

You're bleeding more than I am, Vortex said with a worried whine.

Gwin hurried to apply salve to all of Vortex's scratches. She seemed to understand that Will wouldn't accept any treatment for himself if his dragon hadn't been seen to first.

As Vortex flinched under her gentle touch, she shook her head with a sigh. "Will, I swear by the White Dragon you were never supposed to come down this trail."

"This is the trail you sent us down!"

"The grass slide is supposed to turn left at the second hill and lead to the finish line. Nobody ever turns off the trail. I didn't think you would even know how to!"

Will wiped a trickle of blood from his forehead and opened his mouth to argue some more, then he stopped. After a moment, he said, "We veered off to the right. You mean this isn't part of the same trail?"

"It's part of the same network, but this is a more advanced slide. We won't start playing on this one for months yet. And only after Freefall and I go over it to make sure it's safe."

Will stretched out a hand to caress Vortex's velvety soft ear.

His dragon leaned into the touch and rumbled as Gwin finished applying salve to the last of his cuts.

When Gwin finally started smearing the burning medicine over the scratches on Will's face, she sighed and shook her head. "I'm sorry this happened, Will. It's my first year doing flapling training. Maybe I wasn't ready for it."

Will winced, but not because of the burning medicine. Maybe he was the one who'd gotten carried away. Nobody told him to leave the main path, he'd decided to do that on his own. He'd just assumed that everything would be fine without thinking it through first. "I think maybe this was my fault."

She gave him a wry, unconvinced smile. "But you know what? From what Freefall and I saw, Vortex is going to be an amazing flier."

Chapter Twelve

"You saw that? I almost thought I imagined it. He really did almost fly, didn't he?" Will glanced at Vortex, eyeing his dragon's loosely folded wings. He remembered how they'd snapped open, catching the wind. Even though his dragon was still far too small to carry his weight in flight, he'd felt the power behind those wingbeats.

Gwin finished wrapping a bandage around his bleeding arm and stood back, gazing at Vortex with her hands on her hips and a proud smile. "Yes, Freefall and I saw how the two of you hurtled that fallen tree. Vortex showed very good reflexes and nice form, especially for his first time." Her gaze flashed to Will, and she arched her eyebrows. "That was the first time, wasn't it?"

"Yeah! Of course! I mean, he's been flapping his wings every day, like all the others, but he's never tried flying before. Tumi said it's dangerous for them to practice flying before they're big enough."

Gwin eyed him with wry suspicion for a moment, then nodded and chuckled. "A lot of yellow flaplings decide to start flying early in secret. The temptation is just too great. And our dragons won't stop begging for the chance to try." She rolled her eyes at Freefall.

The big yellow dragon rumbled in his chest and blew out a puff of air.

"That's right. You are a bad influence on me!" Gwin said, playfully smacking her dragon's leg.

"The yellow flaplings learn to fly early, too?" Will wondered if Corin had been taking Leika out to practice flying when nobody was watching.

"Not officially, because it really is dangerous," Gwin said, wrapping a new bandage around Will's hand. "Tumi is right about that. Some dragons have died because they pushed themselves too hard. Straining a wing muscle at high elevation. Poor judgement flying past obstacles. Misreading a change in the wind. Any of these things can lead to disaster." Her voice was low, somber. But then her mouth quirked up at the corner. She secured the last bandage and leaned back with a grin. "But yellow dragons and their riders usually dismiss danger in the face of great adventure."

"Well, we don't! I mean didn't. I mean . . . Vortex hasn't been flying in secret. He really wants to, but I couldn't let him risk it!" Now that he thought of it, though, if all the greens and most of the yellows were practicing, that meant that more than half the flaplings were learning to fly already. It didn't seem fair at all.

Vortex tilted his head, swiveling his ears as he listened to Will's train of thought.

Gwin pursed her lips and shrugged, her expression slightly disappointed. "Perhaps not. In that case, Vortex might just be naturally gifted at flying. He managed that hurdle with the form and strength of a dragon twice his age."

Will couldn't help but smile proudly at Vortex. Vortex lifted his head and shuffled his wings happily.

"So, do you want to try the slide again?" Gwin asked with a crooked grin. "You might make it to the finish line this time."

They made it back uphill without any problems. The other kids exclaimed in alarm and admiration when they reached the top again.

"We thought you fell off the mountain!" Corin laughed, gripping Will's shoulders and giving him a shake.

"Nah. I did that once before. It's not as fun as it sounds," Will joked, waving his hand dismissively.

The rest of the kids laughed or rolled their eyes in disbelief.

Will shrugged. Anri would have gotten the joke. But of

course, Anri would have scowled at him for making the joke too.

Will watched as the other kids took their turns sliding down the hillside. Each dragon, saddled with a rider, crouched on a burlap sheet and whisked down the slippery grass hill.

"Are you ready to try again?" Gwin asked.

Vortex looked anxiously down the hill, studying how it steeply descended before leveling out into a grassy field. He glanced back up toward his rider with a nervously scrunched expression.

"What do you think about trying one more time?" Will asked, patting his head.

"You know," Gwin said gently, coming alongside the creamy white dragon. She continued in a soft voice that only Will and Vortex could hear, "they say if you fall off a cormant—then it's best to just get right back on."

I didn't fall off a cormant. I fell off the trail, Vortex said, looking at Will in confusion. *Cormants aren't scary. I eat them.*

Will chuckled. "What Gwin means is that if something scares you, it's best to try again right away. If you don't, you might go on being scared of it forever."

As Vortex gazed down the hill, the wind picked up, flowing over his wings and making his ears twitch. It seemed to give him courage, because a moment later, he shook his shoulders and lifted his head.

I will try again. I don't want to be afraid of hills forever.

Vortex crouched on the burlap sheet again. Will straddled his dragon's shoulders, fighting down his own nervousness, and then they were off.

It was easier this time, knowing what was coming. The dry grass whooshed under them, and the wind whistled in their ears as they slid through dips and turns and over hills. Vortex automatically leaned into the turns, but they stayed on the main path.

Will's skin prickled with electricity as they whisked over the ground. The hair on his arms and neck stood on end as the charge grew.

Together, they soared over a jump. Vortex squawked happily and tiny crackles of static zapped all around them as they landed on the far side.

"Yeah!" Will shouted. "That's what I'm talking about! It's fun, right?"

Vortex didn't answer, but Will could sense the fear and fun warring in his dragon's mind.

The end of the trail was fast approaching. At the bottom of the hill, the copper wire glinted in the sun over the finish line, and the yellow riders cheered them on.

"You can do it, Vortex!" Corin shouted, hands cupped over his mouth. "Hit the wire! Zap it!"

Next to him, Corin's dragon Leika reared back, fanning her yellow wings and bugling encouragement.

"You got this, buddy," Will said. "Go for it!"

Vortex braced himself, tensing his muscles and swaying his tail to keep his balance. He focused on the shining wire.

Just as they slid under it, he tapped the wire with his nose. There was a small flash and a popping sound, then they skidded to a halt among the others, breathless, giddy, and laughing.

"You did it!" Will shouted, clapping Vortex's neck. "I saw that! You made a spark!"

I did! I really did! Vortex trumpeted proudly and fanned his wings.

The other kids bustled around them, thumping Will's back and shouting praise. Their dragons warbled and chirped, playfully butting heads with Vortex.

"Look, hear come Tato and Goldwing!" Corin said, pointing up the hill.

Will could hear the whooshing sound of burlap sliding over the grass. He turned to see the pair riding down the grassy slope.

Goldwing held his wings slightly open and kept his legs in a half-crouched position, absorbing the bumps on the ground with his knees as they whisked down the hillside.

They veered right and left through the turns, around bends and over mounds. Tato whooped joyfully as they took a jump, sailed through the air, and landed on the downward slope of the next grassy mound.

"Go, Tato!" the other kids cheered. "You can do it, Goldwing! WOOHOO!"

Goldwing leaned into the final bend, taking the last hill at its steepest point and building immense speed.

Will and the rest backed up, clearing the area around the finish line.

As the pair made their final approach, Goldwing narrowed his eyes at the copper wire in concentration. He opened his mouth slightly and . . .

BAM!

While they were still a good ten feet away, a flash of white-hot electricity bolted from Goldwing's snout, shot through the air, and struck the wire. Tendrils of crackling electricity shimmered along the wire before arcing to the ground.

Tato and Goldwing skidded into the clearing. The rest of the kids jumped into the air and cheered as they rushed forward to surround them.

"Wow," Will breathed. His hair was still standing on end from the residual static of Goldwing's lightning bolt.

"That one was pretty good!" Corin said, thumping Tato's back. "Goldwing is getting pretty strong. But he's still not as strong as Leika."

"Oh, stuff it, Corin!" Tato said, grinning. "Goldwing could zap the claws off Leika, and you know it!"

"We'll believe it when we see it." Corin chuckled and draped an arm over Leika's neck. "You are faster today. I'll give you that much. Leika and I will have to work hard to keep ahead of you."

"Was . . . Was that what we were supposed to do?" Will asked. He blinked, still trying to get the shimmering purple afterimage of the lightning out of his vision.

"Nah, it's not really a race." Corin shrugged. "Trying to be the fastest just makes it more fun and gives us bragging rights. That's all. You don't have to try to beat anyone."

"No. Not that. I—I mean the lightning. I thought . . . I didn't know it was supposed to be . . . Wow!"

As he spoke, Freefall soared overhead and landed in the field beside them. Gwin slid down his shoulder and approached the group.

"Don't worry about it," Corin said with a crooked smile. "All our dragons had weak sparks at first. Maybe Vortex just needs some practice."

"Vortex did make a spark," Will said. "I saw it. You all did too. That means he must be a yellow, right?" He turned to look imploringly at Gwin.

She furrowed her brow at the ground, pressing her lips together like she didn't want to say something unpleasant. She took a breath before speaking. "The burlap you ride creates static electricity while it slides on the grass. A lot of electricity. When yellow dragons feel that charge, it helps them find their own electricity for the first time. That's why this is the first training exercise we use with yellow dragons."

Will's throat tightened. He had to swallow before he could speak again. "So, are you saying Vortex didn't make a spark after all?"

"All I'm saying is that I don't know. The static alone could generate a weak spark, but Vortex could have made some electricity too. You're both welcome to keep trying."

The rest of the kids joined in, encouraging them to try again. So Will and Vortex went down the hill again. And again. And again. Each time, Vortex struck the wire with a sharp crack of electricity, but it was nowhere near as bright or as loud as what the yellow dragons could produce.

After a while, they stopped and waited at the bottom of the hill, watching the others go through their runs, hoping to learn the secret of making a strong spark.

The yellow flaplings slid under the wire, shooting miniature bolts of lightning from five, ten, or even fifteen feet away. Crackling electricity flooded the field, shimmering in jumping arcs along the yellow dragons' wings and horn nubs as they strutted around, proud of their newfound powers.

Even though Shara and Rone looked smug sometimes, sauntering by after their dragons shot jolts of lightning that cracked through the air like fireworks, none of the yellow riders were actually mean to Will or Vortex. But Will was starting to feel distinctly out of place, and Vortex was disheartened as well. Though the class wasn't over yet, Will decided they were done with the experiment.

"Do you want to go back now?" he asked his dragon.

Yes. I'm hungry. Let's get some food.

Will chuckled. "You're always hungry. Where do you even put all that food?"

In my stomach, Vortex said matter-of-factly.

Will laughed again and rubbed his dragon's head. "You got me there. I'm hungry too. Let's get some lunch."

Nobody stopped them as they trudged back up the slopes toward the dragonhold. As they reached the top and turned down the trail that would lead home, Will heard a crackle and pop of electricity echoing over the hills, followed by a joyful whoop from Corin.

"So, what do you think, Vortex?" Will turned to his dragon. "Did it feel like you were making electricity? Or was it just static?"

Vortex wiggled his ears and cocked his head to the side. *I don't know. What does it feel like to make electricity?*

"Beats me." Will shrugged and tucked his thumbs into his belt. "I don't have a clue what it's supposed to feel like."

As they rounded the last bend that led toward the dragonhold, they passed by a wide alcove in the mountainside. The squawks of young dragons filled the air, mingled with booming shouts that sounded like they came from the green wing instructor, Joric.

"Hey, this must be where the greens are learning to

fly." Will and Vortex exchanged a look. Then, overcome with curiosity, they walked closer to listen.

"You can do better than that!" Joric barked. "Kick off harder. Don't open your wings until the top of your jump! Now try again!" The sharp commands echoed off the rocky walls, followed by the loud squawk of a young dragon.

Will nudged Vortex's shoulder with his elbow. "Want to get closer and watch?"

Vortex perked up and hopped on his front claws excitedly. *Yes! Let's watch!*

Together they crept along the wall, staying hidden behind rocky outcroppings and prickly bushes, until they came to a place where they had a good view of the green dragons and their riders.

Will froze and his jaw dropped.

Chapter Thirteen

The large oval-shaped area was lined with heavy boulders that had been pushed aside to make room for the greens and their riders. The space had to be at least as big as a football field.

The green riders were lined up in a neat row, each holding a wooden spear. Joric walked among them, giving instruction and correcting their grips with a stern expression on his face.

"Hold that spear in the middle. You've got to keep it balanced!" he shouted, stalking past the line of kids.

"But I have a longer reach when I hold it further back," one of them argued.

"When you're on dragonback, reach won't matter. What's a few inches when you're flying at speed? Holding it too far back throws the balance off. Your arm will get tired, and your aim will suffer. Now do it right!"

The boy shifted his hand to the correct position.

Joric marched down the line. When he reached the end, he turned and lifted his arm toward the mountaintop.

Vinna, Joric's dragon, perched on the cliffs overlooking the arena. Her claws clutched long ropes fastened to straw bales, each painted with a red bullseye.

At her rider's signal, the green dragon spread her wings and dropped off the wall, gliding down the cliff side with the straw bales trailing under her.

The kids clutched their spears, preparing to strike.

As Vinna passed overhead, the kids stabbed at the straw bales, aiming for the red targets.

Some might as well have been blindfolded and flailing sticks at a piñata. Others struck the tightly bound straw, only to have their spears rebound uselessly. But one boy, it looked like Albin, became so focused he didn't notice when his weapon stuck fast in the red center. Vinna soared past, and the spear wrenched itself free of the boy's grip.

He yelled in pain, shaking out his fingers and squeezing his hand against his belly.

Joric marched over to him. "Don't forget to rotate your spear as the target passes. Like this." He held out his own spear in demonstration, twisting the point around his body so an imaginary target would slide right off. "In the dragon games, a mistake like that could cost your victory, and maybe break your hand. But at least you hit the target." He turned to the other kids. "Unlike the rest of you!"

Continuing down the line, Joric snapped instructions to the rest of the green riders, telling one to strike harder, another to stop swinging the stick as though it was a rug beater, and another to try changing hands. Anri stood among them, listening intently.

At the far end of the field, the young green dragons were gathered together. Their practice didn't seem to be quite as organized as the instruction their riders were getting. They were taking turns stretching out their wings, jumping into the air, and flapping a few times before gliding to the ground with clumsy landings.

Now and then, one of the greens would put in a little extra effort to gain some altitude before making a slow descent.

"Look at that. They really are learning to fly," Will murmured.

Vortex gave a soft rumble.

As they watched, Jade jumped, flapped her wings, then dropped too hard on her right side. The awkward landing caused her to roll onto her wing, and she squawked in protest.

Anri shot a worried glance across the field, but her dragon righted herself quickly and tried again.

"They aren't learning any elemental powers. Just fighting and flying," Will said.

I could do that. I could learn to fly, Vortex said.

After what had happened at yellow training, Will was

certain that Vortex was right. He could probably glide through the air better than a lot of those greens.

He was also sure that hitting targets with a spear wouldn't be too difficult to learn. He could stab a bale of straw just as well as any of those other kids.

He ran a hand down Vortex's neck and gave his shoulder a pat. "Well, we haven't had any luck with the other classes. We might as well try joining these guys. What do you think?"

You'll let me learn to fly? Vortex asked, excitement bubbling up in his mind. His wings trembled, as though itching to open up to the wind.

"Promise to be careful?" Will aimed a solemn finger at his dragon's nose. "I don't want you showing off and getting yourself hurt, got it?"

I will be careful! I promise I will! I'll be so careful, and I won't get hurt! The thoughts were paired with a high-pitched whine of eagerness as Vortex shuffled his feet and curled his tail, lowering his head pleadingly.

Will shook his head and snorted, grinning. "All right, all right. You don't have to lay it on so thick." He rubbed Vortex's nose and his dragon rumbled happily.

Later that night, Corin sauntered into the barracks, dusty from training and with little specks of grass clinging to his tunic. "Why'd you leave so early?" He asked, flopping next to Will on his cot. "I thought you and Vortex were having fun!" Behind him Leika crawled over to her bed of springy straw. She looked thoroughly exhausted but also pleased with herself as she collapsed onto it.

"We just weren't getting it," said Will. He gave an awkward half smile and shrugged his shoulders. "I almost thought that Vortex made a spark that first time, but it had to just be static electricity. He couldn't make lightning like the others. Besides, we were starting to get hungry."

Corin's expression shifted from concerned to excited again in a flash. "Oh, is that all? Then when you come back tomorrow, you should—"

"Corin, wait."

Corin stopped, mouth open, and hand raised in a gesture for words he hadn't spoken yet.

"We aren't going back tomorrow."

Corin's brow furrowed, and he dropped his hand.

Leika lifted her head and swiveled her ears forward, blinking at them.

"Really?" Corin asked. "Weren't you having fun?"

"Sure we were. But I don't think Vortex is a yellow. If he was, wouldn't he be able to zap electricity the way Leika does?"

Corin snorted and stood up, yanking off his dirty tunic and tossing it into the laundry pile before sitting on his own bunk. "Yeah . . . well, I still don't think you should quit. Yellows get to have all the fun, you know. Why wouldn't you want to play with us as much as you can?"

Will rolled his eyes. "Not everything is about how much fun you can have. You know that, right?"

"I guess so."

Will thought that was the end of the conversation, but Corin seemed determined. The next morning at breakfast, he approached Will again with a new set of arguments.

"Why does it matter if Vortex isn't a yellow dragon?" He plopped on the bench next to Will. "We have the best games. And where else would you go to live when we're done with training? Lightning Cliffs Dragonhold won't freeze your tail off like Frozen Peaks or burn you to ash like Fire Mountain. Don't even get me started on Poison Plains. Just the thought of going there makes my skin crawl." He shuddered dramatically.

Will took a bite of his egg tart and swirled the kaffa in his mug thoughtfully. "Something tells me there might be a lot of lightning in Lightning Cliffs Dragonhold. Am I right?" He arched a skeptical eyebrow at his friend.

Corin ran his fingers through his blonde hair and gave a sheepish grin. "Well, I've never actually been there, but I've heard stories . . ."

"Listen, Corin, Vortex and I had a lot of fun playing with the yellow wing. But I want to find where we really belong. It doesn't seem like we fit in anywhere, and the only group we haven't tried yet is the greens."

"What?" Corin stared with his egg tart halfway to his mouth. "You're not being serious, are you? The greens?

Those guys are nothing but a bunch of nasty, snooty, stinging shufflo—"

"Watch it!" Will warned. "One of my best friends is a green rider!"

Corin gulped and shrugged his shoulders with a light chuckle. "I . . . I mean, I'm sure they're very nice in their own way. But why would you join them when you can play games with the yellow wing?"

"Because I don't think Vortex is a yellow dragon."

"That doesn't matter to us!"

"I know that. The red wing welcomed us too. We appreciate it, really, but it matters to me." Will paused to take a gulp of kaffa, then sighed. "It's my job to take care of Vortex. He's counting on me to do what's best for him. How can I do that if I don't even know what kind of dragon he is? So far he can't make fire or ice or electricity. If that means he's a green dragon, then he's going to get green dragon training. And none of the snobby green riders are going to stop us!"

Corin leaned on his elbow and eyed Will. "You know, you almost sound like a green rider."

Will lowered his mug and blinked at Corin, not sure if he should be offended or not. "What do you mean?"

"I don't mean that you're snobby." Corin laughed and gave a casual shrug. "Just . . . determined. Focused on your goals. That kind of thing. It's very green rider-y of you."

Will paused, mulling over Corin's words for a moment. Maybe he had a point.

Can I have another bucket of meat? Vortex asked, licking the drippings from his snout.

"Another? You already ate two!"

But I'm still hungry.

"I can hardly believe how much you little dragons stuff into your bellies." Will went to the counter and filled a bucket, plopping it on the ground in front of his dragon.

Vortex immediately began devouring it. *I need food if I'm going to fly.*

"Unless you're so full of meat, you can't get off the ground!" Will scolded, halfheartedly.

"Leika ate three whole buckets for dinner yesterday too." Corin popped the last bite of his breakfast into his mouth. "I didn't think she could get it all down, but she did."

"Is anyone sitting here?" Rin appeared at Will's shoulder, carrying her plate of food. Before anyone could answer, she sat on the bench next to Will and leaned an elbow on the table. "Tumi says the dragons are about to have another growth spurt. That's why they're eating so much."

"Since when do red riders join the yellow table?" Corin laced his fingers together behind his head and leaned back with a smirk. "Let me guess. You and Ember heard how much fun Will and Vortex had and want to join the yellow training too?"

"We'd totally do that," Rin said with a toothy grin. "Only I heard Gwin doesn't even bring snacks to the training ground for you."

"Rin, I'm pretty sure Tumi is the only one who brings snacks to his training sessions," Will muttered around a mouthful of egg tart.

"Really?" Rin shot Will a scandalized look, as though learning without snacks was unthinkable. "Well, it doesn't matter. I'm not here to join the yellow wing. I came to ask Will how his training went yesterday."

Will took a long drink of his kaffa, watching as Vortex picked up clumps of meat in his teeth and swallowed them whole. Then he put down his mug and leaned against the table. "It didn't go how I wanted it to."

"Oh?" She frowned in sympathy. "What happened?"

"Vortex couldn't make electricity. It was just like what happened with the red and blue wings."

"I saw a spark," Corin jumped in. "I'm sure of it. But Will won't listen to me."

Will shrugged. "He made smoke and mist too. But that's not the same as making ice or fire, is it?"

"Why not try the red wing again? You and Vortex handled the heat of the training cavern pretty well. Ruby is going to teach our dragons how to make fireballs today."

"Really? Wow!" Corin said, leaning forward with eyes

wide and an awed smile. "I've never seen a red dragon make fireballs before. I wish I could come, but that far into the dragonhold, the ground burns my feet through my boots."

"You mean you've tried going there?" Rin asked. "Why would you do that?"

"I've heard stories," Corin said, leaning in. "Somewhere inside Fire Mountain there's a system of caves. Molten pools of magma, lava falls, fire erupting from the earth all around, everything glowing red and orange with heat. Red dragon riders challenge each other to race through the caves for fun. Oh, I wish I could see it!" His eyes sparkled with joy, as though he wasn't describing a literal pit of doom. "If Leika and I could handle the heat, we'd even be able to join one of those races someday. It would be amazing!"

On the other side of the table, Anri set a plate down and looked at Corin with a flat expression. "I always thought yellow riders were as mud-brained as sunstruck cormants. Now I'm sure of it."

Trouble hopped off her shoulder and landed, tail twitching, on the bench. Anri offered the kisnit a chunk of her egg tart.

"Do you have any idea how foolish it is to expect a yellow dragon to fly through the magma caves?" she asked. "The heat in the air would blister the flesh off your bones."

"You're exaggerating!" Corin waved his hand dismissively.

"No, I'm not," Anri said. "My father was a blacksmith. My brother still is. Have you ever stood near an open forge? Red dragons are made to handle that kind of heat. They don't burn, and neither do their riders."

"Well, yeah . . ."

"You wouldn't expect Jade to fly into a lightning storm. Or Ember to bathe in the pools at Poison Plains, would you?"

Corin shrugged. "Vortex might try it."

Anri's eyes turned sharply to Will. "What?"

"They've already tried all the other dragon wings," Corin went on. "What'll you do if Vortex does well with green training, Will? Keep training with them and go to Poison Plains Dragonhold?"

Anri slammed her fist on the table, making Will jump. The movement startled Trouble, too. The kisnit jumped up to her shoulder, chittering with her fur puffed out. "What is he talking about?" she demanded.

"Well . . ." Will shot Corin an annoyed look, then reached out a hand to rub Vortex's neck. His dragon was licking the last meaty drippings from his bucket and growling happily. "Vortex didn't have any luck with the other dragon wings, so we thought we'd try training with the greens today. Maybe we'll do well there."

Anri's eyes sparked with fire. "Oh, you'll do just great!"

she snapped. "Our dragons are learning to fly. And we're learning to stab things with sticks. But what happens when we're done here? When we go to our dragonholds, what will you do, then? Do you plan to live in a swampy bog filled with deadly, toxic pools?"

Corin leaned toward Will. "I can see why she's your best friend. She's such a joy to be around," he muttered.

Anri's eyes flashed to Corin. She sucked in a sharp breath and leaned back.

"Well, what if Vortex is a green dragon?" Will said. "What if that's the reason he can't breathe fire or ice or make electricity like the others?"

Anri's gaze traveled to Vortex.

The little white dragon was watching them all intently with his amber-colored eyes.

When she spoke again, her voice was much gentler than it had been. "But, Will, what if he isn't? If you stay here, he can tell you if he's getting too hot. If you go to the Frozen Peaks, you can keep him warm with a nice fire. But if you bring him to the Poison Plains, he could die from the toxic vapors before you even know something is wrong. Is that a risk you want to take?"

A shiver ran along Will's spine at the thought.

He turned and studied his dragon. Vortex's skin had lost a lot of its early translucency, filling in and brightening as he matured. The creamy gray undertones it used to have had all but vanished. There wasn't a hint of a regular dragon color on him anywhere.

"I never believed he was anything but a white dragon," Anri said. "He's not a red, not a yellow, not a blue, and definitely not a green."

Corin narrowed his eyes at her. "Are you saying Vortex isn't good enough to be a green dragon?"

"No," Anri said, still looking at Will. "I'm saying Will couldn't possibly be a green dragon rider. As far as I can tell, he's nothing like them."

Chapter Fourteen

Will thought about Anri's words as they walked to the green training arena together. He knew she had a point, yet if this worked, he and Vortex could finally find their place among the dragon riders.

He could tell Anri wasn't happy with the situation, but since he wouldn't be dissuaded from training with the green wing, she walked with him in quiet resignation.

"Vinna has been teaching the green flaplings to fly," Anri said in a low voice. "It's a lot more work than I realized."

She raised her hand to her shoulder to fluff Trouble's cheek fur with her fingertips. The kisnit wrapped her tail around Anri's neck and watched Will with big dark eyes.

"I know," Will said. "Vortex can't wait to try flying. He's going to be great at it." He turned and smiled at his dragon. "I warned him not to push himself too hard."

Anri snorted. "That's not what the others are doing. Most of the other green riders are pushing their dragons to try harder and be better than all the others."

"Really?" Will glanced back at Jade, green as a spring leaf as she walked alongside Vortex. "Is that what you do?"

"No. Jade is already trying her hardest. She doesn't need me to push her. Besides, she doesn't need to prove anything. I already know she's the best dragon there is." She smirked. "Not that it keeps her from trying to outfly all the others."

Jade lifted her head and tipped her ears back, looking rather smug.

As they followed the path, several other green riders came into view, walking ahead of them. Will recognized Albin and Snakebite, flanked by their friends.

"You know," Anri continued, "we can't ride our dragons while they learn to fly. We're too heavy. So we're learning other green rider skills. Spears, staves, and swords—"

"Wait—swords?" Will cut in, stumbling midstride.

Anri shrugged. "Green training is all about the Dragon Games. We're preparing to be champions someday. It's all Joric cares about. Our dragons have to be the best flyers so they can win the technical flying competition. They have to have the most endurance so they can win the coastal race. We have to practice with spears and swords so we can win the weapon skills contest. It's . . . a lot. And none of it is easy."

"Okay, but seriously?" Will picked up his pace to keep up with her. "You're fighting each other? With swords?"

Albin turned back and noticed Will. For a moment, his nose wrinkled in disgust, then a wicked grin spread across his face.

Will suspected this had something to do with the other boy's threat. He'd said Will would regret joining the green wing. He knew Will would come in as a newbie, trying to fight the others who'd already had a lot of practice. Maybe they'd been practicing with this in mind, getting ready to gang up on him. He'd have to be on his guard.

"Yes," Anri said, pulling him out of his train of thought. "It all goes back to when dragon riders fought swarmers. Greens don't have distanced attacks like the other colors, they had to get close to fight with tooth and claw so their poison can work. Even though a green dragon can survive getting stung by a swarmer, they could still get pulled to the ground. So it was the rider's job to fight them off. They'd use spears when they could, but swords for backup if the swarmers latched on."

"Wow," Will said, staring into the distance.

Anri lifted one shoulder in a dismissive half shrug. "These days, the only sword fighting we do is at the Dragon Games. Anyone can join. But Joric says it'd be a stain on our reputation if someone other than a green rider won, so we have to start training now."

"Fighting? Each other? With swords?" He choked out a laugh. "You've got to be kidding me! That's awesome!"

"Are you even listening to me?" Anri snapped.

Trouble chittered at him and twitched her tail, matching Anri's mood.

Will lifted his hands defensively and backed up a step. "Okay! Okay, it's just . . . I wasn't expecting actual sword fighting. Are you using real swords? Did anyone get stabbed yet?"

Anri pinched the bridge of her nose and closed her eyes, then took a deep breath and looked at him. "We use practice swords, of course, but it still hurts to get tagged. I've got a dozen purple bruises to prove it. We might not be training with swords today, though. Yesterday, we only worked with spears."

As the trail opened to reveal the arena, her eyes traveled ahead, and she winced. "Never mind, this is even worse."

"What?" Will followed her gaze and saw, propped along the rock wall of the mountainside, a row of wooden sticks with leather grips wrapped tightly around their middles.

"It looks like you'll be fighting with a staff today," Anri said. "Are you sure you don't want to back out now? It's not too late."

Will couldn't help grinning when he saw the row of weapons. He was going to learn to fight with a staff! How cool was that?

Anri seemed determined to make green rider training sound like torture. Her expression was grim as she surveyed the arena. But smacking someone with a stick had to be safer than stabbing them with a sword, right?

Joric was waiting for them, legs braced and fists planted on his hips as he watched the young riders and dragons approach. As the students fanned out to form a semicircle around him, he noticed Will and Vortex. He said nothing as they took their place among the students, but his brow wrinkled in displeasure.

Will lifted his chin and pulled his shoulders back, determined to do his best to fit in no matter what anyone thought of him or his dragon.

"Listen everyone," Joric said. "Yesterday, you worked on target practice with spears. It could have gone worse, but it also could have gone a lot better. It's clear that you lack grip strength and the ability to aim beyond the tips of your noses!"

A few kids sniggered at this. Others blushed and stared at their shuffling feet.

"As for your dragons, they've had enough fun gliding around like lazy seabirds. They need to get flapping and work on those shoulder muscles. They'll be practicing gaining altitude from takeoff today."

"But why?" one of the kids asked. "Whiplash says his wing muscles still ache!"

"If he wanted to laze about and sleep all day, he should have been hatched a red! We hold green dragons to a higher standard." For a moment, Joric's hard gaze fell on Will and Vortex.

A shiver ran up Will's spine.

"When you get to the Poison Plains, your drekhem will be on the ground, remember that! You won't have the luxury of gliding off a perch from a hundred yards up. You won't even have offshore winds to lift your dragon's wings. It'll be their own muscles picking them up or nothing at all. Get used to it."

Will could almost hear the other kids swallowing down their objections and the silent whining of their dragons as they tried to look stoic and strong. He could feel Anri's eyes on him, waiting for him to give up and take Vortex back to the dragonhold.

You still feel like doing this? he asked Vortex.

His dragon lifted his head and pushed out his chest. *Yes. I want to try flying. I don't think this man is as angry as he sounds.*

Joric split the kids and dragons into separate groups, just as they had been the previous day. Vortex walked across the arena with the green flaplings, shooting a few glances back at Will as he went.

Will gave him an encouraging smile and a thumbs-up,

then joined the riders as they gathered around the wooden staves.

"Everybody pick a staff and pair up. I'll be making rounds to see how you're coming along. Remember what you learned last time. Don't forget your footwork. Alternate striking and blocking."

While the others stepped forward to choose their staves, Will hesitated. "Hold on . . . I . . ."

Joric turned away without so much as a glance in his direction.

"I wasn't here last time," Will finished lamely.

"Come on," Anri said.

Will turned to see her approaching with a staff in each hand. Her satchel rested against the wall with Trouble's tiny face and huge bat-like ears poking out of the top.

Anri tossed a staff at him, and he barely caught it before it smacked him in the face.

"I'll show you what we learned so far," she said.

"Hey, thanks!" He smiled at her.

Anri pressed her lips together and nodded, then went right into the lesson.

She showed him how to block a strike from above, planting her feet and holding his staff up in defense. Then she showed him how to protect himself from an underhand swing aimed at his legs. They practiced these simple attacks and blocks against each other over and over, adding in a few side strikes and picking up speed until sweat dripped off their faces.

During one of their brief breaks, a familiar squawking caught Will's attention.

The young green dragons were practicing leaping into the air and flapping to get a little height. Vortex's brilliant white wings stood out from the various shades of green, and it was his voice that had caught Will's attention.

Vortex jumped, his white sails beating the air, and flew a full body length higher than any of the surrounding greens before dropping to the ground with a heavy thump.

A loud *thwack* and a burst of pain in his ankle made Will cry out. The next thing he knew, he was on his back in the dirt with Anri's staff poised warningly over his belly.

"Don't lose focus," she warned, looking him in the eye.

"Hey." He slapped her staff away and scrambled to his feet. "You didn't have to do that!"

"Do you think any of the others would be nicer? You think they would have held back? I could have knocked the wind out of you. Maybe it would have been better for you if I did. It might finally convince you that you don't belong here!"

Will ground his teeth together. "Fine. If you don't hold back, neither will I."

Anri laughed. "Oh, you've been holding back? Please show me your amazing staff fighting skills, off-lander!" She bowed in invitation, then readied herself in a defensive position.

Feeling kind of betrayed, Will knitted his brows and rushed at her, using the attacks she'd taught him, but anger wasn't enough to overcome skill. Anri blocked every one of his attacks, and with a swift sweep of her staff, she knocked his feet out from under him again.

He landed hard on the ground with a stinging ankle and a bruised ego.

"Ungh . . ." Will coughed and rolled to his side, shaking the dust out of his hair.

"You have to watch out for that," Anri said. "It isn't easy to block attacks when you're lying in the dirt. Of course, you could be eating snacks with the red wing or playing in grassy fields with the yellow wing if you wanted to."

Will groaned. "Why would I do that when this is so much fun?" His ankle throbbed where her staff had repeatedly struck him, but he jumped up and swung his own staff over his head.

For a split second, he was terrified that he'd acted rashly and was about to seriously hurt Anri. But she was quick on her feet. Before his strike landed, she blocked it and swung back with an attack of her own.

For the next few seconds, their two staves swung and struck so quickly they sounded like firecrackers.

Strike.

Block.

Strike.

Swing.

Block.

Crack, crack, crack!

Anri made another low sweep with her staff, but this time, Will was ready. He jumped, and the weapon whooshed under his feet.

Taking advantage of Anri's momentary surprise, Will made an attack of his own. He pivoted his staff and struck her arm, sending her off balance, then swung around to sweep her ankle.

But whether it was because he didn't want to hurt her, or because Anri was just that agile, she jumped back in time, staggering a little instead of falling to the ground.

Regaining her footing, Anri circled to the side and scowled at Will.

"What?" he demanded. "You knocked me down twice already, and I don't get to do it back?"

She didn't answer, but he could see the spark of anger and frustration in her eyes.

"I don't get it, Anri. We were friends! Why are you trying so hard to get rid of me? Are you ashamed that I'm an off-lander? Or is it because Vortex isn't a green? Why aren't we good enough to be friends with you anymore?"

"You're right. You don't get it." Her anger didn't fade. If anything, it grew hotter. But her eyes glistened. "You don't belong here. The green wing isn't for you. You and Vortex deserve better."

Before he could process her words, and with no further warning, she rushed forward, striking in a blinding flurry.

It was all Will could do to keep up, blocking the sharp cracks of her staff.

Agony burst in the knuckles of his right hand. He yelped in pain and released his grip reflexively, trying to shake out the throbbing sting.

At that moment, Anri swept his feet out from under him again. This time, she followed up with a sharp blow to his belly, knocking the wind out of his lungs.

Will's abdomen clenched in tight pain and tears sprang to his eyes as he tried to gasp in a lungful of air.

From the other end of the field came a sound that Will had never heard before: a deep roar from Vortex.

Chapter Fifteen

Will fought to take in a breath, but his lungs wouldn't cooperate.

You're hurt! Vortex's frightened thought came loud and panicked. *I'm coming. I'll help!*

Will tried to cough. He shook his head, blinking moisture from his eyes. *I'll be fine in a minute. Don't attack anyone, okay?*

He'd had the wind knocked out of him before. Loads of times. Landing hard from jumps on his mountain bike always sent the handlebars right into his belly. It was never a fun experience, but he knew it would be over soon.

As he lay there, trying to suck in enough air to clear his head and stand up, Anri crouched over him, leaning on her staff.

"Listen," she said in a low voice, her expression somehow angry and sad at the same time. "Vortex isn't a green dragon, and you aren't a green rider. You can't stay here."

Her words hurt far more than the jab to his belly. He wanted to ask what the problem was. Why was she so opposed to them joining the green wing? It wasn't like they fit in anywhere else. Was she ashamed to be his friend now that she was an elite green rider?

"Impressive!" Joric boomed. Will focused on the sound of his voice and realized that not only the green instructor but also all the other students were watching them intently.

Will wiped his sleeve over his eyes to clear the dust just as Vortex's white head pushed through the crowd. His dragon crooned anxiously.

Will half expected Joric to offer him a hand up, but he didn't. Maybe green riders thought offering help was somehow an insult.

He heaved himself to his feet and halfheartedly slapped the dirt off his trousers.

"I'll admit, I had my doubts about you, boy," Joric said, clasping Will's shoulder.

"Huh?" Will gasped.

"Was this your first time wielding a staff?"

Will nodded, gripping his belly as he fought to take another breath.

"Until now, I would have said that Anri was my star

pupil. If you can hold your own against her on your first day, you must be a born fighter."

"Thanks," Will said. Or that's what he tried to say. It came out more like a choked "hnghs."

Whining anxiously, Vortex forced himself farther through the crowd and nuzzled Will's shoulder.

Will patted his dragon's muzzle. "I'm fine," he gasped, sucking in a tight breath. "All part of learning."

"Him? A born fighter?" Albin scoffed, crossing his arms and looking Will up and down. "Not likely. I bet I could take him."

Immediately, the other kids cheered and shouted encouragement.

"Yes! Fight!"

"Go, Albin! You can do it!"

"Beat that off-lander!"

"Oh, great," Will groaned under his breath. He could feel the bruise blossoming on his belly, and his ankle still throbbed.

He glanced at Anri, but her expression was unreadable. She looked lost in thought.

"All right, Albin. I like your spirit!" Joric clapped the boy on the back. "Partner up with Will. Anri, you can put Dal through his paces. The rest of you, back to practice! And I don't want to see any lazy footwork, understand?"

"Awww!" a chorus of whining voices answered.

"But I want to watch!"

"Let us watch the off-lander fight!"

Joric didn't bother scolding the green riders for arguing. All it took was a sharp look, and they scurried away to continue their own training.

Vortex grudgingly returned to the far side of the field with the rest of the greens, but he kept glancing back toward Will as he went.

When they were alone, Albin gave Will a wicked grin. "I warned you I'd make you regret this, didn't I?"

"I don't know what your problem is," Will said, then forced himself to take a deep breath despite the pain in his belly. "Is Snakebite any less a green because Vortex is here?"

Albin snorted and brought his staff up to a ready position. "Your dragon doesn't belong here and neither do you."

His words, filled with indignant fury, sounded so much like what Anri had said that Will flinched.

Albin's staff whipped forward in a sharp strike.

Will hastily blocked the blow with his own staff, staggering to the side under the force of the attack.

Albin swung again.

Will blocked, stronger now that he had a chance to brace his feet.

Albin struck again and again and again. Their staves cracked together, the popping sound echoing off the surrounding rock walls.

After a few seconds , Will got his bearings. He could see that, although Albin was angry and determined, he wasn't as good at fighting as Anri. His strikes almost always came from above, aimed at Will's head or neck. He never tried to sweep Will's feet. His staff came in a steady, predictable rhythm, back and forth.

Arms trembling and aching all over from sparring with Anri, Will decided that if he was going to best Albin, he'd have to do it now before he was too tired to fight anymore.

Albin shifted his weight to swing at Will's head again. Rather than blocking the blow, Will dodged to the side and whipped his staff forward, cracking the end against Albin's bony elbow.

"Ow!" Albin twisted his body to protect his arm.

Without hesitating, Will swung again, this time aiming for Albin's feet.

But he'd underestimated the other boy.

Albin saw the blow coming and jumped over Will's staff. In the same movement, he brought his own down, striking the side of Will's neck with a sharp *thwack!*

A flash of hot pain shot through Will's body, spiking from his head all the way to his toes. He crumpled to the ground.

Vortex shrieked in outrage.

Will forced himself to open his eyes, straining to see through the colorful splotches dancing in his eyes. He pushed himself to his feet and his vision cleared just in time to see Vortex leap into the air.

His dragon's white sails stretched wide, catching the air and beating down as he strained to fly to Will's side. But his wings faltered. One side came down too fast and he fell. His front claws skidded over the ground, dragging him into a tumbling somersault. He flopped in the dirt, kicking up gravel and debris as he slid until he came to rest in a cloud of dust.

"Vortex!" Completely forgetting about Albin and the pain in his neck, Will leaped to his feet and raced across the arena to where Vortex slowly unfurled his mass of wings, tail, and legs.

Through their connection, Will could feel Vortex's pain in his own mind. It almost felt more real than his own.

"Vortex! Are you okay? Where does it hurt the worst? Your wings? Your claws?"

Vortex pulled his head out from under his belly and sneezed the dirt out of his nose. A trickle of blood followed. Then he gingerly shook out his wings and crawled to his feet.

Will cradled the joint of one wing in his hands, examining a raw, bloody patch in the skin. "This is even worse than what happened on the trail yesterday," he said. "We need salve! Does anyone have salve?"

Behind him, some of the other kids sniggered.

"His dragon can't even fly across the field," one of them muttered.

"Shut it, Dal!" Anri snapped. "Whiplash couldn't even get his claws off the ground on the first day."

Will was barely listening to them. "Doesn't someone have medicine? My dragon is bleeding!" He patted down Vortex's wings and examined the rest of his body, checking for broken claws and brushing the dirt from his eyes and ears.

Joric came up beside them, opened a clay jar, and scooped out a glob of salve.

"Thank you!" Will said with a relieved sigh.

"Part of being a green rider," the man said as he dabbed the medicine into the various cuts and patches of road rash, "is teaching your dragon to accept it when you're hurt, and accepting it when your dragon has to suffer as well."

"What?" Will said, not sure what he was hearing. "You mean I should just leave him alone when he gets hurt?"

"There's a difference between being hurt and being injured," Joric said. "Ignoring injury can lead to weakness. But coddling mere hurts can also lead to weakness. If you coddle your dragon, you'll won't be able to push him to be the best he can be."

Will stared at Joric, not knowing what he could say.

"If your dragon jumps to protect you at the first sign of pain, you won't be able to push yourself either."

Will made a face. "I don't think—"

"Look what just happened," Joric said, eyes as cold as ice. "You got smacked with a stick. And instead of learning from the experience and trying again, you're over here smearing salve on your dragon's nose."

Will's jaw snapped shut, and he looked at the ground with a frown.

"This is a waste of time and resources. And it's because your dragon couldn't let you feel a little pain, and you felt you had to run over here when he fell three feet into soft dirt."

"But . . . he's bleeding!"

"And I'll take care of it. Do you think it's a coincidence I carry a jar of salve with me?" Joric gave Will a stern look. "If you're going to learn with the green wing, you need to train like a green rider. Your dragon will not race across the arena every time you get knocked down. And unless Vortex is seriously injured, he can brush the dust off his own wings and sneeze the blood out of his own nose. Do you understand?"

Will licked his lips and swallowed. He glanced at Vortex's wide, frightened eyes, then back at Joric. "I understand."

He understood that he'd never bring Vortex to this awful place ever again. What kind of monsters let baby dragons bleed and cry all alone just to toughen them up?

Will remembered his Uncle John, who'd taken him out to biking trails when he'd seen how much Will loved downhill racing. Will had fallen lots of times, and his uncle had always been ready to help him get back onto his bike, treat his cuts and scrapes, or drive him to the ER if that's what he needed. He'd always been there to encourage him to try again, no matter what happened.

A lump formed in Will's throat at the memories of his uncle. He hastily wiped away a tear and stood. "Come on, Vortex. Let them have their stupid flying practice and stick fighting." He draped an arm over his dragon's neck and led him away.

"Ha! See?" someone jeered. "They're giving up already! Can't even handle one day of training with us!"

Will snorted and shook his head. "Don't listen to them."

Are we giving up? Vortex asked, sounding meek and ashamed.

Will's jaw tightened, and he massaged the bruise on his neck. What else could they do? Vortex couldn't make ice or electricity or fire, and Will didn't want him spending another minute with those cruel bullies in the green wing.

I don't want to give up. I want to be a good dragon.

Will stopped walking and grabbed Vortex's chin, tilting his face up so he looked him in the eyes. "You are a good dragon! You're the best dragon there is! The most special, the most loved, the bravest and smartest dragon in all Avria."

Vortex closed his eyes and pressed his head against Will's chest.

"And you're right," Will agreed with a sigh. "We shouldn't give up. I have to figure something out, because the way we've been doing this isn't working."

When they returned to the dragonhold, they went straight to the bathing chamber. Vortex only complained a little while Will scrubbed the caked blood and dirt out of his wounds and applied a fresh layer of salve. Will tried to be gentle, but he knew from experience that road rash could lead to a nasty infection if not cleaned thoroughly.

All the while, he struggled to think of a solution to their problem. They'd tried all four dragon wings with no luck at all. Will felt frustrated, but also guilty for feeling frustrated. Vortex had tried his hardest to fit in with all the others. It wasn't his fault. He was only a baby dragon. He shouldn't feel like anything was his fault.

If anything, it was the dragonlords' fault. They could see Vortex wasn't a usual dragon color, and instead of coming up with lessons to help him figure out what he was good at, they expected him to just fit in with everyone else.

Finally free of dirt and blood, they returned to the flapling barracks and eased themselves onto their beds.

"Man, these bruises are really going to hurt in the morning," Will muttered, staring at the dark stone ceiling.

Vortex grumbled in agreement.

The sound of boots tapping against the stone floor

caught his attention, and Will sat up stiffly, expecting to see Corin entering the room.

But it wasn't Corin. It was Rin, with Ember trailing close behind her.

"Hello, Will," she said. Her eyes found the raw red patches on Vortex's wings, and she frowned. "I heard you were back and . . . came to see how things went today." She noticed the dark purple bruise on Will's neck and bit her lower lip with a grimace.

"It was fantastic," Will grumbled. "Joric said I was the best student in the class. And Vortex flew all the way across the arena, even though it was his first day!" The words snapped out of his mouth like bitter accusations.

Rin exchanged a silent look with Ember.

They don't believe you, Vortex said. *Ember can feel how angry you are.*

Will snorted and pulled his legs into a crisscross position on the bed.

"It was that bad, huh?" Rin asked.

"Those green riders are jerks. Not Anri, but . . . even Anri wasn't—" He cut himself off before he said something he didn't mean.

Rin let the silence between them stretch on for a while. Then she asked, "Are you going back with the green wing tomorrow?"

"No." Will stared at the floor.

"Well . . . I think . . . maybe you should stick to one thing for a while."

Will shot her an annoyed look, but she didn't seem to care.

"Listen, maybe Vortex just needs more practice at something before he gets it. Remember how he was able to make smoke? No green or yellow dragon can make smoke. And you both handle the heat of the training cavern really well."

Will leaned back against the wall and closed his eyes. "I don't want to take him back to any of the classes. It's just a waste of time."

Rin took in a breath, and he continued before she could say anything, "He tried his hardest, Rin. He really did."

"I know, but—"

"Vortex isn't a red dragon," Anri's voice surprised them both.

Will's eyes snapped open. He and Rin turned to see Anri entering the room with Jade at her side and Trouble balanced on her shoulder.

Chapter Sixteen

"He isn't a red dragon!" Anri gestured at Vortex while looking pointedly at Will, as though she was tired of trying to explain that water is wet. "He isn't a red, and he isn't a green either. I don't know why you want to make him into something he isn't."

Will stared back at her and folded his arms. After how she'd treated him in the training arena, how could she think he'd listen to her about how to raise his dragon?

Anri caught his look but didn't back down. She stepped closer, looking between Will and Rin. "Vortex is a white dragon. Just look at him! Why is that so hard to believe?"

Rin looked at Vortex. He lounged on his bed, looking like a pale ghost in the shadows. "Even if he is white, he should still be allowed to learn from the instructors, shouldn't he?" she asked. "I mean, what if he does well learning with the red wing?"

"He shouldn't be pretending to be something he's not!" Anri said, waving her arms in exasperation.

"I don't think he is pretending. He's just learning. And what if he's a red dragon, after all? I never heard of a green dragon that could breathe smoke."

"He isn't a red, Rin!"

"Just stop!" Will lurched to his feet, wincing at his aching bruises, and stared at both girls. "You two are arguing about us like we're not even here."

Anri lifted her chin and pursed her lips.

Rin at least blushed and looked away.

"Look, I'm not bringing Vortex to any of the wings anymore. We're done with that."

Both girls looked up in surprise.

"But that doesn't mean we're giving up. I'm going to train him myself. We'll figure it out as we go."

"Yourself?" Anri looked at him like she was sure she'd heard him wrong. "You don't know anything about training dragons."

Rin's eyes sparkled with excitement. "Oh, that's a great idea! But Anri has a point. You'll need someone to help you."

"Who's going to help him?" Anri asked. "All the instructors are busy with their own classes."

"I will!" Rin said. "Ember and I can teach you everything we learn in the red wing. Maybe some of it will work after all."

Anri placed a fist on her hip and frowned at Rin. "Fire breathing? Really?"

Rin lifted her chin with a small smile. "It doesn't hurt to try, does it? Vortex did make smoke. Maybe he just needs more practice." As Anri shook her head and rolled her eyes, Rin clapped her hands together. "Why don't you and Jade teach him what you learn in the green wing?"

Will flopped back onto his bed, running his hands over his face. These girls were treating his life like a lump of clay they could mold however they wanted. He didn't have the energy to argue with them about it anymore. And anyway, they had some good ideas.

While Anri and Rin yammered on about their plans, Corin and Leika strolled into the barracks looking weary but pleased with themselves.

Corin froze in his tracks when he spotted the two girls and shot Will a dumbfounded look.

"It wasn't my idea." Will shrugged. "They just waltzed in here like they own the place and started making plans to teach Vortex everything they know."

"Really?" Corin asked. "Why?"

Rin sat on the edge of Will's bunk and leaned her elbows on her knees. "Because Vortex isn't learning anything by practicing with the regular dragon wings."

"But Vortex doesn't need to learn any of the dragon

skills," Corin said. "That stuff doesn't matter. The elemental attacks were for fighting swarmers, and it's not like we have to fight swarmers anymore."

Anri jabbed a finger in Corin's direction. "You don't think so? Well, let me tell you! The swarmers aren't gone. They were never destroyed, only blocked from Avria with some kind of spell. Fishermen in the north still see them offshore in the spring, and they come closer every year. The swarmers could come back!"

"Whoa, hey!" Corin held his hands up in a sign of surrender. "I'm not trying to pick a fight, green rider. Will's my friend. I just want him and Vortex to be happy."

"Anri and I want to teach Vortex whatever he can learn," Rin said, her eyes darting between Corin and Anri as though she were trying to defuse a bomb. "Is the yellow wing learning anything useful? Something Vortex could practice on his own, I mean?"

"Well, sure." Corin leaned against the wall and scratched behind Leika's ear. "Gwin says sliding down the grass slope is great practice for flying. It teaches balance, path visualization, and risk assessment. Also, it's a lot of fun! Leika and I can teach Vortex those things. Of course, it'd be better if he came to our lessons."

"Vortex doesn't need to be goofing off with the yellow wing," Anri said under her breath.

"Enough," Will said, frowning at Anri. His gut still

hurt where she'd jabbed him with her staff, and he didn't feel like being patient with her. "Stop arguing. We'll do it all."

"What?" Rin asked.

Corin tilted his head in confusion.

"Anri," Will sat up to face her, "will you teach me and Vortex what you learn from Joric? I need to practice fighting, even if it's just to protect myself from kids like Albin. And Vortex really wants to learn how to fly."

Anri nodded gravely.

"And Rin," Will turned to face the other girl, "will you teach us whatever you learn from Tumi? You're right about Vortex making smoke. I think he got closer to breathing fire than to anything else, so maybe there's something to that."

"Of course." Rin smiled.

"And Corin, I want to practice whatever you learn from Gwin and Freefall. Vortex and I had more fun with the yellow wing than anywhere else. There might be something to learn from that."

"Brilliant!" Corin said, slapping his hand against his knee.

For the next few weeks, Will spent his days practicing with his friends in their spare time between meals and chores.

Some days Corin took him and Vortex out to the grassy slopes to ride the slides, and while Vortex didn't worry about making electricity, he did learn how to balance, lean into the turns, and visualize his path to make better time. He and Leika also had fun trying to beat each other to the bottom.

Sometimes, Rin and Ember showed him what they were learning in the red wing. Ember helped Vortex feel where his fire sac would be if he had one and explained how to make a clean flame. Vortex still couldn't make fire, but he discovered he could make his vapor hot and smoky or cold and misty if he concentrated. Rin seemed to think this was a promising sign.

Anri brought Will a wooden training sword, a spear, and a staff so he could learn the fighting techniques of the green riders. Sometimes Anri would disarm Will with a clever twist of her weapon and knock him flat on his back, only to help him up and spend hours teaching him how to do it himself. Will practiced lunges, blocks, and attacks every day. He could feel his muscles getting stronger and his reflexes getting faster.

And then there were days when all four of them let their dragons play together while they talked and compared the different lessons they'd been learning.

Now and then, Anri and Jade brought Will and Vortex out to the training field to practice flying. Jade demonstrated wing exercises, gliding poses for various wind conditions, and different launching techniques.

"Can't he just flap harder?" Will asked while Jade

practiced a confusing figure-eight wing pattern for taking off vertically. "That seems way too complicated. Vortex could just jump and flap like usual."

"Dragons don't fly the same way birds do," Anri said. She folded her arms and didn't take her eyes off Jade as the green dragon launched herself straight up into the air.

"What do you mean, they don't fly like birds? And what does that have to do with anything?"

"Feathers aren't flexible like dragon wings. Not only that, but dragons have muscles all through their wing membranes. They can change the shape of their wings more than birds, which means they can do things in the air no bird could ever dream of, if they practice and are strong enough. According to Joric, this exercise strengthens their membrane muscles and teaches them how to use their wings more effectively."

Jade landed, then reared back to demonstrate the takeoff again, pointing her nose straight up into the sky with her tail aimed at the ground. Her wings beat forward and back, flipping almost upside down so that her upstroke lifted her into the air, giving her an extra boost as she gained altitude.

"What do you think, Vortex?" Will turned to his dragon. "Can you do that?"

I'll try, Vortex said, sounding uncertain and shuffling his wings.

They practiced the maneuver every day, building

strength and endurance. In time, Vortex could almost hover in the air without dropping at all.

Feasts and celebrations frequently interrupted the grueling training sessions. Red dragon riders loved to celebrate every milestone, no matter how small, with music, dancing, and food. Every dragon rider was invited to join in on the fun in the great hall.

The young dragons grew bigger day by day, eating as much as they could at each meal and growing so fast Will wondered how they didn't split their skin. Soon enough, the flaplings were too large to crowd into the dining hall with their riders, so they had to eat out by the shufflo pen with the adult dragons.

As the dragons grew, all the instructors began teaching them to fly, much to Leika and Ember's delight. They started with the basic jump-and-glide exercise that the greens had mastered long ago.

Vortex and the green flaplings had a clear head start over the others. The reds, blues, and even yellows were clumsy and slow in comparison. Maybe learning to fly early was risky, but Will had to admit that Vortex was stronger because of the amount of practice he'd had.

With the days so packed with activity, Will hardly had a chance to catch his breath. So when he noticed the trees on the lower foothills shifting from deep green to red and gold, it came almost as a surprise. The winds from the lowlands carried earthy aromas of mushrooms and moist wood. Fall was upon them.

Tumi brought in a master leathersmith to measure the kids for their riding gear. They begged to know if this meant they'd be riding their dragons soon. But Tumi only smiled and assured them they still had months before their dragons would be large enough to carry them.

In the meantime, they spent their days developing their skills and strengthening their muscles, doing chores for the dragonhold, and celebrating anything and every-thing with lively music, dancing, and spiced honey wine.

"You know Jade will always be a better flyer than Vortex, don't you?" Anri said one cool evening as they watched their dragons race through the training field.

All the young dragons were practicing short flights together. Launching at one end of the training field, beating their wings to gain altitude, then racing across the open distance to the other side. Jade and Vortex always made it across before the others, but the green dragon always came out in the lead.

Will glanced at Anri.

She side-eyed him with a smirk that told him she was teasing.

"You seem pretty sure about that." Will folded his arms over his chest and grinned at her. "Jade might be faster in a glide, but I think Vortex is stronger. There's no way she could keep up with him long distance."

Over the grassy training field, Vortex beat his wings, straining to gain the lead before they made it to the near side. The downdraft from his wings made eddies in the air behind him, catching a blue dragon off guard and sending him spiraling into a clumsy dive. The blue squawked in frustration.

"Don't worry, Tundra!" Jayda called. "Get back up, you can still make it!"

"Vortex is strong, sure," Anri pet the little kisnit curled into a fuzzy ball in her lap, "but Jade is agile. She can always outmaneuver him."

"Don't forget, it's only a game," Corin said. "Our dragons are supposed to be having fun."

"Oh, we know," Will agreed. "Anri just likes to trash talk. It won't work, though."

"What do you mean?" Anri asked, looking innocent. "What won't work? I'm only telling the truth."

As though to prove her point, Jade tucked her wings, dropped into a graceful dive, then landed at the end of the field with a victorious squawk.

Will was going to make some sort of retort to Anri's bantering, but he couldn't think of anything to say after Jade's clear victory.

Corin laughed and slapped him on the back. "Okay, Will. Whatever you need to tell yourself to feel better. I'm just going to admit that Jade has all our dragons beat in flying."

While Corin and Anri were still laughing together, a dark shadow flashed over the ground.

Tumi's red dragon soared into the field, massive wings temporarily blocking the sun. She backwinged, rear legs touching down in the middle of the clearing. As she folded her wings against her back, Tumi dropped out of the saddle with a grin that Will could see all the way from where he and his friends sat.

"I have good news!" Tumi hollered, waving an arm over his head.

The young dragons and riders looked at one another, then flocked to the instructor.

When everyone was close enough to hear, Tumi tossed his long braids over his shoulder and beamed at them with a bright, toothy smile. "Do you all remember what happens on the cliffs of Charramor every summer?" The way his eyes twinkled when he asked, it was clear that he expected everyone to know.

"The Dragon Games!" the others shouted before Will could look around in bewilderment.

Tumi clapped his hands and rubbed them together in anticipation. "There is a big change coming to this summer's Dragon Games, and it has to do with all of you. Do you want to know what it is?"

"Yes! Tell us!" they all cheered.

"Normally, the games are only open to full-grown dragons at least two years old. But this summer . . ." Tumi paused for dramatic effect, ". . . we're going to have the first-ever junior tournament!"

Chapter Seventeen

Shocked silence flooded the area as everyone looked around, wondering whether they'd heard Tumi correctly.

"So . . . we can join the Dragon Games after all?" Will asked.

"Does that mean we'll be able to ride our dragons by then?" Corin pressed.

"Now hold on," Tumi said, shaking his head with a laugh. "It's an experimental thing. Teams of young dragons will get to compete in a series of riderless contests. There's even going to be a cash prize for the winning team."

Will gasped. His parents! If he won enough money, maybe he could help them. "A cash prize? How much?"

He wasn't the only one interested. A lot of the other riders murmured together excitedly, already planning how they'd spend the prize money.

Tumi shrugged. "I'm not sure. The prizes for the Dragon Games are always generous. It would be more than enough for a few of you to nicely furnish your new drekhems when you move to your dragonholds. The usual prize for winning an event is twenty silver pieces."

Someone gasped. Anri stared at Tumi with wide eyes and her hand over her mouth.

The excited chatter kicked up a notch, with murmurs of "twenty silver pieces!" scattered through the crowd.

Will didn't really understand how Avrian money worked. He hadn't even had the opportunity to pay for anything yet. But from everyone's reaction, it seemed like that much silver was a lot.

Would it be enough to pay his parents' debt and get them out of Elder Madoc's farm? He remembered the dark shadows under his father's eyes and how thin and weary his mother had been the last time he'd seen them. It was worth it just for the chance.

"We'll all get to attend the dragon games this year," Tumi said, talking loudly to be heard over the chatter. "Even if you don't join the tournament, there will be plenty to do: fireworks, food, dancing, feasting, entertainment, snacks, gift shopping! Even if you choose not to compete in the tournament, I guarantee you'll have fun. So, who wants to enter?"

Will whooped with joy and rushed forward with the rest of the kids. Vortex bugled a loud note, giving his wings a good flap. Tumi didn't seem to mind the rush, though. He laughed and held up his hands fending off the surge of eager competitors.

Everyone started asking questions at the same time, jostling to get in front and grab Tumi's attention.

"How long do we have to train?"

"How many of us can team up together?"

"What will we be competing in?"

"Is there an entry fee? I don't have any money!"

"Okay, okay! Settle your wings, everyone!" Tumi waved everyone off and waited for them to quiet down. "Now, listen. This might be hard to take, but you'll need to form teams of three."

Will quickly did the math in his head. There were twenty eggs at the hatching, which meant that there would be six teams of three and two dragon and rider pairs would be left out. He frowned, hoping he and Vortex wouldn't be one of them.

The rest of the kids immediately started murmuring again. All six of the red riders huddled close, talking in low tones. They'd easily be able to split into two teams.

"There is a small entry fee," Tumi continued, "but I'll be happy to pay for anyone who can't afford it."

Just then, Timmin stepped away from the red wing with his orange-red dragon following. His eyes darted around, and he hugged his dragon's neck close to his side. "Um, what if we don't want to compete?"

"Timmin!" Rin protested, grabbing the boy's sleeve. "What are you doing?"

"Sorry," Timmin said, scuffing his feet. "I—I just don't like being in front of crowds! Everyone watching us and judging us . . ." he grimaced.

Some of the green riders smirked and whispered to one another.

Tumi just nodded in understanding. "That's not a problem, Timmin. No one will make you compete if you don't want to."

Timmin's shoulders relaxed, and he let out a small sigh. The other red riders didn't say anything, but it was obvious that they weren't happy with his decision.

Will wondered what the problem was. If Timmin didn't join a team, the others could find someone else to take his place, couldn't they? Maybe it was just because Timmin was their friend, a member of the red wing, and they were used to training with him every day.

"When you've formed your teams, come find me and I'll get you signed up." Tumi produced a roll of papers from his hip bag. "Your dragons will be competing in three skills: target hitting, elemental attack—or claw strikes for greens—and technical flying. Consider who is strong in each skill when you're forming your teams."

The kids immediately clustered together in four separate groups, talking quickly and bartering with one another to make teams with the best chances at winning.

"Well, I don't know what claw striking is or how you're supposed to hit a target," Will patted Vortex's head, "but if greens can compete in the tournament, you have as good a chance as anyone. What do you say?"

Could we help your parents if we win?

"I think so. But I don't want to make you do this if you'd rather not."

Vortex thought about it for a moment, then flicked his ears and gave a little huff. *I want to help them. I don't understand what a tournament is, but I'll try to do it if I can help.*

Will's heart swelled and melted at the same time. "Thanks, buddy. You're the best!" He hugged his dragon and wiped some moisture from his eyes. "I'll be here to help you the whole way. Don't worry. Now I guess we just find someone to team up with."

They looked around to see who hadn't teamed up yet. Anri was thick in the group of green riders, and all the red riders seemed to be arguing together. "Hey, there's Beck and Icicle! Maybe they'll want to be a team."

The blue dragon and rider were walking away from the crowd to a shady spot by the mountain wall.

"Hey, Beck!" Will waved an arm to get the boy's attention as he and Vortex trotted over.

Beck and Icicle turned to sit in the shade with their backs to the wall. The other boy smiled and waved in greeting. "Oh, hello, Will. Hi, Vortex."

"Hi! So, um, do you and Icicle want to join the tournament?"

"Of course. It will be a good opportunity to experience the Dragon Games to the fullest."

"Oh, that's great! I was worried no one would want to team up with us." Will chuckled in relief and ran his hand through his hair. "We just need to find someone else to make three . . ." He faltered when he saw Beck's face fall.

"Oh." Beck exchanged an uncomfortable look with his dragon. "I didn't know . . ."

Will blinked in confusion and looked at Vortex.

Icicle feels sorry and Beck feels . . . embarrassed? his dragon said, confused.

"We're teamed up already," Beck explained. "There are only three blue flaplings. It makes sense, you see? Tumi said teams of three, so . . ."

Heat rose in Will's face, but he tried to brush it off. "Hey, don't worry about it." He chuckled and waved a hand dismissively, rubbing the back of his neck. "I, um, we'll go see if anyone else hasn't teamed up yet."

Before Beck could offer any more condolences, Will and Vortex scurried back to the rest of the crowd. Most of the kids seemed to be in teams already, some lining up to sign their names on the registration list.

Vortex tapped Will's side with a wing and aimed his nose at the edge of the crowd. *Corin and Leika are unhappy.*

Will saw his friend some distance from the other yellow riders, shuffling his feet, with Leika resting her head against his arm.

"Corin!" Will shouted, waving his arm as he jogged over.

Corin looked up and waved back with a weak smile. "Hi, Will."

"What's the matter?"

Vortex chirped to Leika, and the dragons bumped noses in greeting.

Corin frowned and scraped his toe in the dirt. "Tato, Vala, and Rone teamed up. Shara doesn't care, because she doesn't want to compete at all. She says she just wants to see her friends and play games of chance, but I was hoping I'd get to join."

Will looked around. "You could team up with someone else."

"Didn't you hear what I said? Shara doesn't want to compete. Even if she did, there are only five yellow flaplings."

"Why don't you team up with us? Vortex wants to join the tournament, and we aren't in a team yet."

Corin stopped shuffling, and his eyebrows shot up. "I thought we had to make teams with dragons of the same color."

"Tumi never said that. And if that was the case, Vortex wouldn't be able to join at all, would he?"

Corin's bemused expression cleared, and a grin spread across his features. "That's a great idea! Hey, Rin!" Corin jumped up and waved both arms. "Anri! Come over here!"

Standing together on the other side of the crowd, Anri and Rin looked at each other, shrugged, and walked over to join the boys.

"Do you have teams yet?" Corin asked.

Anri shook her head, arms folded defensively.

"No," Rin said. "Since Timmin backed out, there aren't enough of us to make two teams."

"Will has a great idea," Corin said, smacking Will's arm. "Dragons of different colors could team up! Would one of you like to be a part of our team?"

The girls looked at each other uncertainly.

"Are you sure we're allowed to do that?" Rin asked.

"Tumi never said we couldn't." Corin wrapped an arm around Leika's neck and rubbed her head. "Our dragons already play together and practice together. Why can't they compete together?"

"It's against the rules," Rin said, wrinkling her brow. "At least, I thought it was."

Will threw his hands in the air. "If it's a rule, it's a stupid one. We're all friends, even if our dragons are different colors. Why can't we compete together?"

Anri took a breath and looked at Jade. "There's a good reason they keep the greens separate from the others. An adult green could kill another dragon with just a scratch."

"Pfft!" Will made an annoyed face and waved it off. "But Jade doesn't have her poison yet. She's totally safe right now!" He scratched behind the green dragon's tiny horns, and Jade chirped happily.

Anri frowned in thought.

"Do you think we could win?" Rin asked.

"Vortex is one of the best flyers in the hatching!" Corin said. "And don't think I haven't seen Ember practicing fireballs on the side. He's got the target hitting event down."

Rin blushed and smiled. "We have been practicing. He's doing really well."

"Leika is great at making lightning," Corin continued, bouncing with energy. "She'll make a blazing display for the judges. And Jade is the best flapling at maneuvering in the air. She'd do great at the claw-striking event, I'm sure of it!"

"But only one of us could join the team," Anri said. "Tumi might not have said dragons of the same color, but he definitely said teams of three."

"So only three of us compete," Will said. "It's better than none of us. We'll still be able to train together, won't we? And we can share the prize money four ways. With all that money, just think what we could do!" He couldn't help but glance at the southern pass and beyond, to the road leading to Madoc's estate.

"What do you want the money for?" Anri asked.

Will folded his arms and shrugged. "I was hoping I

could get my parents out of Elder Madoc's farm and find them a place of their own. Somewhere they could be safe and happy, you know?"

The girls exchanged another look.

"What do you think, Anri?" Rin asked.

Anri lowered her gaze and sighed, shaking her head. "I won't join the team."

Chapter Eighteen

"You won't join our team? Why not?" Will asked. Though he tried not to show it, Anri's words had stung. She'd never wanted to have him and Vortex in the green wing, but he thought she'd at least still want to be friends.

"Because," Anri waved a hand toward Rin and Ember, "you can only have three on a team. I've seen Ember practicing fireballs. He's neck and wings ahead of the other red flaplings. I don't know what claw attacks are or whether Jade would be better at them than the other greens. You'll have a better chance at winning if Ember's on your team."

"You'd do that?" Rin asked, clutching her hands over her heart. "You'd miss out on the tournament just to give us a better chance at winning?"

Anri gave a dismissive snort and looked away, folding

her arms. "Don't make too much of it. We don't even know if Tumi will say it's okay."

"If I'll say what's okay?" Tumi's deep voice made them all turn. The flapling instructor approached with the stack of papers in his hand and an expectant smile on his face.

Will explained the plan, tripping over his words whenever Corin interjected with how great the idea was. Rin kept hissing at the other boy to be quiet and stop interrupting.

When Will finished, Tumi quietly looked them over for a moment and nodded.

"I've noticed that you all have become good friends. With all the training you've been doing, it makes sense that you'd want to team up."

"So we can be a team?" Rin asked, rocking forward on her toes.

Tumi shrugged and rested his hands on his hips. "I don't see why not."

"All right!" Corin jumped and pumped his fist in the air. Leika tipped her nose up and bugled happily.

"But I can't make the final decision on this," Tumi said.

"What?" Will, Rin, and Anri asked in unison.

Corin tilted his head, puzzled.

"The official rules are decided by the dragonlords. I can put your entry in, but it's up to them whether you'll be allowed to compete together."

"Just because our dragons are different colors?" Will asked.

"Do you think they'll let us?" Rin asked at the same time.

Tumi shrugged and unrolled the papers. "It is unusual, but I don't see why it would be a problem. How about we sign you up?"

***

With the Dragon Games coming, the usual classes all but stopped. The young riders were given fewer chores around the dragonhold, freeing up those who were competing for training.

When the kids and their dragons weren't eating, sleeping, or bathing, they were off with their teammates practicing for the tournament, or begging the instructors to teach them useful skills that would give their dragons an edge.

Will, Rin, and Corin trained in the open courtyard outside the flapling barracks. Since the other teams practiced on their usual training grounds, the courtyard was almost always empty.

To Will's surprise, Anri and Jade usually practiced with them instead of with the green wing. When Will asked her about it, Anri claimed Jade would learn more from their group than from the bunch of shufflo rumps in the green wing.

If he was tempted to be flattered by this, that feeling vanished when Anri appointed herself the drill instructor for the group. A decision that Will found baffling, since she wasn't even joining the team.

"If you're going to compete, you're going to win!" she snapped when he confronted her about it. "Now, Corin, Leika has to make a bigger spark than that if she wants to impress the judges!"

"UUUGGGHH!" Corin moaned. He raked his hands through his blonde hair and scratched his fingers over his eyes like he wanted to gouge them out. "This is SO BORING!"

Leika threw her head back in a mournful bellow, echoing her rider. The iron target that Anri had set up for them leaned against the rock wall nearby. The yellow dragon had been striking it with sparks of electricity for over an hour already.

Anri insisted she should hit it with stronger and stronger electricity, aiming from a little farther back every day. Even though Leika was getting better, Anri still wasn't satisfied with her progress.

"It doesn't matter if it's boring!" Anri jammed her fist into her side and pointed an accusatory finger at them. "You've got to make your electricity stronger. Ember can already shoot a fireball three body lengths away."

On the other side of Corin, Ember lifted his head and puffed out his chest, looking smug.

Rin patted her dragon's head but frowned at Anri. "I'm sure Leika is trying her hardest. Maybe she needs a rest."

"Do you really think not practicing is how you get better at things?" Anri demanded, then turned back to Corin. "If you want to win the prize money you're going to have to—"

"Hold on, Anri," Will interrupted, resting a hand on her arm.

She whirled on him. "They're not taking this seriously, Will! If Leika doesn't—"

"Just hold on," Will said, more firmly. "I think you're going about this all wrong. Maybe Rin is right."

Anri rolled her eyes and let out a huff. "So you think they should be taking naps? Frolicking in the fields?"

Will gave a sideways smile and raised his eyebrows. "Actually, yeah, kind of."

Anri stared at him like he had squids squirming out of his ears. "What?"

"I think they need to have fun."

Corin raised his eyebrows and Leika's ears perked up.

"Seriously, Anri. Think about it! Yellow dragons and their riders all love to have fun, right? It's what motivates them. I think there's a reason for that. It's why their training is all about having a good time and not about technique." He grinned at Corin. "So, do you wanna play a game?"

"Swarms, yeah!" Corin laughed and rubbed his hands together.

"Good. I've got a great idea." Will trotted over to the wall and grabbed the target, a round hunk of hammered metal about the size of a hubcap. A rusted chain hung from a hole in the rim. "Anri, where'd you get this?"

"There are a lot of them in the storage room behind the library," Anri said with a skeptical frown.

"There's a library?"

Anri arched a severe eyebrow at him, as though Will had said he didn't know there were baths available.

"Nevermind. Can you find some more of these targets? About ten should be enough."

She eyed him for another brief moment, then shrugged and nodded. "Come on, Jade. Let's get some more."

"We'll help," Rin said. "Come on, Ember."

"Try to get ones with chains attached, like this one!" Will called as they left.

Anri waved over her shoulder in acknowledgement.

"Okay, so now . . ." Will hefted the metal disc and held it out to Vortex. "Do you think you can wedge this chain into that crack up on the wall?"

Vortex looked up to where a projection in the rock ran alongside a narrowing crevice.

I'd have to hover right next to the wall to do that, he said.

"And you're the best at underwinging! You can hover longer than any other flapling. I bet you can do it if you try!"

Vortex grasped the chain in his front claws, gathered himself on his haunches, and launched into the air.

"Do you think he can do it carrying the extra weight?" Corin asked, watching as Vortex circled higher. "And with the mountain wall messing up the air patterns too?"

"Even if he can't, it's still good practice."

Vortex came level with the crack and tipped his wings back to stall in the air.

Dropping his back half until he was nearly vertical, Vortex flapped hard. With every upstroke, he flipped his wings backward until they were upside down, fanning the air in the opposite direction and giving himself an extra lift. It took a lot of concentration and worked groups of muscles that weren't used to carrying his weight.

Vortex wobbled, but managed to keep his altitude, inching closer to the wall until he could wedge the loose end of the chain into the crack.

"Yeah, Vortex!" Will cheered.

Corin whooped and clapped his hands.

Vortex tugged on the target to make sure it was secure, then dove for the ground and landed in a flurry of dust and wind.

Will rushed to him and hugged his dragon's neck. "You did it! And on the first try!"

Vortex rumbled happily. *It wasn't easy, but it was fun. Can I do another?*

Will laughed and rubbed his dragon's stumpy horns. "Vortex wants to go again," he said to Corin.

Leika picked up her ears and chirped, making Corin laugh. "Now Leika wants to try too. But this isn't the game, is it?"

"Not yet. We do need more targets, though. And here they are!"

Anri and Rin emerged from the main doors with their dragons, each carrying metal discs. Anri and Rin each dragged two by the chains while Jade and Ember balanced precarious stacks between their wings.

"We could use a hand with these!" Anri called.

Will and Corin trotted over to help, and Will explained what Vortex did with the first target, saying all their dragons should do the same with the rest.

"They should be all over the place," he said. "Not too close together, and not too close to the ground either."

The young dragons were eager to prove themselves, finding unique and fun places all over the courtyard where they could mount their targets. Leika dangled one from the top of the stone arch that stretched over the road leading out of the dragonhold. Ember hung one of them from a rock tower over the dining hall. Anri even found a wire cord long enough to string between two spires so they could hang some targets midair.

When they were finished, Will turned to Corin. "Ready to hear what the game is?"

Corin laughed. "I think I figured it out already. But why don't you explain it, anyway?"

"Does everyone feel up to a race?"

All the dragons perked up.

Leika bounced with excitement.

A race? Vortex asked. *A race with who? Where?*

"A race with Leika and Ember, of course," he said. "But not the usual kind. Do you think you can fly all the way to Smoketree Peak and back before Leika and Ember can hit all ten of these targets?"

They all looked up the mountainside behind them. Above the rocky caverns of the flapling barracks, the steep wall stretched until it ended in a sharp peak, skimming the clouds.

Vortex studied the peak, then eyed Leika and Ember, ruffling his wings proudly. *Leika and Ember are good flyers, but I think I can do it.*

Will smiled at his dragon, then grinned at Rin and Corin. "Challenge accepted. What do you guys think?"

Corin folded his arms and nodded. "Leika's ready to show you all what she can do. Let's go!"

"It sounds fun," Rin said. "Ember wants to try."

The dragons took their places side by side in the courtyard. Will counted down, and when he reached one, all three launched into the air in unison.

The wind kicked up from their combined takeoff was nearly as strong as from a full-grown dragon, whipping dust into the air and making smaller rocks skid across the hard ground.

Aiming straight for Smoketree Peak, Vortex beat his wings with all his might, rapidly gaining altitude. He even used the underwing technique to build momentum on his upstrokes. After a few moments, his stamina slackened, and he was forced to turn into an ascending corkscrew pattern.

Ember launched himself to the closest target and blasted it with a well-aimed ball of orange flame before flying on to the next.

Leika made a straight shot for the topmost target, which dangled from the mountain wall over the entrance to the hatching ground. It was the farthest away, but the choice made sense. Once she hit that one, she could take a gliding route through the rest without struggling to gain altitude again.

Anri stood next to Will with Jade at her side, both of them watching the racing dragons in silence. But Will noticed Jade's wings twitching as her eyes followed her friends, like she wished she could join in on the fun.

"You know . . ." Will said in a low voice, leaning over to

nudge Anri with his arm, "we could find a way for Jade to play too. If she wants to, that is."

Anri shrugged and glanced at Jade. "We aren't planning to join the tournament."

"That doesn't mean you can't train with us," Rin said.

"Maybe she could fly to the peak with Vortex next time," Corin added.

Jade's eyes followed Leika. As the yellow dragon approached the first target, her wings swept down, giving her a quick boost in altitude. Then she twisted midair, so the target was directly below her.

A flash of electricity shot from the tip of her nose, striking the target a moment before she zoomed past it.

Leika let out a triumphant screech.

"That's the way to do it!" Corin cheered.

Jade squawked and opened her wings, like she wanted to jump up and follow her friend.

"Come on, Anri," Will said, "even I can see Jade wants to get out there and play."

"She does," Anri said, with a reluctant nod. "She wants to hit the targets with Leika and Ember."

"Oh, but she can't do that, can she?" Rin asked, frowning. "Maybe we could find a way to—"

"Actually, she can," Anri said.

"Wait . . ." Will tore his eyes away from Leika and Ember's aerial acrobatics to look at Anri. "What do you mean she can? How can she hit the targets? I thought you told me everything you learned about green dragons."

"It doesn't matter. Without her poison, she can't—"

"Did Joric teach you a green dragon ability I haven't heard about?" Will asked.

Over the courtyard, Leika wheeled around, heading to her next target. She seemed to struggle to build up enough electricity to make a shock, so she hovered for a few moments, fighting to keep her altitude.

Ember zipped past her, squawking with glee and blasting the target with fire on his way to the next one.

"Don't worry about it, Leika!" Corin yelled. "He won't be ahead of you for long!"

Will wasn't paying much attention to the dragons anymore. He fixed Anri in his gaze, pinching his lips together and crossing his arms. "What happened to teaching us everything the greens were learning?"

Anri bit her lip and folded her arms.

"Why won't you tell me?" Will demanded.

"If Jade can do something, maybe Vortex could do it too," Rin said, sounding a lot less annoyed than Will felt. "We won't know unless he tries."

Anri let out a breath and shook her head. "Fine! It's just kind of gross, that's all."

"Gross?" Will's annoyance fizzled out, replaced by burning curiosity.

Even Corin turned away from the race to raise his eyebrows at Anri.

Jade looked up at her rider and made a curious chirping sound.

"No, dear," Anri said, stroking her dragon's ears, "I love everything about you. You don't need to be ashamed."

"Anri, you're killing me here!" Will whined.

"What is it? What does she do?" Corin asked.

Anri glanced up at Ember, who was circling back to reach his last few targets.

High above them, Vortex was just reaching the tip of Smoketree Peak. He touched it with a claw, then wheeled around to make his descent.

"All right," Anri said. "I suppose we'll just show you. Come on, Jade. We might as well."

Filled with burning curiosity, Will, Rin, and Corin followed Anri and Jade to the lowest metal target, hung at shoulder height on the rock wall next to the barracks.

Anri pointed at it. "Go on. Show them what you can do."

Jade chirped and faced the target. She stared at it for a brief moment, took aim, opened her mouth, and . . .

CLANG!

A thick glob of some clear, viscous substance oozed on the surface of the metal disc.

"Wh-what? What just happened?" Will asked, looking between the target and Anri.

"It's called a poison shot," Anri said. "Green dragons can shoot poison at their enemies. Only Jade's isn't poisonous yet."

"That's amazing!" Corin breathed, then he let out a laugh and grinned at Jade.

"But . . ." Rin blinked in shock. "I thought they couldn't . . . I mean, the whole reason green riders use spears and swords is because their dragons couldn't kill swarmers from a distance."

Anri nodded and rubbed between Jade's horns. "Joric says it probably wasn't very effective unless the poison hit an open wound on a swarmer. And green riders rarely use it now because they think it's undignified." She scoffed. "It is pretty gross, though, right? Like blowing your nose at a target." Jade grumbled and Anri chuckled. "Yes, I know it doesn't come from your nose."

"However she does it, I want Vortex to try learning that," Will said. "I think it's pretty cool!"

Halfway to the courtyard now, Vortex skimmed the mountainside, gaining speed in a swift dive as he raced to the ground again.

With only a few targets left, Ember swiveled on a wingtip to make his final approach.

Everyone backed away from the ooze-coated metal target to give the dragons space.

Leika seemed to pause, whirling in a circle above the last three targets and studying them carefully.

"What is Leika doing?" Will asked.

"She's going to lose the race if she doesn't hurry," Anri said.

"I don't think so." Corin folded his arms and leaned against the wall. He watched Leika, a smile pulling at the corner of his mouth. "Just watch."

Will turned to see how close Vortex was. His dragon glided low over the surface of the mountainside, drifting side to side to avoid protruding mounds of rock. He flapped once to hurtle a small hill, tipped over a ledge, and darted downward like a missile.

Ember blasted another fireball at a target, then flapped toward the last one on the opposite side of the courtyard.

Leika folded her wings flat against her back and dove straight down at breakneck speed.

Everyone watched in silent anticipation.

Leika let out a slow, building screech as she approached her first target. Her mouth cracked open to release a charge of electricity.

Vortex was almost to the bottom. He squawked and flapped, building speed. At the last moment, his wings snapped open, whipping his hind legs forward, ready to catch the ground.

Leika's mouth opened wider, and a blinding flash of light filled the courtyard.

Chapter Nineteen

Lightning shot from Leika's mouth, striking the first target, arcing to the second, the third, and the fourth. It crackled in a jagged streak to strike the fifth right next to the four riders. A mighty, deafening boom roared over them.

The residual crackle of electricity made the hair on Will's arms and neck stand on end. The smell of ozone, like burning plastic, wafted through the air.

Will blinked the dancing lights out of his eyes to see blue and orange flames consuming the ooze that still dripped from the last target. Black char sizzled in a lightning-shaped scorch mark on the ground.

Leika sat smugly in front of them, swishing her tail happily while Vortex walked over and Ember glided in from the other side of the courtyard.

Leika won, Vortex said, sounding tired and a little disappointed.

"What the . . ." Will blustered. "Holy COW! When did she learn how to do that?"

"Stinging swarms!" Anri said. "How?"

Rin just stared, open-mouthed and speechless.

Corin chuckled. "That was a fun game, Will. Does everyone want to play again?"

Will let out a weak chuckle and ran his fingers through his staticky hair, then he grinned at Anri. "Only if Anri lets Jade join this time."

EVEN IF ANRI had wanted to stop Jade, Will didn't think she could have prevented the dragon from joining in the next race. The young green darted from target to target so nimbly, Leika and Ember were hard-pressed to keep up. Their only advantage was that it took Jade a while to build up her poison shot, giving Ember and Leika a chance to catch up while Jade paused before striking her targets.

Leika's ability to shoot a chain of lightning that could strike multiple targets at once also had the drawback of draining her energy. She needed to rest for several minutes afterward before she could make another spark at all.

Ember could shoot fireballs one after another in a seemingly endless stream. But the red dragon was slower and clumsier in the air than Jade and Leika. All in all, it was a pretty even match. Whenever Ember or Leika struck a target that Jade had gotten to first, the glob of poison shot burst into flame and hung on like a blazing torch until it burned out.

When the other riders returned from their own practice, most were amazed at what they saw. The yellow riders exclaimed that they should have thought of that game themselves. The red riders cheered on Ember as he tried to keep up with the others. The blue riders commented on how interesting it was to see the different flying and fighting styles side by side.

Vortex soon grew bored with flying from peak to peak while his friends played on the obstacle course. With some careful consideration, Will decided that Vortex could fly the course, but he'd have to actually touch each target— whether with his nose, claw, wing, or tail—before flying to the next. Vortex agreed to the terms, and all four dragons raced together.

Thanks to Jade's flammable poison shot, a burning target often forced Vortex to change course, making the game that much more challenging for him.

This led to Jade and Ember conspiring to sabotage the targets in his preferred path, forcing him to take round-about routes to keep from burning himself.

The target race quickly became a spectator sport that the whole dragonhold enjoyed. Every evening, red dragon riders converged on the cliffside ledges surrounding the courtyard to watch Vortex and his friends race through the course, cheering when the young dragons managed to pull off difficult maneuvers or strike targets from difficult angles.

The other kids also enjoyed watching the game. Many times, when Will and his friends had finished for the day, the other kids would let their dragons try out the obstacle course for themselves.

Although their dragons were being trained by the flapling instructors, not one of them was as strong or agile in the air as Vortex and his friends. Even Ember now flew as well as most of the greens. And none of the other yellows could produce lightning as powerful as Leika.

Will was certain that Vortex, Leika, and Ember would dominate the junior tournament, and with the prize money, he'd be able to help his parents. They'd finally be away from Elder Madoc, happy and safe.

"If you win the tournament," Anri said one evening, "where do you think your parents will go?"

The four of them were enjoying their evening meal outside while their dragons flew through the obstacle course together.

"I don't know," Will said, taking a bite of his spiced meat roll. "As far away from Madoc's farm as they can get, I guess."

"Maybe they'd like to live in Silverlake," Anri suggested. "That's where my family lives."

"Nah." Corin waved a hand dismissively. "Silverlake is barely a day's ride from Aldlake. If they want to get far away, they should go to Morfield. I could ask my folks to find a place for them to stay."

"Morfield may be farther away, but it's on the other side of the mountains," Anri countered. "They'd have to go through the pass or travel right past the Poison Plains to get there."

"So what? As long as they don't actually go into the Poison Plains, they'll be fine. Morfield is great! We have the best spring festival and the best sunrise market on the western coast."

"I'm sure Morfield is very nice, Corin," Rin said, sipping her mug of kaffa, "but I think Will's parents will decide for themselves where they want to go. And don't we have to actually win the tournament first? None of this matters if we don't get the prize money."

Corin's eyes sparkled. "Just think of all that prize money!" he said, apparently not listening to what Rin had said at all. "What are you going to do with your share?"

Rin made an annoyed face that Corin didn't notice, but she shrugged in answer.

"I'm going to buy a silk bed for Leika," he went on. "And a whole chest full of nice clothes. And a really fancy padded shufflo leather saddle."

Anri snorted. "You seem pretty confident that you're going to win."

"Why not?" Will asked mildly. "Even the green dragonlord thinks we're going to win."

"What?" the other three asked, turning to stare at him.

Will pointed to the stone arch over the main road. A large green dragon perched at the peak, watching as the four flaplings raced through the obstacle course. A familiar burly figure sat on the dragon's neck as he stared in their direction.

Vortex, Leika, Ember, and Jade darted through the obstacle course in the courtyard, hitting targets in rapid succession, flipping back on a wingtip, whirling, and diving. Targets burst into flame and chimed like gongs. Lightning flashed and crackled in a chain reaction to hit two or three targets at once. Bright wings flurried, tails whipped, and the dragons screeched in eagerness, delight, or frustration as they competed to get ahead.

"I'm pretty sure that's Dragonlord Lamar," Will said. "I met him on Hatching Day. He's been sitting there for a while, just watching."

"He thinks you'll win?" Anri asked. "How do you know that?"

Will chuckled and gulped a mouthful of ginger water. "Just look at his dragon. The look on his face says everything."

It was true. Lamar's green dragon watched the group

of competing flaplings with an expression of bitter resentment on his long face.

"Ha!" Corin scoffed. "Let him get an eyeful, then! Green riders always think they have to be better than everyone else."

"Corin!" Will said, frowning at him.

Anri rolled her eyes. "Don't worry about it. He's got a point."

"Sorry, Anri." Corin flashed her a sheepish grin. "I almost forget you're a green rider sometimes."

Anri snorted at this, but didn't comment.

"Leika!" Corin shouted. "Show that big old green what you can really do!"

Wheeling above them, Leika tipped her head to her rider and let out a playful squawk. Then, flapping hard, she shot into the sky almost as fast as Vortex could.

"What is she doing?" Will asked.

"I don't know," Corin said, chuckling. "Whatever it is, it'll be great."

In the lower level of the courtyard, Vortex veered off and looked up, watching Leika curiously. But Jade and Ember were struggling in a neck-to-neck race to the finish, refusing to be distracted by anything.

Nearly level with Smoketree Peak, Leika let herself stall out. Tipping her wings back, she flipped upside down and backward before dropping like a stone in a nosedive.

Rin leaned forward. "Look at her go. I've never seen her do that before!"

Even Anri sat up and watched with wide eyes.

Leika folded her wings flat to her sides and picked up speed, using her tail like a rudder and aiming her snout at the nearest target.

"It looks like she's going to try for all of them," Will said. "Can she do that? Hit all ten targets at once?"

Corin shrugged and shook his head. "She thinks she can."

Leika cracked open her mouth, letting out a jubilant screech, and a burst of white-hot lighting shot into the air. The electricity hit the first target and rebounded, crackling from disc to disc around the courtyard.

Jade and Ember swooped to the side, wingtip to wingtip as they raced to the last target at top speed.

A moment before Jade and Ember reached the final target, Leika's bolt of lightning jumped from the target, zapped through Ember's wing and shoulder, and burst out from his body.

Ember wailed a piercing cry of agony that echoed off the mountain walls. His wings seized up, and he careened toward the ground.

Chapter Twenty

"Ember!" Rin jumped up and raced into the courtyard.

"Jade! Catch him!" Anri cried.

"Vortex! Help them!" Will hollered, running to follow Rin.

Ember dropped like a stone, neck limp, tail trailing like a comet, wings flopping uselessly in the wind.

All the dragons converged midair, but it was Jade who got her claws around Ember. Straining with her wings, she managed to slow their descent. They hit the ground, shaking the earth under Will's feet. Ember still wasn't moving.

A crowd of riders raced into the courtyard and gathered around the fallen red, desperate to help.

Overhead, the sky filled with adult dragons, circling and crying out in agitation. Three of them swooped down to land in the courtyard. Their riders dropped to the ground, and Dragonlord Brom, Tumi, and Nader ran to the fallen dragon.

"Step back! Make room!" Brom called.

Rin didn't seem to notice anything other than her broken and bleeding dragon. She clutched his neck and bent her face over his. "Ember! Ember! No! Please be okay! Please!" Her tears dropped onto his red hide, and her voice cracked with sobs as she caressed his ears and nose.

A dark, blistered wound marred the joint in Ember's left wing. But more alarming was the massive gash in the dragon's chest, as though some molten alien had burst out of him. The smell of burned dragon flesh made Will's stomach churn.

Brom crouched and felt Ember's side, waving back the gathered crowd. "He's breathing, thank heaven. Are the healers coming?"

"They're on their way," Tumi answered. His voice was so low and rough he almost didn't sound like himself.

Leika landed nearby and paced back and forth, making worried chirps as she walked.

Ember's eyes fluttered and cracked open, but his moist inner lids remained closed, making his eyes look cloudy and wet. He croaked a weak, gurgling sound.

"We know you didn't mean to, Leika," Corin said, stroking his dragon's neck. Even though his words were comforting, his voice sounded high and panicked. "It was an accident. Ember knows you're sorry. Look, the healers are coming. Ember will be fine. You'll see. He'll be just fine."

"Move aside!" a deep voice called. "Make space! Let us through!"

The crowd parted, revealing three adults in white and blue silk robes, the traditional garb of healers. Will recognized the old master healer, Uther, who'd treated his own broken ribs and injured foot when he'd first come to Fire Mountain.

The healers positioned themselves around Ember, examining his injuries, looking into his eyes, and listening to his heart and lungs.

"Nader," Uther said, without looking up from Ember, "take Scorch and fetch a litter. We need to carry him to the healer's hall immediately."

"Of course," Nader said, jumping onto his dragon and gliding away.

"Oh, Ember," Rin sobbed, wiping her eyes with her sleeve. "Will he be okay, Master Healer? I can't understand anything he's thinking!"

"We'll do everything we can for him." Uther patted her arm. "Fortunately, red dragons are resistant to burns. His heart is still beating, and he's breathing. Both are good signs."

A moment later, Nader and Scorch returned, Scorch carrying a litter made of canvas and wood in his front claws. He dropped the contraption on the ground next to Ember before landing nearby.

"Let's get this dragon inside where we can treat him properly," Uther said. A few of the stronger riders shifted Ember onto the litter.

"This never would have happened if your dragons weren't mixing together in this inappropriate manner!" a man's voice came from the edge of the crowd.

Will, Corin, and Anri, along with many others, turned to see Dragonlord Lamar stepping forward. He stared down at them with his fists planted on his broad hips. In the courtyard behind him, his dragon watched with mild interest, apparently unconcerned about the injured red flapling on the ground.

"What do you mean?" Will asked.

"There's good reason for the colors to be separated from one another," Lamar said. "I'm appalled that your instructors allowed this to happen!"

Tumi stood and faced off with the green dragonlord. "These four have been training together for months, and this is the first time any of them got injured. But even in the usual training wings, dragons get hurt sometimes. You can't expect us to believe—"

"Watch your tone, Tumi!" Lamar growled. Behind him, his green dragon rumbled. "If I was in charge here, they wouldn't even be housed together. It isn't right to let them mingle like this."

"Then it's fortunate you're not in charge here," Dragonlord Brom said, joining them. He placed a calming hand on Tumi's shoulder and stepped between him and Lamar. "I don't think you came here to air your opinions on how we train our youngsters. So what does bring you to Fire Mountain today?"

Lamar regarded Brom for a cold moment while the healers hauled Ember away.

Rin left with them, stumbling along at her dragon's side and crying inconsolably.

Will shifted on his feet, not sure whether they should follow or not.

Lamar shrugged and adjusted his riding belt. "I've come to assess the green flaplings, of course. If they're going to fly to the Poison Plains next year, they need to be making good progress now. If they're slacking off and overeating with you red riders, they'll never manage the flight."

Tumi's cheeks flushed, and his eyes widened.

Anri spoke up before he could say anything. "I'm one of the green riders! The others are probably in the training arena. All our dragons spend a lot of time flying. We're getting stronger every day."

Jade gave a little chirp of agreement and nuzzled Anri's arm with her nose.

Lamar nodded and almost smiled. "So this is your dragon. That was quick thinking, having her slow that foolish red's fall. And an impressive bit of flying, if I may say so. Joric seems to have done a decent job training the green flaplings of this hatching."

"Actually, Jade does most of her practice here with Vortex, Leika, and Ember," Anri said, twisting her fingers together. Her eyes darted over to the healer's hall where Ember's litter was just vanishing from view.

They could still hear Rin crying in the distance.

Will wanted to walk away from this conversation, to go see what was happening with Ember and Rin, but he didn't know how to do it without appearing rude to the dragonlord. He fidgeted, wishing he'd gone with Rin and Ember when he'd had the chance.

Most of the crowd was dispersing now that the excitement was over. He wondered if he could slip away with them.

"Is that so?" Lamar asked Anri, his forehead creased.

"It is." Brom folded his arms. "These four have become good friends. They train together daily."

"I would have thought such a skilled pair would practice for the junior tournament with her team," Lamar said. Then he laughed. "Or is your team too lazy to practice with you?"

Anri's eyes hardened. "Jade and I aren't on a team. Vortex, Leika, and Ember are the team. We're just helping them train."

Lamar looked around, bemused, as though Anri had

told a joke and he didn't get the punchline. "You mean a green is . . . with a yellow and a red and . . ."

"That's right," Will said. The disgusted look on Lamar's face nettled him. "We're all training together. We'd have Anri on our team if we could, but only three were allowed."

At Will's words, Lamar's eyes flashed, and he stared at Tumi. "How could you allow this? It's bad enough having a yellow and a red flying together. But to allow a green to team up with whatever that mutant is!" He flung a hand toward Vortex.

"Hey!" Will squared his shoulders and fumed. He had to remind himself that punching a dragonlord in the face would probably be a bad idea.

"They're only flaplings, Lamar," Brom said. "They're used to training together. The greens don't even have their poison yet. What could be the harm? Now that Ember is injured, if Anri wants Jade to take his place on the team, I see no reason to stop her."

Corin made a soft choking sound and edged to the side, like he wanted to slip away unnoticed.

"This is unconscionable. Disgusting!" Lamar waved his arm as though swiping the idea away. "I refuse to allow it. We're going to get to the bottom of this now!" He turned and stalked toward the main doors of the dragonhold. Brom and Tumi followed.

Will exchanged a nervous look with Anri and Corin, and the three of them trotted after the adults.

"Nothing in the rules forbids—" Brom began.

"The rules?" Lamar snapped. "It shouldn't have to be in the rules!"

"But why?" Will asked breathlessly. "Everyone else is already teamed up. Why is it so bad if dragons of different colors want to compete together?"

"I'll tell you why," Lamar growled, arms stiff as he marched ahead. "Not only is it dangerous to have them training together, as today's accident proved, but it's madness to let careless and foolish riders hold back a talented green!"

"Hold her back?" Tumi asked with a scoff. "Vortex, Leika, and Ember are among the most skilled dragons of this hatching!"

They passed through the massive doors to the main hall, their boots tapping against the tile floor and echoing through the cavernous space. The high, arched ceiling was carved directly out of solid rock, and recessed wall sconces flickered with orange light along the walls.

"You saw how Vortex flew," Anri said once the doors closed behind them, "and how strong Leika's electricity is . . ." She faltered and bit her lip, as though regretting her words.

"Yes, and how well did that work out for them? A red dragon perhaps fatally injured, and a yellow dragon traumatized. Didn't it occur to you, green rider, that it could have been your dragon in the healer's hall right now?"

Anri's face went pale. Her mouth opened wordlessly, and her wide eyes moistened. She took a half step backward and shook her head, as though rejecting the very thought.

Corin gasped. His eyes shifted between the three of them as he wrung his trembling hands.

"Let's just be thankful that didn't happen," Brom said gently.

"You may want to brush this incident aside, Brom," Lamar said, "but I don't think the other dragonlords will see things the way you do. We need to discuss this together." The dragonlord turned on his heel and marched away.

Chapter Twenty-One

"Come on, guys." Will nudged Anri and Corin. "Let's go see how Ember and Rin are doing."

Anri blinked and nodded. "You're right. That's more important right now."

Corin swallowed and nodded shakily.

They left the main hall and made their way across the courtyard to the healer's hall, their worried dragons trotting behind.

Finding the room where Ember was being treated was easy. The bustle of healers and apprentices rushing about like bees around a damaged hive gave it away immediately. That and the low, pained moans of Ember and the muffled sobbing of Rin carried through the long halls.

As they drew near the open doorway, the sharp smell of medicine filled the air.

Leika gave an anxious whine, and Corin placed a

comforting hand on her shoulder. "They're taking good care of him, Leika. Don't worry." His voice sounded strained.

As they turned to enter the room, an apprentice, her arms loaded with bloodied strips of cloth, almost collided with Will.

"Oh! I'm sorry," she said, blowing a loose strand of hair out of her face. "No visitors please. We need to keep the room clear, and you'll only get in the way."

"How is he?" Corin blurted. "Will Ember be okay? Will he live? How bad is it?"

The girl's face fell a little. "I'm afraid he's badly hurt. It's too soon to tell, but he's suffered severe burns on his wing and chest. The master healer fears that there's damage on the inside as well. We're doing everything we can to make him comfortable."

"He's not going to die, is he?" Tears trickled down Corin's cheeks.

Will's heart sank at the words. The hallway suddenly felt dark and cold and empty.

"Shh!" The apprentice grabbed Corin's shoulder and guided them away from the open door. "He needs to rest as well as he can. We don't know how things will turn out yet."

"You said he's burned," Anri said. "How could he be burned? He's a red dragon. I thought red dragons were fireproof."

The girl shook her head. "Red dragons can handle a lot of heat. They can even swim in lava if they want. But a yellow dragon's lightning is hotter than lava. Many times hotter. It was too much for him." She pressed her lips together and glanced back at the room. "We're applying medicine and bandages now. Wait somewhere out of the way if you like. When we're done, they might be ready for visitors."

The three friends nodded and backed farther down the hallway, where a stone bench sat under a window overlooking the courtyard.

When they sat down, Leika rested her chin on Corin's lap with a soft whine. He wrapped his arms around her neck miserably.

"It wasn't your fault, Corin," Will said. "It wasn't Leika's either. It was an accident."

"But it was," Corin said. "It was our fault. We should've been more careful. Or maybe Dragonlord Lamar is right, and we shouldn't have been practicing together at all."

Will felt a twinge in his gut. "Leika never meant to hurt Ember. Anyone can see how sorry she is."

"That doesn't change anything!"

Will raked his hands through his hair and leaned back against the wall, not sure what else he could say. He glanced at Anri, and she gave him a sad smile.

Vortex stretched his neck out to bump noses with

Leika, but the yellow didn't respond.

Rumbling softly, Vortex lay next to her on the floor instead.

They waited in silence, listening to healers bustling in and out, rolling carts laden with supplies and sharp surgical tools and hauling away soiled bandages, towels, and jars of bloodied water.

After a while, a cook came by with meals for all three of them: cold meat, sliced vegetables, soft white cheese, and bread. Corin didn't feel like eating and Will discovered that he'd lost his appetite as well. Anri picked at her food and offered little tidbits to Trouble, who stayed nestled in her leather shoulder bag.

After what felt like an eternity, Master Healer Uther emerged from Ember's room. His expression was weary and resigned, and his forehead glistened with a thin sheen of sweat. As he walked down the hall toward them, he examined a scroll.

"You waited out here all day? Good friends, I see." He blinked but didn't look up from his scroll.

Will stood and clasped his hands together. "Yes, sir. We're waiting to find out how Ember is doing."

"And Rin too," Anri added.

Corin didn't move. He stayed on the bench, face pale, and hardly looking up from Leika's yellow head resting in his lap.

"Yes, yes. It's very sad." Uther frowned as he read

something on the paper. "Most shocking . . . er, pardon the expression." His eyes finally lifted to look at them. "We have cleaned and applied salve to his burns. The damage to his chest and wing are not too severe to heal, provided he survives."

Will swallowed hard, then asked, "Will he survive?"

"He is resting now," Uther said, rolling up the scroll and tucking it under his arm. "But there was serious damage to his left lung. As the tissue breaks down, it will poison his blood. We have medicine that will mitigate that, but it's far from a certain cure. Even if he survives, his lung may never be the same."

Corin let out a soft sob, and Leika whined, pressing her wings into her sides and curling her tail.

"I'm truly sorry." Uther sighed, folded his hands, and rocked back on his heels. "I wish we had better news. You're free to visit your friends now, but please let Ember rest as much as he can. And I'm afraid your dragons will have to wait in the hallway. There's simply not enough room for them inside."

"Okay." Will nodded. He felt numb, like he was walking through a dream.

Anri tugged on Corin's sleeve. "Come on, Corin. Let's go see Rin."

Corin stumbled to his feet, and together, they walked down the hallway. Somehow, it seemed longer than before.

When they reached the door, Will pushed it open to

reveal an oval-shaped room illuminated by oil lamps. The temperature inside was as hot as the hatching ground and hotter by far than the flapling barracks. Corin gasped and Anri hissed under her breath as the wave of scorching air hit them, but Will only paid attention to the unconscious dragon lying on the ground and Rin, with her tear-streaked face pressed to his neck.

Thick white bandages wound around Ember's chest and shoulder. Pale blood seeped through the gauzy fabric, and his damaged wing joint was smeared with a thick green poultice. His shallow breathing sounded moist and wheezy.

"Rin?" Anri whispered.

Rin lifted her head, making no attempt to wipe away her tears or hide her scrunched-up face. "He's . . ." She started to speak, but her voice tightened. "He's . . . Oh, Ember . . ." She stifled her sobs against her sleeping drag-on's neck and stroked his ears and budding horns.

"Rin, I'm sorry," Corin blurted. "This is all my fault. I shouldn't have told Leika to show off like that. I don't know what I was thinking."

Rin shook her head and sniffed, seeming beyond words.

Behind them, Leika's yellow head poked around the corner. She gazed at Ember with wide eyes and drooping ears. Vortex and Jade followed, crowding the doorway with their curious and sorrowful faces.

Will, Anri, and Corin stayed with Rin until one of the healer apprentices ushered them out. Rin, of course, stayed at her dragon's side. Nobody would have been able to make her leave.

As soon as they were in the cool night air of the courtyard, Anri let out a sigh of relief. "I would have stayed even longer for Rin and Ember, but I'm glad to be out of that heat. I feel like my brain was cooking in there. I can't wait to take a bath."

Corin took a deep breath and shook out his shirt. "I know what you mean. They probably keep it hot in there so red dragons are comfortable. I don't know how red riders stand so much heat."

Will looked at them curiously. After the initial blast of scorching air, he'd forgotten about how hot it was in Ember's room.

"What?" Anri asked him. "Didn't you feel hot in there?"

"I am a little thirsty," he admitted, "but I didn't notice the heat that much. I was thinking about Ember."

Corin wrinkled his brow skeptically. "I felt like I was going to pass out!"

They entered the dining hall, filled with the smell of spiced meat and fresh bread. It was so late, the place was nearly empty, but Tumi stood from a nearby table to join them.

"How is Ember doing?" he asked in a low, worried voice. "I hope he's resting well."

Will and Anri told him what Uther had said about Ember's condition, explaining how his lung injury could be life threatening. When they finished, Tumi shook his head and rubbed his fingers over his eyes. "Yes, Uther said the same to me. Red dragons are hardy creatures, though. With plenty of rest and care, he might pull through."

They stood in awkward silence for a moment. Corin shifted his weight, like he was waiting for Tumi to berate him for his horrible mistake.

"I had some other news for you as well," Tumi said with a slight grimace. His eyes traveled to the doorway, looking out to the healer hall across the courtyard. "I'm not sure it makes any difference now."

"What is it?" Anri asked.

Tumi sighed and shook his head. "Without the approval of the dragonlords, your team won't be allowed to join the junior tournament. They'll need to vote on it if you want to compete together."

Anri's jaw tighten, and she lifted her chin.

Corin looked confused. "We wouldn't compete without Ember, anyway."

"I thought you would feel that way." Tumi folded his arms behind his back. "Like I said, it doesn't matter now. Let's just hope Ember recovers. There will be other Dragon Games to join when you're older."

Chapter Twenty-Two

In the weeks following Ember's injury, Will and his friends didn't bother with training their dragons at all. Somehow, it just didn't feel right. So Vortex, Jade, and Leika flew whenever they felt like it, took naps on sunny ledges as often as they wanted, and joined the adult dragons at the shufflo pen whenever they were hungry.

Will and Anri still sparred from time to time, but they only took up staves or swords when they were having an argument about something. Will thought it would be better to talk things out, or settle disputes with a game of rock paper scissors, but Anri seemed to prefer knocking him down with a stick.

The friends visited Ember in the healer hall every day after finishing their chores, and every day, the visible burns on the dragon's wing and chest healed a little more. But even as his scorched hide improved, his condition worsened.

Ember developed a horrible cough and his temperature dropped dangerously. He refused to eat solid food, so the healers put him on a liquid diet of shufflo blood to keep him alive.

Master Healer Uther said this was all to be expected. With his internal tissues breaking down, Ember's blood was growing too acidic and damaging every organ in his body. He mixed a concoction of boiled herbs that would help. If only they could get Ember to swallow it. But, much like a stubborn, sick child, Ember couldn't bear the taste of the medicine and refused to take it.

"Please, Ember," Rin begged, holding the bucket of brownish green liquid. "I know you don't want it. But if you drink this medicine, you'll feel so much better!"

Ember turned his nose away and whined miserably. Then he coughed, hacking up a spray of bloody fluid from his damaged lungs.

Will and Anri exchanged a worried look, but neither said anything. Will knew that if anyone could convince Ember to take his medicine, it would be his rider. They would only make things worse if they tried to intervene.

"I know it smells bad," Rin said, "but you have to trust the healers. Drink it, please!" She thrust the bucket under his nose imploringly, and the dragon thrashed his head back, screeching in defiance.

"Now you stop that!" Rin scolded, almost sounding severe.

Ember froze and stared at her with moist, anguished eyes. His breaths came in shallow wheezes and his wings trembled.

"You have to drink this medicine," Rin insisted. "You have to, or you'll keep getting worse."

Ember tentatively stretched out his neck and sniffed the liquid. He dipped his tongue in, only to cringe and throw his head back in a croaking wail.

"No, you can't have more blood now," Rin said with a sigh. If she was trying to sound stern, she failed entirely. "You need to drink your medicine first. That's what the healers said."

Anri wiped a sheen of sweat from her forehead and leaned closer to Will. "I don't understand why medicine always tastes so disgusting."

"I know," Will said. "Even the stuff that's supposed to taste like berries or bubble gum is still really gross."

Anri arched a brow at him. "What?"

"Oh, that's right." Will chuckled and shrugged. "In the off-lands, doctors mix stuff into medicine to make it taste better. Sweet like candy, you know? Otherwise kids won't drink it. It doesn't always work very well, but it's better than nothing, I guess."

Anri pushed away from the wall with a gasp. "That's it!"

Rin and Will stared at her. Even Ember seemed to forget about the bucket sloshing with disgusting green medicine and blinked curiously.

"Ember wants to drink some shufflo blood, so let's get it for him," Anri said.

Rin sighed. "But the healers said—"

"No, I get it," Will said, smiling. "That's a great idea, Anri. Come on, let's get some!"

They raced to the shufflo pen where a team of older dragon riders were carving up meat for the day's meals. It didn't take much to convince them to part with a bucket of drippings for Ember.

With their prize in hand, they carried the sloshing bucket back to the healer's hall and plopped it on the floor in front of Ember.

Ember immediately perked up at the meaty smell. His ears flicked with interest, and he snuffled his nose over the thick red liquid.

"Wait a minute, Ember. Not yet," Will warned.

Anri took the medicine from Rin and poured every last drop into the fresh blood. "Try to drink it now."

Ember lowered his snout and sniffed the mixture. He opened his mouth and lapped up a mouthful, then growled in disgust.

Rin sighed in disappointment and ran her hands over her face.

But Ember didn't draw his head back. Instead, he

dipped his beak in and sucked up a gulp. Then another. And another.

He narrowed his shining green eyes and grumbled as he drank, but he didn't stop.

Rin watched. Her mouth opened amazement, and she slowly leaned in. "That's it! Don't stop drinking, Ember. Keep going. It'll help you. You'll get better!" Her smile widened, stretching her tear-stained cheeks.

When Ember finished slurping the last of the medicine from the bottom of the bucket, he licked his muzzle clean and curled up on his mat with a begrudging grumble.

"I know it didn't taste good. But you did it!" Rin said, stroking his nose. "I'm so proud of you."

Ember coughed and shuddered, then drifted into a restless, twitching sleep.

A wave of relief washed over Will, and he sighed. Ember might not be out of the woods yet, but he was at least on the right path.

Next to him, Anri was watching Rin and Ember with a relieved expression that matched how he felt. The corner of her mouth pulled up in a small but genuine smile.

She caught him looking at her, and the smile shifted to a puzzled expression. "What?"

Will shook his head and rubbed the back of his neck. "It's nothing. I'm just happy Ember took his medicine. That was a good idea."

Ember's recovery turned a corner after that day. His

cough slowly improved, and his color, which had faded to a pale reddish orange, brightened to its usual vibrant red.

Soon he was able to walk outside and nap in the sunshine and fresh air. With the cool wind of early spring blowing through the mountain peaks, Ember chose warm volcanic ledges to rest on and watch his friends as he regained his strength.

"Don't you think Ember is looking better today?" Rin asked one sunny afternoon. She ran a hand gently over the pale scar on her dragon's chest, then scratched behind his ears.

Rin, Anri, and Will were all lounging on a sun-bathed rock at the edge of the courtyard with their dragons. Having just fed, the dragons were happy to spend the warmest hours of the day huddled together.

"You say that every day," Will reminded Rin with a laugh. "But yeah. I do think he's looking much better."

"I bet he'll be able to fly again soon," Rin said with a grin.

"His color is almost back to normal," Anri said. "And I can hardly hear any difference in his breathing anymore."

"That's right!" Rin beamed. "He almost never coughs anymore. You know, if he can start flying soon, he might still be able to do the target portion of the tournament with you."

Will and Anri exchanged an uneasy look.

"It won't be a problem if he's slow," Rin said. "The

target contest is scored on accuracy, not speed. Ember could still hit the targets. He'd just have to take his time, that's all. Or . . ." She looked from Will to Anri and back. "Did Anri already take my place on the team?"

"No . . . it's not—" Will started.

"I don't mind if she did. Really," Rin said, shaking her head. "I understand why. With Ember still recovering—"

"No, Rin," Anri said. "It's not that. It's just . . . when Ember got hurt, Dragonlord Lamar saw the whole thing. He convinced Brom that we couldn't be a team unless the dragonlords voted on it."

Rin paused in stroking her dragon's ears. Her forehead wrinkled, and she cocked her head to the side. "Because Ember got hurt?"

Will snorted. "I don't think that had anything to do with it. Lamar seemed angrier that Anri and Jade were hanging out with us. He was worried that she'd join our team. A talented green dragon training with a bunch of lesser colors was just too much for him to accept."

Anri folded her arms against her chest and scowled at the ground. "He thought training with you would hold us back." She scoffed. "It's ridiculous! None of the other green riders wanted us on their team, anyway. They think I'm too soft."

"Soft? You?" Will asked, bemused.

Anri didn't stop. "Even if Vortex doesn't have elemental powers, he's still the strongest flyer in the hatching. He's even stronger than the greens. And Leika and Ember are more skilled with their elemental attacks than any of the others."

"Wait a minute," Rin said. "The dragonlords have to agree to let you be a team? So you could still compete, as long as they vote on it?"

"Well, yeah, I guess so," Will said. "But we didn't want to bother you with any of that while Ember's still recovering."

"Let Anri join your team, silly!" Rin laughed. "It's not that hard. Of course, you should still compete! Ask them to vote on it."

"But . . ."

"Do you think we want to split up the whole team just because of Ember's accident?" Rin asked. "He'd do his best for his friends. But Jade can outfly every dragon in the hatching! We don't mind sitting out."

Anri pulled her mouth up in a half-nervous smirk. "You want us to call all the dragonlords here just to decide whether the three of us can be a team? Lamar will love that."

"And what about Corin?" Will asked.

The girls frowned.

"He hasn't been the same since the accident," Anri said. "Leika has hardly used electricity at all since then. They might not want to compete anymore."

Rin lifted her chin. "He's probably still blaming

himself for what happened. I should talk to him." She pressed her lips together for a moment and turned to her dragon. "Ember, do you know where we can find Leika and Corin?"

Ember lifted his head lazily and yawned, then blinked at her.

"All right, that's not too far," she said with a smile. "Why don't we go find them?"

Ember hefted himself to his feet and shook out his wings with a huge stretch and another yawn. Then he and Rin started off through the courtyard with Will, Anri, Vortex, and Jade following.

Rin and Ember led them through the training ground and beyond, to the trail that led to the grassy hills where the yellow flaplings trained.

Before they got that far, though, Ember fluttered his wings and led them down an offshoot of the mountainside trail. They found Corin lying on his back in a grassy hollow with his hands folded behind his head, staring at the deep blue sky. Leika lay at his side with her eyes half closed and her yellow ears twitching as a cool breeze swept over the grass.

"Corin?" Rin said.

Corin turned his head to look up at her but didn't sit up. "Hello," he said, then turned back to stare at the bright, cloudless sky and breathed in a deep lungful of air. "It's peaceful out here, isn't it?"

Rin pressed her lips together, then marched the rest of the way down the trail, until she was right next to him. She sat down.

"Anri and Jade said they'd compete in the tournament instead of me and Ember. Will Leika still be on the team?"

He tilted his chin toward her and pursed his lips. "But we can't. Dragonlord Lamar said—"

"Tumi told us they'd have to vote on it," Will reminded him. "But they never did."

"You want to ask them to vote?" Corin finally sat up and faced Rin. Dry grass crackled under him as he drew his feet in. "But Leika . . . I mean . . . are you sure Ember's okay with Jade taking his place?"

"Ember is fine with it, and so am I," Rin said firmly. "You don't think a red rider would want to break up a whole team on their account, do you?"

Corin grimaced and looked away.

"Come on, Corin." Rin rested her hand on his shoulder. "They can't do it without you."

He stroked Leika's head, and the pale-yellow dragon gazed into his eyes. After a silent moment, Corin nodded. "All right. We don't want to be the reason anyone misses out on the tournament. If you think we should still compete, then we're in."

"Thank you!" Rin threw her arms around Corin's neck in a delighted embrace.

Corin chuckled nervously, peeling her arms away. "All

right. But listen," he said. "Leika . . . well, she doesn't think making lightning is much fun anymore."

"What?"

"Well, you see," Corin shrugged, running his hand through his blonde hair, "whenever she tries to make a charge, she starts thinking about how Ember got hurt. Or, I don't know, maybe it's me. Maybe I'm the one who keeps thinking about it. But either way, it sucks all the fun out of it, and she can't . . ." He ran his hand along Leika's neck with a haunted expression on his face. "We just don't want that to happen again."

"Nobody does," Will assured him. "I'm sure we can find a way to make training safe for everyone."

"Assuming the dragonlords will let us compete together," Anri said wryly. "I'm not too sure that's going to happen."

Rin folded her arms and smiled confidently. "It won't hurt to ask."

Chapter Twenty-Three

At Rin's suggestion, they waited until after Dragonlord Brom had finished dinner and was relaxing in the great hall. With a few horns of mulled ale in him and the resident bards playing lively music, he'd be in a cheerful mood and more likely to agree to their request.

While their dragons took their evening meal at the shufflo pen, the four friends made their way to the head table of the great hall.

Dragonlord Brom chatted with the senior dragon riders, leaning his elbow against the table and sipping from his ale horn while the bard strummed a lively melody on his lyre.

After Will made their request, the dragonlord set his ale horn in its cradle and brushed a sleeve through his beard. "You want them to vote on it, do you?" He cleared his throat and nodded. "It's been a long time since I've had the other dragonlords here to dine with us. Too long. We haven't all come together since the hatching."

"So you'll do it?" Will asked.

Brom took another drink of ale and regarded them thoughtfully. "I can't promise they'll vote in your favor, but I'll send out the invitation. They should at least consider it."

Seated a few spaces down from Brom, Tumi leaned against the tabletop. "I already know how Lamar will vote. There's no changing that man's mind."

"True," Brom said. "But the others may be more agreeable. We shall see. Regardless, it will be pleasant to host the other dragonlords here again."

The summons went out the next day. Three red dragon riders flew off to the three other dragonholds early in the morning. Will wondered how they contacted the holds that could be hazardous to red dragons. Did they actually go into the Poison Plains where the toxic fumes could kill them? Wouldn't the Frozen Peaks be far too cold for a red dragon to stand?

But there must have been some sort of system in place because all three dragons returned unharmed. And one week later, the other three dragonlords soared into the courtyard of Fire Mountain Dragonhold.

Brom, wearing his traditional robes, and his mighty dragon, Bronzehorn, stood in the courtyard with open arms to welcome the others. Tumi and the other flapling instructors flanked the dragonlord, ready to join the conference and give their testimony regarding Will and his friends.

Dragonlord Lamar's green dragon landed first, followed by Trinley's yellow and Perrin's blue.

Will and his friends watched from a discreet distance by the barracks while the leaders of all the dragon riders came together. Their steeds launched back into the air to perch on the surrounding ledges.

"I don't think Dragonlord Lamar is too happy about being summoned here," Corin said, sounding worried.

"I didn't think he would be," Anri scoffed. Holding Trouble in her arms, she scratched behind the kisnit's fuzzy ears. "It serves him right."

"You might want to reconsider how you talk about him," Rin said. "He's your dragonlord, after all. Not that I disagree with you."

Anri snorted. It looked like she was about to say something else, but she stopped herself with pursed lips.

"There's Dragonlord Perrin." Will pointed as the youngest dragonlord offered a formal bow of greeting to Brom. "Did I ever tell you that he and Boreas rescued me on the way to the hatching?"

"Yes," Rin and Anri said.

"What? No!" Corin gasped and gave Will a scandalized look. "What happened?"

"Well, it's kind of a long story. I got into a fight with this worthless punk on the way to the hatching ground. He'd stolen Vortex's egg, you see. I ended up falling over the cliff with the egg and landed in the river."

"Is that why you looked like you'd lost a fight with a cormant that first week?" Corin asked.

"Pretty much," Will said. "Boreas and Perrin found me. If it wasn't for them, we never would've made it. Perrin's a good guy. I'm sure he'll be on our side."

Brom greeted the arriving dragonlords with a warm smile that Perrin and Trinley returned. Lamar ignored the gesture and bowed stiffly, gesturing for them all to proceed to the conference room.

As the group marched into the dragonhold together, Tumi sidled up to Perrin and gave the dragonlord an enthusiastic and playful hug, thumping the blue dragonlord on the back.

Perrin returned the embrace, a little awkwardly, and the two chatted together as they entered the hold.

"What was that about?" Corin asked.

"Didn't you know?" Rin said. "Dragonlord Perrin is Tumi's brother."

"Really?" Will said. "But they're so different!"

"Not that different," Rin said. "From what you told us, Dragonlord Perrin is a nice person, just like Tumi."

"Then he'll vote in our favor," Anri said with a satisfied smile. "That means we only need Dragonlady Trinley to vote for us, and we'll have the majority!"

"Do you think she will, though?" Will asked, looking at Corin.

"How should I know?" Corin shrugged. "She's a yellow rider, so she's eager to let people have their fun. But she's also a dragonlady. I'm sure she takes her job seriously. Only her dragon knows what she's really thinking."

"Hey that's an idea!" Will brightened and turned to Vortex, who was lounging in the sun next to him. "Can you tell what Dragonlady Trinley thinks about all this?"

Vortex lifted his head and looked to the dragonhold, focusing on the conference room where the meeting was just beginning. *I can't hear her thoughts like I can yours. But she's happy to be here. She's amused by something that's happening, and she's hungry.*

"Hmm. That's not very helpful. What about her dragon? Can you ask her dragon what she's thinking?"

"Will!" Anri scolded.

Vortex was silent for a moment.

On a ledge overlooking the courtyard, Trinley's yellow dragon turned her gaze toward Will and rumbled a deep growl.

Skydancer says no dragon will share their rider's secret thoughts. She says we should know that already.

"Oh, oops," Will winced. "Is she mad at me?"

The huge yellow dragon shuffled her wings and blinked in the sunlight, turning her nose away again.

Vortex's thought came small and abashed in Will's

mind. *She thinks we're funny, like hatchlings trying to steal food unnoticed from an adult dragon's mouth. We don't know how ridiculous we are.*

Will snorted and threw his hands into the air. "Well, that's just great!"

"What did Vortex say?" Anri hugged Trouble close to her chest.

All three of Will's friends watched him with expressions of mingled horror and curiosity.

"Skydancer is laughing at us," Will said.

Rin sighed in relief. "At least she's not mad! How did you expect that to go? Asking a dragon to tell you what her rider is thinking?"

"It seemed like a good idea at the time!" Will said. "Avria has so many rules that nobody ever talks about. I never know when I'm about to do something wrong by accident."

"Well, I don't think we'll have to wait long," Rin said. "They'll let us know as soon as everyone votes. We already know how Dragonlord Lamar will vote. It seems like Brom and Perrin will be on our side. So all we have to do is wait for Dragonlady Trinley to decide. She seems nice, so I don't think she'd vote against us."

Despite Rin's confidence, the four friends and their dragons waited in the little alcove by the barracks for hours, watching the tall doors leading into the dragonhold.

The other flapling riders went about business as usual,

heading off in groups to train, taking breaks for meals, and doing their daily chores.

Halfway through the day, while the sun was at its highest and the young dragons napped on the warm rocks, the green wing strolled past them, chatting and laughing together on their way to the training field.

"Hey, Anri!" Albin called, sniggering. "How's your team doing? Oh, that's right, you don't have one!"

"Your mouth is talking again, Albin. You might want to check on that," Anri answered in a bored tone.

Albin didn't seem to hear her. "Isn't it tragic?" he said, faking a frown. "With your dragon, you could've been great. But instead, you chose to associate with these rejects."

The other green riders nodded.

"Hey!" Corin shouted.

"Shut your face, Albin!" Anri snapped, cheeks reddening. On the rock beside her, Jade woke with a snort, blinking bleary eyes.

In Anri's arms, Trouble fluffed out her fur and made tiny growling noises, laying her ears flat against her head.

"You should just give it up now," Kade said at Albin's shoulder. To Will's surprise, this boy looked like he was genuinely concerned for Anri. "These riders will only hold you back. Nobody in Poison Plains will take you seriously if you do this. You'll never amount to anything."

"That's it!" Will rose and faced off with the green

riders. "Leave Anri alone. She's braver than any of you, and a better fighter than all of you put together. Jade can outfly every flapling in the hatching. If the dragon riders in Poison Plains look down on her because she's our friend, then they're just as stupid as you are!"

"Oh, listen to him!" Albin said, waving his hands in mock fear. "It's the off-lander with the freak dragon who almost didn't make it to the hatching. We should all be scared!"

Dal laughed with him, but Kade and Eris looked thoughtful, giving Will hope that at least those two weren't completely brainless.

Will squared off with Albin, fists clenched at his sides, but he didn't strike. He just glared at the other boy, waiting to see if he would make the first move.

Corin stood and joined him, and Anri stepped up to his other side with Trouble chittering on her shoulder and her arms folded across her chest. "When we beat you at the junior tournament, you'll see what kind of rejects we are," she said.

Albin snorted and rolled his eyes. "Whatever. You're all delusional."

The green riders sauntered off, chatting together and occasionally looking over their shoulders at Anri and her friends.

"They're total jerks," Will grumbled and settled on the ground against Vortex's side.

"They're green riders," Rin said, as though that explained it. Then she shot Anri an apologetic smile. "Not that all green riders are bad."

Anri laughed and shook her head. "No. I'm a jerk too. I'll admit it."

"You're not!" Rin said, looking shocked. "You're rough around the edges sometimes, but you mean well. It's easy to see that you're a good friend once people get to know you."

Anri bit her lip and looked away, cheeks flushing.

Jade butted playfully against her side.

"Rin, cut it out," Will said, chuckling. "You're embarrassing her!"

Rin lifted her chin smugly. "If she's going to associate with a red rider, she's got to get used to being complimented. Red riders take friendliness very seriously."

"Maybe that's why this conference is taking so long," Corin said. "Brom is probably keeping them so busy with food and entertainment that they're not getting around to the voting part."

"But Dragonlord Lamar doesn't seem like he'd take that for very long," Will said. "I think they're just arguing with each other."

When the wafting aroma of seared meat and seasoned vegetables announced that it was dinnertime, the dragonlords still hadn't emerged from the conference room. Will and his friends gave up waiting and made their way to the dining hall while their flaplings ate with the adult dragons by the shufflo pen.

The four friends sat together as usual to enjoy tender slices of roast meat with thick brown gravy and herbed vegetables in a butter sauce. Will's mood improved as he ate, putting out of his mind the confrontation with Albin and worries about the conference of dragonlords.

They stayed at their table, sipping mugs of creamy spiced kaffa and chatting together long after the other kids left for the evening, when the sound of heavy boots clacking on stone drew their attention to the doorway.

Will and Anri turned to look. Corin cut off in the middle of telling a joke. Rin licked her lips and gulped.

Tumi strode across the floor with a calm, neutral expression.

"Are they done?" Rin asked. "Have they decided?"

"They have decided," Tumi said. "Come with me. You'll hear the verdict in the conference room."

Chapter Twenty-Four

The four friends jumped to their feet, leaving their mugs of kaffa unfinished on the table, and scrambled to follow Tumi out the door.

"It took them long enough," Corin muttered under his breath.

"I bet Dragonlord Lamar wouldn't stop arguing with them," Will whispered back.

Pale moonlight flooded the courtyard, enhanced by braziers and oil lanterns which cast flickering shadows on the ground as they walked to the main doors of the dragonhold.

Will felt Vortex's sleepy thoughts in his mind. He wanted to share the long-awaited verdict with his dragon, but having finished his dinner long ago, Vortex nestled on his mat in the barracks, dreaming soundly.

Oh well, he'd just have to tell his dragon the news when he woke up.

The group trotted up the steps and through the double doors into the dragonhold. They passed through the anteroom and entered the conference hall, where the dragonlords and flapling trainers waited around a long table, set with a pitcher of wine, dried meats, bread, and preserved fruit. All of them looked weary after the long day.

"Ah, good. You're here." Brom rose and nodded at Tumi. "Thank you for bringing them."

"Of course, Dragonlord," Tumi said with a small bow.

Brom cleared his throat and pulled at his beard as he paced the room. "I suppose you four have been waiting all day to learn the results of our meeting, so I won't make you wait any longer. We've voted, and you will not be allowed to compete together in the tournament."

"What?" Will asked, looking between Brom and the other dragonlords in disbelief. "Why not? Our dragons are just as good as the rest of the flaplings. Why can't we be a team?"

"Will!" Rin hissed, shooting him a scandalized look.

The dragonlords and flapling instructors reacted with expressions ranging from amused to insulted.

Dragonlord Brom cleared his voice again before answering, "I understand your shock, young rider. But the decision has been made. After the incident with Ember, it's too risky to allow dragons of different colors to train together."

Lamar grumbled and shifted in his seat. "It was inappropriate for a green to fraternize with other colors to begin with! If this girl joins your team, you'll be holding back a green rider from achieving her best."

"Lamar," Brom shot the green dragonlord a severe look, "I will ask you to exercise some tact while you are a guest in my dragonhold."

"I speak the truth as I see it," Lamar said. "If coming to Fire Mountain means I need to lie through my teeth, we'll hold the next meeting in Poison Plains."

Dragonlady Trinley rolled her eyes and Dragonlord Perrin just shook his head wearily.

As they left the conference hall and made their way across the courtyard, Will couldn't restrain himself any longer. "I can't believe it! They voted against us? I thought Dragonlord Brom was on our side."

"Well, we don't know for sure how he voted." Rin bit her lower lip.

"It makes sense that Dragonlady Trinley wouldn't trust us," Anri said. "She doesn't know us at all. But Brom has seen our dragons training together for months. He knows that working together is making them stronger and faster than the others. Jade was already the best flyer, but now all of our dragons can outfly the green wing."

Corin scuffed his feet as he walked, keeping a little

behind the others. "Maybe they're worried Leika will hurt one of your dragons again," he said in a subdued voice. As they approached the entrance to the barracks, he turned aside and leaned against the wall, staring at his boots. "It makes sense. Lightning is hard to control. Once it's released, Leika can't take it back."

"That's ridiculous!" Will scoffed. "It's the same for all the dragon abilities. You don't think Ember could call back his fire, do you?"

Corin twisted his mouth to the side. "No."

"I admit we made a mistake. We should have been more careful. But just because Ember got hurt once doesn't mean the team should have to break up. The dragons don't have to all compete at the same time in the tournament, so they don't have to train at the same time either, right? Leika could just stay in a separate area when she's using her electricity or something."

The tall doors of the dragonhold opened once more, and the dragonlords stepped out into the night.

In unison, three massive dragons dropped from their ledges and glided to the ground in descending spirals, landing in the open space among swirling eddies of dust and sand.

Will paused, debating with himself for a moment, then ran out into the courtyard.

"Hey! Where are you going?" Anri called.

Ignoring her, Will ran to the massive blue dragon

Boreas just in time to catch Dragonlord Perrin as he prepared to climb into his saddle.

"Wait!" Will panted, stumbling to a stop.

Perrin paused, regarding Will, then stepped back from Boreas's foreleg with a nod. "I was wondering whether you'd come find me after the meeting."

"I can't believe they're all being so unreasonable," Will blurted, waving an arm in exasperation. "Couldn't you explain it to them? Make them see that it's stupid to keep the dragon colors apart? You're smart, so why won't they listen to you?"

Perrin gave a little wince.

"Even Dragonlord Brom! Why would he turn on us like that? He always loved to watch Vortex and the others race together."

"There are a couple of things you need to understand, Will," Perrin said. "First, just because someone is intelligent, that doesn't mean everyone will listen to them. People usually decide things based on their own understanding. If they are unwilling to understand, or incapable of understanding, no amount of explanation will sway them."

Will pressed his lips together and scowled in frustration.

"Second, you should not lose your regard for Dragonlord Brom. He didn't vote against you tonight."

Will blinked and looked into Perrin's calm, patient

eyes. "Wait, what? He didn't?" Then he gasped and took a step back. "But that means you did!"

Dragonlord Perrin nodded. "I did. And I argued with the others to do the same, though not for the same reasons as Lamar. Dragonlady Trinley took quite a lot of convincing."

"You—you made them vote against us?" Will demanded, voice cracking. Over the past few months, Will had come to see the tournament as his one chance to free his parents and prove that Vortex was as good as any other dragon. But now Perrin, his first real friend in Avria, the one dragonlord he thought he could count on, had betrayed him!

"Allow me to explain why," Perrin said, holding out his hand in a calming gesture.

Will felt too angry to speak. He stared, waiting in silent resentment.

"Do you recall that there are rumors of swarmers off the northern coast?"

Will nodded, wondering what this had to do with anything. Their dragons weren't training with swarmers. What did it matter to them?

"We are working hard to prevent these rumors from turning into mass panic. My dragonhold has verified many of these reports. Frozen Peaks is in the north of Avria, within sight of the coastline. With my own eyes, I've seen the dead bodies of swarmers washed ashore. In fact, some of them haven't been entirely dead when we arrived."

"Whoa, really?" Will asked, intrigued despite his anger.

Perrin nodded gravely. "Boreas is one of the few living dragons who's killed a swarmer. Granted, it wasn't far from death by the time we arrived. But the fact that any swarmer has made it to our shores alive is a matter of great concern."

Will nodded, remembering the pictures of swarmers he'd seen in tapestries: huge flying bugs with whip-like stinging tails, sharp grasping legs, and horrible mandibles.

"We've been working with Master Bard Kelree to research the phenomena for some years now. Not long ago, the reports were few. In past years, only the fishermen who sailed far offshore returned with tales of swarmers. And they only reported dead and decomposing corpses. But every spring, the reports grow in number and come closer to shore."

"That's . . ." Will frowned and shook his head to clear his thoughts. "That's scary, all right. But what does it have to do with the junior tournament? Why does that mean we can't be a team?"

"I believe the dragons may soon be called upon to defend Avria from swarmers again."

"Anri thinks so too," Will said.

Perrin nodded and continued, "If that day comes, we'll

need every dragon available in the skies, and in top fighting condition. The dragons of Avria haven't battled swarmers for many generations. Nobody alive remembers the training and techniques necessary to be effective against them. I believe we could lose many lives in our first encounter, leaving the common folk vulnerable."

Will listened with bated breath, a sense of nebulous dread growing in his gut.

"If you three set a precedent that dragons of different colors can train side by side—and especially if you win the junior tournament by doing so—other riders will follow your example. Other dragons would be injured the way Ember was, or perhaps die in tragic accidents. That risk alone is almost too much to tolerate. With the added threat of coming swarmers, and the lives of so many on the line, it's simply unacceptable."

Will felt like he'd been punched in the gut. He still didn't agree with Dragonlord Perrin, but he understood him.

Perrin took a deep breath and added in a gentle tone, "Also, I believe dragons excel when they train with their own kind, without fear that a poorly aimed ice-bolt or fire-ball will hurt their companions."

"What about Vortex, then?" Will asked in a choked voice. "Who can he train with? He doesn't fit in with any of the colors."

Perrin glanced up at Boreas, and the great blue dragon

gave a soft rumble. "That's a question that needs careful thought. If you're dedicated and persistent, I'm sure you'll come to the answer eventually." He patted Will on the shoulder and climbed into the saddle on Boreas's neck. "Until we meet again, young dragon rider. Clear skies!"

Perrin clipped into the saddle, buckled his riding cap, and lowered his goggles while Boreas settled on his haunches. Then the dragon leaped into the air, beat down with his wide blue wings, and kicked up whorls of dust and sand as he took to the sky.

Shielding his face with his arm, Will watched them go. He wasn't sure what to think anymore, but a nagging, uncertain dread grew in his mind.

Chapter Twenty-Five

"I can't believe Dragonlord Perrin would do that!" Rin said at breakfast the next morning. "Nobody else wants to train with other dragon colors. They all think we're crazy for doing it. And if he really wants your dragons to be in top condition, he wouldn't stop you. Our dragons are so much stronger because they've been competing with one another."

"Yeah." Corin swirled his spoon in a bowl of hot, creamy porridge. "Blue riders like to think things through."

Anri nodded. "Dragonlord Perrin might be friendly for a blue rider, but he's still a blue rider. He'll do what he thinks is best, no matter how anyone else feels about it."

"Maybe we could keep training in secret?" Rin asked. "What if we can figure out a way to join the tournament when we get there?"

Anri rolled her eyes at her. "Haven't you thought about this at all?"

Rin's eyebrows pulled together, and Will frowned at her in confusion.

"Just take a moment to think about what he said." Anri looked pointedly at Rin. "Or did you forget what Master Bard Kelree told us in Silverlake?"

"What did she tell you?" Will asked.

Rin fiddled with her spoon, twirling it between her fingers. "The same thing Dragonlord Perrin told you. She's been keeping records of swarmer sightings over the years. She's even ridden north to investigate them herself. It's not just rumors."

"Then we should keep training together," Rin said. "If we need to fight the swarmers one day, we shouldn't stop."

"I don't know about that," Corin said, still mixing his porridge without eating any.

"Why not?" Will asked.

"What Dragonlord Perrin said makes sense to me. If we win the junior tournament, everyone else will try to mix dragon colors too. They'll want to copy us. What happens when an adult green dragon trains with a blue or a red? What happens if another yellow loses control of its lightning? What happens when training together means some dragons die?"

They all went quiet. Will grimaced into his mug of kaffa, remembering the man he'd met on his way to the

Hatching Ground, long ago. The former dragon rider with the haunted look in his eyes and the dark solitude that had hung around him like a cloud.

The old man had gone into the town tavern to catch a glimpse of a dragon egg, seemingly unable to keep away. But just being in the same room with the egg had been too much for him, and the man had fled in misery.

Will tried to imagine what his life would be like if anything ever happened to Vortex. He shuddered and his mind recoiled from the horrifying thought.

"I agree with Corin," Anri said. "I'll still teach you everything I learn about fighting with staff and sword. And Jade will fly with Vortex for as long as it's safe. But no tournament. I'm sorry, Will."

Will sighed and nodded, taking a deep drink of warm kaffa. "I guess you guys are right."

That night, the red dragon riders threw one of their many parties, complete with a bonfire, lively music, dancing, kegs of frothy ale, sugar bread, ginger water, and eye-watering flame steaks. This one was in celebration of the apple blossom rain, the time in late spring when apple trees dropped their flowers, making it look like white and pink petals were raining from the sky.

There were no apple trees in the dragonhold, of course, but buckets full of blossoms were brought in to decorate the tables and dance floor. And there was enough apple blossom tea for everyone to enjoy.

Normally, Will would have joined in with the festivities. But that night he didn't feel like it. He sat a little apart from the crowd, watching the orange glow of the distant bonfire. Vortex was content to lie at his feet with his wings and tail tucked in close.

"You're not hungry, are you?" Will asked. "I could grab you a flame steak if you want."

Vortex made a small grumbling noise. *Flame steaks smell horrible. Like burned meat with plant stuff on it.*

"You mean cooked, seasoned meat?" Will chuckled at his dragon's description. "Or are you worried it would be too spicy for you?"

I could eat one if I wanted to. Vortex's thoughts sounded smug. *But I'm not hungry.*

Will grinned and rubbed his dragon's nose.

"Hello, Will."

Will lifted his eyes to see Anri and Jade approaching in the bonfire's light. "Hi, Anri."

Jade touched noses with Vortex and settled down next to him while Anri sat on the bench at Will's side.

"I just came to say . . . to tell you I understand," she said.

"You understand?"

"About the tournament. I understand why it was so important to you."

Will didn't know what to say, so they sat in silence for a moment.

"It isn't just a game for you," Anri said. "You needed the money to help your family."

"Yeah," he said, voice low. "They weren't doing so good the last time I saw them. The man they work for . . . he's just awful. I need to help them get out of there."

"I wish it could have worked. The junior tournament, I mean. But there still might be other ways to help them."

"You think so?"

Anri shrugged and shifted in her seat. "There will be more options when our dragons are bigger. Maybe we could find a silk mine and sell silk. Or we could do what Nader does and collect death peppers from the mountaintops to sell at markets. I know someone back in Silverlake who'll pay top price for them."

In a rare gesture that surprised Will, Anri placed her hand over his and gave it a gentle squeeze. "We'll figure it out. When our dragons are big enough to fly with us, we'll be able to do a lot more." She smiled at him in the warm orange light of the fire.

Will smiled back. "Thanks." He glanced down at their dragons, lounging side by side on the ground. "It's hard to notice it day by day, but they're getting huge, aren't they?"

"I think they'll be able to carry us soon," she said. "I even heard Tumi talking about fitting them for saddles."

"Really?" Will's heart jumped with excitement.

"Summer is coming. Don't forget that they'll have to fly

us to our dragonholds in the fall. Except the red dragons, of course. They're already at their dragonhold."

"Lucky dogs." Will snorted and eyed the festivities before them. "Parties every week, good food every night, and they don't even have to fly to a new dragonhold."

Anri cocked an eye at him. "You could live here with them if you wanted to."

Will shrugged. "Yeah, I guess we could go anywhere."

"Except to Poison Plains," Anri said wryly. "I know you're not considering that."

"What if I am?" Will joked. "Vortex is as likely to be a green as a red."

Anri withdrew her hand and planted her fists on her hips. "You shufflo-brained dolt! You'd throw away Vortex's life on a hunch that he's some color other than white? Stinging swarms! If I have to—"

"Hey, take it easy," Will said, laughing. "It was a joke. Of course I'm not taking him there!"

Anri didn't seem to think it was funny. She huffed and stood abruptly. "Good! Don't even think about it. I'm going back to the party. Jade, you can stay with Vortex if you want to." She turned on her heel and stalked away.

Jade lifted her head, hesitated for a moment, then scrambled to her feet to follow her rider.

Will sighed and rolled his eyes at his dragon. "Girls are so dramatic."

Or maybe she believes you're stupid enough to go to Poison Plains.

"Ha!" Will snorted. Then he frowned thoughtfully. "Wait, she does think that, doesn't she?"

THE NEXT DAY, Will's friends went back to training with the flapling instructors, leaving Will and Vortex with nothing to do for hours on end but explore the dragonhold. Miles of passageways and hundreds of rooms hid within the stone walls. At first, they started wandering between eating meals and doing chores out of boredom. But Will remembered that Anri had mentioned a library, and he was curious about what other interesting things they might find.

Walking through the dimly lit passageways, going ever deeper into the dragonhold, they passed many rooms they'd never seen before. Many were vacant and boring, but others were beautiful or mysterious.

They found storerooms filled with random objects and supplies, gleaming marble dance halls with ornate carved walls, and lavish guest quarters with velvet cushions and gilded furniture.

As they made their way farther in, they found staterooms and a large steamy arboretum with a domed glass ceiling. Fragrant flowers erupted from stoneware pots all around.

Deeper still, they came to rugged tunnels leading into deep, dark chambers that smelled of sulfur.

They met fewer and fewer residents of the dragonhold as they went on. And the deeper they went into the mountain, the hotter the floor and walls grew. The air smelled of char, and Will's nostrils felt hot with every breath he took.

"Phew! It's scorching in here." Will shook out his shirt, but that only helped the sweat dry on his skin. "It's not too hot for you, is it?"

It is hot. But I'm still comfortable, Vortex assured him.

"All right. Let me know if you need to go back. With all this sweating, I'll probably get thirsty real soon, anyway."

They came to a room that looked like an old library. Metal boxes rested on shelves and covered ceramic containers were arranged in neat rows on the ground.

"This looks interesting." Will stepped inside and looked around. "Let's check it out. Maybe we'll learn something." Finding an oil lantern, Will lit it using the wall sconce in the hallway. "There, now we can see better." He adjusted the wick so the lantern shone brightly.

Vortex sniffed the nearest shelf and sneezed. *These things smell old.*

"Everything's all dusty too. It's like nobody's been in here in ages." He lifted the lid of the nearest metal box.

Old scrolls and books bound in a thin metal that gleamed in iridescent colors sat inside. Taking one of the scrolls, he opened it and ran his thumb along the material. "This doesn't feel like paper."

Vortex sniffed it. *It smells like the colorful robes the dragonlord wears.*

"Dragonlord Brom's ceremonial robes? Those are made of silk. But why would someone make so many scrolls out of silk and just forget about them here? It's supposed to be really expensive stuff."

Carefully, he unrolled the scroll to see what was written on it. It was covered in neat, close-spaced writing, but the language was completely foreign to him. He couldn't understand it at all.

He tried a few more scrolls with the same result before he shelved that box and tried another.

In the next box, he found a small scroll written in English. It was a record of yearly tributes offered by surrounding cities. They'd sent portions of fruits, grains, animals, fabric, medicine, and other supplies in thanks for the dragonhold's protection.

The next scroll recorded the names of red dragon riders and their positions within their fighting wings. The next described the six key festivals, the names of prize winners in various competitions, and recipes for the celebratory pastries, preserves, and beverages.

Will walked around the room, peeking into multiple

boxes and cracking open a few of the books on the shelves in an attempt to figure out how everything was organized.

This place was obviously a treasure trove of ancient information. Perhaps, hidden somewhere in a book or tightly bound scroll, he would find the answer to why Vortex was so pale and why he couldn't produce an elemental power.

He found a book titled "Anatomy of the Red Dragon" and started thumbing through it. He stopped when he came to one of the most detailed illustrations he'd ever seen. It was a cross section of an adult dragon, as though split nose to tail. Even though it was hand drawn in black ink on off-white silk, the picture showed all the dragon's insides—bones, organs, even the brain—in spectacular detail.

The dragon's lungs looked unusual, twin organs surrounded by a complicated network of chambers. The fire sac, positioned just behind the lungs, looked like it was actually two separate organs that worked together.

On the following page, Will found a technical description of the chemical and biological processes necessary for a red dragon to breathe fire. In the margin, the author had written a side note.

When it comes to producing dragon flame, the complicated and dangerous processes involved necessitate that the feat must be accomplished instinctively. It is fortunate that this instinct is firmly ingrained in the dragon psyche as teaching the skill would otherwise be impossible.

"Well, go figure," Will muttered with a snort. He carefully put the book back and rummaged through a few more boxes on the same shelf, hoping to find similar books about blues, yellows, or greens. He didn't find any. "I guess Fire Mountain doesn't need books about other dragon colors."

Farther down the wall, he came to a thick tome that immediately grabbed his attention. The title, scored into the thin metal cover, read, "Legends of the White Dragon."

"Look at this, Vortex. Do you think these stories are about you?" Will chuckled.

That book is very old. I was only hatched last summer. How could it be about me?

"Okay, so it's not really about you. But what if Anri is right and you are actually a white dragon, like the one the legends are about? Maybe we could learn something from it."

He unfastened the buckle closure and opened the book. The silk pages within were covered in black ink script written in many different hands. Some of the earliest writings, near the beginning of the book, were so faded it was hard to make them out at all.

Flipping ahead, Will found some clearer text. But, like

the old scrolls he'd found, the writing was in an ancient, unfamiliar language.

Grumbling, he grabbed a thick stack of pages and flipped them over, finally arriving at some stories written in English, and settled in to read.

The collection of legends was in short, disconnected snippets. Reading them in the order written, it was difficult to paint a full picture of the fabled White Dragon's history. On top of that, the stories all sounded so fantastical that Will had trouble believing any part of them could be true.

One story claimed that dragons used to eat humans whenever they could and that humans waged war against the dragons. But one day, the White Dragon came and befriended the humans. He negotiated a truce and set himself up as ruler over both human and dragon kind for hundreds of years.

The next story claimed that the White Dragon flew by himself into the heart of an advancing cloud of swarmers. Instead of being killed, he called fire down from Heaven that killed all his enemies in a single blow.

Another claimed that the White Dragon, deciding to end the threat of swarmers forever, dove into the heart of Fire Mountain, binding himself to the land so that no swarmers would dare attack Avria again.

"Wow." Will shook his head and exchanged a look with Vortex. "Can you believe this? No wonder nobody wants to call you a white dragon! They must think this dragon was like a god. Listen. 'He could tap the heart of the mountain and drink the fire of earth and sky.' What does that even mean?"

I can't do those things. I can't even breathe fire.

"I know. But you don't need to do any of that to be the best dragon in the world."

Vortex rumbled happily, and Will almost didn't hear boots tapping along the hall as someone walked past the open door.

The steps stopped, and a woman poked her head inside. Will recognized her as a red dragon rider, though he didn't remember her name.

"Is someone in there?" she asked.

"Yeah," Will said, lifting the lantern. "I just came in to do a bit of reading."

Her eyes found him and slid to Vortex, widening in alarm. "Are you okay?"

Will frowned in confusion. "Yeah . . . Is it okay for me to be here? I was just reading some of these old books."

The woman stepped through the arched entrance, still looking worried and confused. She placed a hand on Vortex's head, as though feeling for a fever. "You're not hurt? Are you sure you're all right?"

"Of course we're all right," Will said with a laugh. "Why wouldn't we be? This place isn't radioactive or anything, is it?" He uneasily eyed the metal boxes housing the stacks of books. Was that why this place was buried so deep in the mountain?

The woman lifted her hand from Vortex's head, relaxing a little. "Well, no. You've found the archive room."

"Oh, so it's not a library?"

She shook her head. "No, we keep the library near the main entrance, where anyone can enjoy it. This is where we keep valuable records. Stored here, on specially treated silk in the heart of the dragonhold, they don't wear out over time. The heat and dry air preserves them, you see."

"Oh. So why did you think . . ."

Her eyes were scanning him again, like he was a puzzle she couldn't figure out. "I've never heard of anyone else coming this far into Fire Mountain Dragonhold. Only red dragon riders can survive the heat here."

Chapter Twenty-Six

The next morning, Will told the others what had happened in the archives. Anri and Corin stared in amazement.

Rin gasped. "Does that mean Vortex is a red dragon?" Eyes shining, she grabbed his hand.

"I . . . don't know," Will said, chuckling and pulling his hand away to rub the back of his neck nervously. "All I know is that the red rider who found us said we shouldn't have survived being there if Vortex wasn't a red dragon."

Anri leaned against the table and took a drink of kaffa without meeting anyone's eyes. "He's not a red dragon."

"How else can you explain what happened?" Rin demanded. "Have you tried going deep into the dragonhold? I bet you couldn't make it to the archives. You'd pass out from the heat before you got close!"

Anri shrugged. "That doesn't mean he's a red dragon. It just means he and Will can survive the heat."

"He can also make smoke." Rin pointed a finger at her. "I've seen him do it."

"Come on!" Corin moaned dramatically. "It's too early in the morning to argue. Besides, Will and Vortex can still go to whichever dragonhold they want. I still say they should pick Lightning Cliffs."

"Of course you think so," Anri said, smiling wryly.

"Well, why not? Yellow dragons are as good at flying as greens."

"Excuse me?" Anri's brow arched.

"They practice flying in storm clouds and over the windy cliffs. I bet green dragons never do that!"

Anri opened her mouth to argue, but Corin cut her off. "And yellow dragons have a lot more fun. Besides, the cliffs are a comfortable place for anyone to live, no matter the color of your dragon. It's not scorching hot like Fire Mountain or snowy all the time like Frozen Peaks or toxic like Poison Plains."

"You have a point," Will said. "But I'm not sure how well Vortex would do flying in a thunderstorm. We could get struck by . . . Well, we might not do as well as yellow dragons."

Even though Will had quickly corrected himself to avoid the painful topic, Corin winced at his words. His eyes flashed to Rin, then dropped to the tabletop. "Yeah, I guess you're right," he said quietly.

"Don't get me wrong. It sounds like a lot of fun. I'm sure we'd love living there."

"Corin," Rin placed a hand on his arm, "stop being so hard on yourself. Everyone knows it was an accident. Ember is doing much better now. He's even flying again!"

Corin flashed a quick smile that didn't reach his eyes. "Thanks, Rin. We know you forgive us."

"Hey everyone!"

They turned to see Shara, a girl from the yellow wing, burst into the dining hall.

"Tumi just said we're going to ride our dragons today. We're going to start flying!"

There was a second of stunned silence, followed by a collective gasp from everyone in the dining hall. Then everyone started moving and talking at once. Kids stood, carrying their dishes with them as they hurriedly shoveled their breakfasts into their mouths on the way across the room.

Will jumped to his feet, gulped the rest of his kaffa, and ran for the barracks.

Vortex! Vortex, we're going to fly today! he thought.

Across the courtyard, where the shufflo pen sat adjacent to the concourse, his dragon abandoned the fresh shufflo he'd been eating and leaped into the air, soaring in a sky-bound dance of delight. *Yes! We will fly! I will carry you and we will fly together!*

Will made it to the barracks with Corin, and they frantically pulled on their riding gear. Will wasn't sure whether they'd need the thick leather trousers or jacket, but he buckled his wide riding belt, stuffed his feet into his tall sturdy boots, strapped the goggles over his face, and yanked on his gloves.

As they raced through the courtyard to the training ground, young dragons dropped from ledges all around them, swirling in a rainbow storm of colors, squawking and roaring in excitement. Will easily spotted Vortex's shining white wings among the reds, blues, yellows, and greens.

In the middle of the training grounds, Ruby lounged with her tail curled around her feet. Tumi sat in front of her on a large wooden chest with one foot resting on the opposite knee.

The young riders converged, taking their positions in a semicircle around Tumi and Ruby, with the young dragons landing behind them.

"It looks like word has gotten around," Tumi said, flashing a bright grin.

The kids laughed and nudged each other in anticipation.

"Does this mean you're all ready for today's lesson?"

"Yes!" a chorus of voices answered.

"Well, then, if you want to learn how to ride your dragons, you'll first need to learn how to saddle them. And look at this!" He stood and popped open the lid of the huge chest. "I just happen to have a chest full of dragon saddles right here, fresh from the leathersmith!"

Smatterings of nervous laughter mixed with the lively chatter as Tumi handed saddles to everyone. As the folds of thick leather dropped into Will's arms, a thrill of excitement mixed with nervous anticipation rushed through him. It was a familiar sensation. He'd felt the same way every time he took his bike on an untested, steep mountain trail, or ridden an extreme roller coaster for the first time.

He was really going to fly with Vortex!

Are you scared? Vortex asked, sensing his emotions. He crooned in encouragement. *Don't be scared. I won't let you fall.*

"Of course you won't." Will took a deep breath, which didn't settle the butterflies in his stomach at all. "I'm just really excited. Okay, nervous too. I've seen the things you can do in the air. I hope I don't pass out or puke or do anything else really embarrassing."

Vortex nudged his shoulder in comfort while Tumi handed out the rest of the saddles.

"Now," Tumi called so everyone could hear, "the saddle you have is yours to keep until your dragon needs a larger one. I want to remind you how important it is to care for your flying gear. All the gear we use in flight is for our safety. Your riding cap protects your ears from the wind and prevents hearing loss. Your goggles keep debris from blinding you. Even your jacket and trousers protect your skin from drying out and cracking in the wind. But as useful as all of that is, your saddle is far more important. Care for it properly, and it will save your life."

When Tumi was satisfied that everyone was paying attention, he lifted his own, much larger saddle from the ground and approached Ruby. The big red dragon was already on her belly, holding her neck low in wait.

Tumi stepped on her foreleg, hefted the saddle, and tossed it over her neck. Then he grabbed the dangling leather straps and turned his attention back to the crowd of kids. "These straps are all that stand between you and a swift plummet to the ground. If you don't care for your saddle properly, the leather will crack and fail when you need it most. There is a reason you've been learning how to care for leather every day since coming here. Your lives are in your own hands. Don't forget it."

"Wow," Corin muttered in Will's ear. "Tumi is a lot more serious today than usual."

Will only nodded. He ran a hand over the thick leather straps of the saddle in his arms, the ones that would fasten it to Vortex's neck. The leather felt soft and supple under his fingers, just as it should.

They all paid close attention while Tumi showed them how to saddle a dragon, adjusting the position of the seat, fitting the straps so they wouldn't rub against bone or hinder movement. Then it was their turn.

Will struggled at first, afraid that if he fastened it too tightly, he'd hurt Vortex or interfere with his breathing.

"No, just the opposite," Tumi assured him. "If your straps are too loose, they'll rub his skin as he flies, and he'll end up with painful sores on his neck. It's better to get them too tight than too loose. He'll let you know if you're hurting him."

"Oh, okay." Will pulled on the leather straps with shaking hands, tightening them further.

Vortex patiently waited while Will adjusted and readjusted the knots. Through their bond, Will could feel the eager anticipation and happiness bubbling up in his dragon. There wasn't even a shadow of anxiety mixed in.

"Aren't you nervous at all?" he asked.

Why should I be nervous? You are doing well with the saddle. And it will be much nicer to fly together than to walk everywhere.

Will tied off the lower strap and tugged until the cinch tie didn't budge. "You're being more sensible than I am. I want to fly with you, but I also feel like I could lose my breakfast any moment. Is this too tight?"

Vortex assured him the saddle was perfectly comfortable.

As soon as everyone was ready, Tumi instructed them

to mount up. The young dragons crouched down and their riders swung their legs over their outstretched necks.

Having ridden on Boreas and Scorch before, Will was surprised at how different it felt to be mounted on the neck of his own dragon. Aside from being so much smaller, the connection between their minds made the anticipation that much greater. Through Vortex, he could feel the sun on his wings, the breeze over his skin, and the vast blue sky above, like a deep pool just waiting for him to dive into it. Will found himself instinctively studying the sunlit walls for updrafts and noticing swirling eddies of dust over the ground—clues for the steadiest flight path.

Will clipped his riding straps in and patted Vortex on the neck. "You're doing great, buddy. Don't let my nerves make you worried. I'm just being silly."

I know that, Vortex said, fluttering his wings in amusement.

Will laughed, catching curious stared from the other kids.

Mounted on Ruby's neck, Tumi led everyone on a march across the training grounds.

Gathered on the surrounding mountain walls, red dragon riders clapped and cheered for them. Dragons in every shade of red imaginable took to the sky, circling far above as they watched the flaplings. A few of them blasted quick breaths of bright flame in celebration.

The procession stopped at the base of a long rock

jutting from the mountain wall. A well-worn path, made by countless generations of young dragons flying with their riders for the first time, led to the peak of the stone.

Ruby turned so she and Tumi faced them.

"This is a momentous occasion," Tumi announced with a proud smile. "Today, your flaplings ascend Flugspíra and carry you in flight for the first time. When you land, they will be flaplings no more but full dragons."

Chapter Twenty-Seven

A fresh swell of cheering rose from the watching dragon riders. Many of the kids joined in.

"First, Ruby and I will demonstrate what we expect of you," Tumi said. "When we land on the far side of the training field, fly to us one at a time."

Everyone watched as Ruby climbed up the rock, looking comically large on the jutting spire. Then she launched herself with a quick kick of her hind legs, spread her wings, and glided smoothly across the field.

When they landed, the kids looked around at each other.

"So, um, who's going first?" Will asked nobody in particular.

"We should have the strongest fliers go first," Kade said.

"Should we form a queue?" one of the red riders asked.

Anri leaned forward and patted Jade. "We'll go," she said.

Without waiting for anyone else to agree, Jade climbed the path to Flugspíra, wings lifted proudly.

"Show them what you can do, Jade!" Corin cheered.

Everyone watched as the young green dragon perched on the rocky point. She gathered her feet under herself, spread her wings, and dropped into the air.

Everyone cheered. The circling red dragons roared in approval. It didn't matter that Jade wobbled in her flight path or that her wings didn't flap quite in sync like they usually did. She flew! Jade landed on the other side of the field, front-heavy and awkward, but turned and let out a joyful bugle of triumph. Even from across the field, Will could see that Anri's face was beaming with joy.

After that successful first flight, everyone else was eager to take their turn. The dragons jostled for position, nudging their way into better places in the line and growling at each other.

Will kept Vortex back, refusing to take part in the commotion. He knew that they'd get their turn eventually, and it wasn't worth it to fight for a position in the front of the line.

As a result, they ended up in the back of the line with Rin and Ember. The pale scarring on Ember's wing joint and chest was still clearly visible, but he'd been flying for longer periods of time lately, though nowhere near as much as he used to.

Rin bit her lower lip, face pale, and she kept absently stroking Ember's arched neck. She looked like she was even more nervous than Will.

"Are you okay?" Will asked, frowning in concern. "The healers said it was okay for Ember to fly with you today, didn't they?"

Rin licked her lips. "They did. I'm okay, really. The healers said it would be good for him to try it. Even if he doesn't—well, you know, the healers are ready, just in case." Her voice was high and unnaturally chipper, and her words came out in short, rapid clips.

Will looked around and, for the first time, noticed the three adults in blue robes standing outside the healer's hall. They seemed to be on standby just in case Ember needed them.

Ember gave a little whine and arched his head back so Rin could rub his ears.

"See?" Rin gave a nervous laugh. "He wants to fly with me. And he'll do great. Won't you Ember? You'll do just fine."

"Rin . . ." Will gave Vortex a mental nudge, and they sidled up to Ember. Will rested a hand on Rin's arm. "Ember will be fine. You know Tumi wouldn't let him fly with you if it would be too much for him."

Rin nodded, eyes glistening. She didn't look convinced.

The rest of the dragons took their awkward, wobbling first flights with their riders. Each one landed heavily on the other side of the field, occasionally ending up with a nose full of sand. The greens tended to do better than the others, having flown longer and more strenuously in training.

No matter how awkward or weak each flight was, the young riders whooped and shouted with joy. The adult riders cheered, and their dragons roared and bugled. Tumi applauded each one with a bright grin that Will could see all the way across the field.

"Okay, Ember. It's our turn now, isn't it?" Rin said after Timmin and Strawberry had taken their wobbling flight. She buckled her riding cap under her chin and adjusted her goggled with trembling fingers.

Suddenly, Will felt a little ashamed at how nervous he felt. Rin's hands were shaking because she was genuinely afraid that this flight would hurt her dragon. He was only afraid that he might embarrass himself.

He frowned at his own foolishness, then gave Rin an encouraging smile. "Ember will do great. You'll see. In a minute, he's going to be a full-fledged dragon, and you're going to be a dragon rider. Clear skies, Rin."

She smiled at him in acknowledgement of the traditional dragon rider saying. Somehow, it seemed to help. Her shoulders loosened and her posture relaxed a little. "Clear skies, Will."

Ember marched up the smooth path to the top of Flugspíra. He spread his wings and leaped.

The wobbly glide lasted less than a minute, and Ember only flapped his wings once. He dropped a little faster than the others, but evened out near the end and landed amidst the cheering crowd at the far end of the field, squawking with joy. Rin slid out of her saddle and grabbed Ember's head in a tight embrace.

"Phew!" Will blew out a quick breath. "He made it."

Ember is stronger than Rin thinks he is, Vortex said.

"She's just worried about him, that's all. It looks like it's our turn. Are you ready to fly?"

Yes! Let's fly! Vortex hopped on his front legs, jostling Will, and lifted his wings eagerly.

"All right. All right!" Will laughed, buckled his riding cap under his chin, then lowered his goggles over his eyes.

Vortex climbed the trail until they were perched at the peak of the rock overlooking the training field. The drop to the ground looked much farther than it had from below.

Will gulped and took a steadying breath.

Vortex raised his wings, so much bigger and thicker than they had been when he was little. They shone creamy white. He arched his neck, and his small horns flashed in the sun.

A faint breeze swept over the field, rushed up the wall, and brushed over Vortex's wings. Will could swear that he felt the sensation himself, as though they were his own wings poised for flight.

I'm ready. Will leaned forward. *Let's go.*

Vortex released the rock with his front claws, thrust forward with his back legs, and caught the air in his outstretched wings.

Flugspíra slipped away behind them. The ground surged upward. Will's stomach flipped, and his breath caught in his throat. He gripped the saddle handles in tight fists but refused to close his eyes.

The field zipped past them as they glided forward, as smooth and swift as the wind itself. It was wonderful. Exhilarating. More fun that Will would have thought possible. His awareness snapped into sync with Vortex's mind, and he could feel the wind pooling under his dragon's wings, the subtle differences in the air temperature around them. He could sense the curved path ahead that Vortex planned to take, just like when they'd slid down the grassy hill with the yellows. He was also subtly aware of the other air currents swirling over the ground, lifting in the sun, surging before the mountain walls. All of it mingled in with their combined joy. They were finally flying together!

The cheering of the waiting crowd, muffled by Will's riding cap, surged as Vortex backwinged powerfully to bring his rear legs forward and catch the ground without jarring his rider.

"That was amazing!" Will shouted, clapping his hand against Vortex's neck.

The other dragons bugled and roared, flapping wings in excitement. The watching adult riders, along with most of the other kids, cheered and applauded.

With his cheeks aching from how hard he was grinning, Will lifted his riding goggles and looked around for Tumi. To his surprise, he found the instructor off to the side of the crowd, talking with Dragonlord Brom, Dragonlord Perrin, and a woman who looked familiar, but Will couldn't quite place where he knew her from. She was silver-haired, slender, and somehow managed to look elegant even though she was wearing dusty riding gear.

Anri and a few of the other kids were standing with them, listening to their conversation.

Will slid to the ground and walked closer until he came alongside Rin. "What's going on?" he asked.

"I'm not sure," Rin said. "The dragonlords and Master Bard Kelree just showed up right before you and Vortex flew. Ember and I were watching you, so I didn't hear what they said. But it looks like it's important."

Anri's face was severe, and Perrin looked worried.

Dragonlord Brom was gesturing with his hands like he was trying to calm everyone down and reassure them.

The woman, Master Bard Kelree, kept looking in Will's direction. He wasn't sure whether she was watching him or Vortex, but her gaze was clear, calm, and calculating.

The bard looks calm, Vortex said, *but she is scared and angry. Anri is scared too. I don't understand why.*

Will glanced at Anri. Her jaw was tight and her eyes dark. She looked anything but frightened. She looked like she was about to punch someone in the nose.

"I'm going to find out what's going on," Will said, giving Vortex a reassuring pat on the neck. "You did wonderful on your flight, pal. Better than anyone else. You even remembered to backwing on your landing!"

Vortex rumbled proudly and arched his neck. *I didn't want to smash my nose into the ground like the others.*

Will snorted a laugh and pushed his way through the crowd until he was close enough to hear what the adults were saying.

"It's nothing but fishermen's tales, surely," Dragonlord Brom said, chuckling. "Why give it more credit than any other tall tale from the north?" He gripped his wide belt with his thumbs and smiled jovially. "Stories like this always pop up in the springtime. The weather gets better, folks gather for festivals, and stories inflate to fill the egos of the storytellers. That's all this is. Master Bard, I hold you in the highest respect, but please don't give in to such childish fancies."

The woman's face looked as cold as ice. "Dragonlord

Brom, if you will not take my word, will you at least listen to Dragonlord Perrin?"

Brom looked scandalized. "You misunderstand me. I do believe you. I do! There are surely reports of swarmers. There always are this time of year. Fishermen sometimes find them. I've seen a few decaying bodies myself. Horrible creatures! Perhaps a fisherman collected one and is pretending the thing is still alive and dangerous. It would be a handy way to impress his friends."

"Whoa! Wait a minute!" Will stepped forward. "Did someone catch a live swarmer?"

Chapter Twenty-Eight

Will stared at the gathered adults in a silent standoff while he waited for an answer to his question.

Finally, Dragonlord Perrin turned to look at him. His features were smooth, but under the calm exterior, Will could see his tension building.

"After hearing reports that a fisherman in Fallshore had caught a live swarmer, Master Bard Kelree asked Boreas and me to bring her there to investigate. Apparently, the man had the thing caged and was charging people to see it. Boreas and I took her north, but by the time we arrived, the swarmer was gone. The fisherman claims he sold it to a rich elder from some other city for a handsome price."

The blood drained from Will's face. A rich elder? What if it was Elder Madoc? Would he bring it to his estate? Would it be dangerous to his parents? He would bet anything that Elder Madoc wouldn't feed a swarmer himself. He'd ask one of his lowly servants to do that dirty work. Someone like Will's mom or dad.

"So you never actually saw a swarmer!" Dragonlord Brom said to Perrin, nodding in satisfaction. "Maybe the fisherman never had one to begin with. Or maybe it was only a dead swarmer, like I said. Once he realized a Master Bard and a Dragonlord were investigating, he changed his story to get out of the consequences."

"What of all the people who said they saw it?" Perrin asked.

"He could have rigged it up to move a little when he pulled a lever or something!" Brom waved his hand dismissively. "Or it could be that he found an immature silky. They sometimes wash out to sea and wind up on the shore. Hideous creatures too! Anyone might think they're swarmers if they don't know better."

Anri shuddered. "Silkies are horrible, but they don't look like any pictures of swarmers I've ever seen."

"The people of Fallshore know what silkies look like," the master bard said in a clipped tone. "Even before they pupate. Fallshore has more silk mines than anywhere else in Avria. People in southern cities might think of them as cave monsters and speak of them as myth and legend. But northerners know them well. Nobody in Fallshore would be duped by someone claiming a juvenile silky was a swarmer."

"Very well, Master Bard," Brom said with a long-suffering sigh. "What would you have me do? Shall I send out search parties to find this swarmer and destroy it? Even if it exists, it isn't ours. According to your fisherman, an elder purchased it. What right would we have to destroy this man's property?"

"What right?" Dragonlord Perrin demanded. "Have you forgotten what it means to be a dragonlord?"

Master Bard Kelree held her hand up to speak. "I haven't come to tell you what to do. I'm only here to tell you what I know. That is my role as a master bard. I intend to fulfill my role with the dragonlords, no matter how stiff-necked they may be. Your role, which you seem to have forgotten, is to protect the people of Avria from swarmers. How you fulfill that role is up to you."

Following the master bard's visit, Will and the other young riders could hardly talk about anything else. A rogue swarmer, possibly loose and rampaging through cities, violently murdering everyone it saw, was practically the only topic of conversation at mealtimes.

The other kids, who'd grown up in Avria, dredged up their favorite horrifying stories of swarmers. Nightmarish tales they'd heard around the bonfire at egg hunting festivals or birthday parties. Comparing their stories with his memories of horror movies in the off-lands, Will had to admit that the swarmers were far more terrible. Maybe because he knew they were real.

As the weeks passed, spring gave way to summer without any new reports about the rumored swarmer, and the focus of conversation shifted back to the upcoming Dragon Games.

Disappointed that he and his friends still couldn't train for the tournament, Will and Vortex spent a lot of time exploring the archives they'd found deep within the dragonhold.

Will started out looking for anything that would tell him about the fabled White Dragon, but eventually, he lost himself in books describing waves of off-landers washing ashore in Avria and the horrors of swarmer attacks.

The highlight of every day was flying practice on the training grounds. Every day, their dragons grew stronger and steadier as they glided from the rocky spire of Flugspíra to the far wall of the dragonhold.

Even though their dragons continued to grow every day, the change was getting harder to notice. An additional pound on a tiny dragon was easy to see. But now that they easily weighed over a thousand pounds each, gaining ten pounds a day was hardly noticeable. The only time Will could tell was when he tightened the saddle straps on

Vortex's neck. He had to leave a little more slack each time.

Opening day of the Dragon Games finally arrived. The young dragons and their riders prepared to travel to Charramor, the traditional festival grounds for the games.

Charramor wasn't far from Fire Mountain Dragonhold, but the distance was too great for the young dragons to carry them. So everyone dressed in their best clothes and sturdiest shoes, filled their water skins, and packed lunches from the dining hall. Dragonlord Brom was even generous enough to give everyone a little money to spend while they were there. Before the sun rose over the mountain peaks, they set off, Tumi leading the way.

"Just wait, Will. This is going to be great!" Corin said, half jogging alongside Will, Rin, and Anri.

In the sky above, the young dragons circled on currents of air as they followed their walking riders.

"I don't know. I'm still disappointed that we can't join the tournament," Will said.

"Yeah, that would've been nice." Corin shrugged, then turned around and jogged backward in front of them. "But there's still going to be so much to do! You're an off-lander, so you've never had the chance to go to the Dragon Games before, or you'd understand."

"I've never been either," Anri said, trying to settle Trouble into her leather bag. The little kisnit squirmed and wiggled out, insisting on riding on Anri's shoulder instead.

"My father was always too busy to take us. After he died, we didn't have enough money to go."

Corin stumbled on a root and nearly fell. "What? You've never been to the Dragon Games?" He stared at her incredulously. "Just stick with me. I'll show you both the best games and the best food! Oh, I hope Madame Maxeem comes this year. She can juggle ten balls at once and breathe fire like a dragon! You'll love it!"

Will smiled and exchanged a glance with Rin and Anri. Ever since Ember's accident, Corin had been stuck in a melancholy mood. But it seemed going to the Dragon Games was finally lifting him out of it. He was more like the fun-loving boy Will remembered from before.

Their three-hour hike started out over rugged terrain and steep switchbacks, but they'd started early enough that the morning air remained pleasantly cool.

Eventually, their path merged with a wide dirt road crowded with travelers of every age and situation from nearby towns. Some were walking, others rode on cormant back or drove teams of shufflos on carts laden with goods. The festive procession reminded Will of his journey to the Hatching Ground the previous summer.

The travelers were surprised and delighted to see the young dragon riders. Their children squealed with joy, pointing at the dragons flying overhead.

The adults seemed equally interested, but mostly about Vortex. Over and over again, Will heard people exclaim when they saw his white wings flapping among the others.

"A white dragon!"

"A white dragon?"

"I thought it was just a story!"

"There really is a white dragon!"

Will pretended not to hear them and stayed close to his friends for the rest of the journey.

In his mind, Will pictured Charramor as a level field surrounded by sloping mountains, a big tent like a circus in the center.

When they got there, the reality was very different.

The winding road passed between two mountain walls with a stone arch stretching overhead. Strange letters were carved into the stones, along with depictions of dragons in flight.

Beyond the arch, the road opened up to a level stone clearing as big as several football fields put together, walled off on one side by the mountain and on the other by a sheer drop.

Hundreds of tents and canopies in every color imaginable were scattered over the whole area. Banners hung from doorways, and streamers fluttered from tent peaks. Some tents were even decorated with thousands of tiny jewels, sparkling in the light.

A low stone barrier ran along the rim of the drop-off, probably to keep clumsy people from tumbling over the edge. Colored flags, red, blue, green and yellow, marked four launch pads where dragons stood ready to take flight.

In the open air along the cliffside, a handful of greens were performing acrobatic flying tricks with their riders. The gathered crowd cheered and whistled as the dragons spun and whirled, dove and flipped like autumn leaves in a gale.

Will stared in amazement. He'd never seen dragons flying like that before.

Vortex landed and came up beside him. *I want to fly like that. It looks fun!*

"Yeah. But how do their riders keep from getting sick? I feel queasy just watching!"

"All right, everyone!" Tumi called, waving his hands to draw them close. "Those of you in the tournament meet at pad four in an hour for the first contest. You're free to get some food or play games until then. The rest of you are welcome to do as you like. Our reserved viewing area is at the end of the row by pad four."

The kids cheered, and the dragons warbled. From a nearby tent, a lively tune began to play. A breeze carried the smell of sweet breads and hot spiced drinks through the air.

Will's spirits lifted despite the fact that he and his friends weren't competing in the tournament. This was going to be fun!

"Well, what do you guys want to do?" Will asked, turning to his friends. "Should we go watch the games?"

"That's what I want to do," Anri said. "Did you see what those greens were doing? I can hardly believe it!"

"I'd rather go play bucket ball," Corin said. "If you make the ball in, they give you honey candy!"

"Why don't we watch the greens first, since they're flying now?" Rin suggested. "Then we can go get snacks and play games."

They all agreed on Rin's plan and made their way to pad four to watch the flying dragons.

Every moment, Charramor grew more crowded with people and animals pouring in from the roads. Shaggy shufflos pulling carts, cormants carrying riders, families walking together, laughing children scampering about with toys.

Everywhere they went, people stopped to stare at Vortex. Some openly gaped and pointed when they saw him, nudging their companions or even shouting, "Look! It's the white dragon!"

Vortex didn't seem to care, but Will blushed and tried to avoid eye contact with them.

The viewing area was on a ledge right up against the rim of the cliff, with only the stone barrier separating them from the sheer drop on the other side.

They found their seats and watched as a group of competing greens flew in tight circles, then plummeted past the viewers. Before crashing into the ground, the dragons snapped their wings open and skimmed the rocky walls, careening over the treetops and back into the sky like twin rockets. Beating the air with their mighty wings, they gained altitude faster than Will thought any dragon possibly could as they each fought to get ahead of the other.

"Wow," Anri breathed, leaning forward as she watched the dragons fly. Perched on her shoulder, Trouble twitched her whiskers and tail. When the dragons swooped in close, sending a gust of wind over the crowd, the kisnit scurried into the safety of Anri's bag.

"I bet Jade will be flying like that in no time," Will said.

Anri flashed him a grin. "It will take work to get that good, but she won't give up, will you Jade?"

Jade pulled her wings back and lifted her head proudly. It looked like she was up for the challenge.

When the junior tournament started, the first competitors were three blue dragons racing from one ledge to another. At the signal, they jumped into the air and flapped hard in the swift mountain air, straining to make headway.

After seeing what the adult green dragons could do, the young blues looked awkward and heavy, barely able to fly straight in the blasting wind.

Icicle made it to the second ledge first, turning and

squawking in victory with upraised wings as the other two touched down next to him.

The crowd cheered and applauded. But it was the kind of applause that adults give at preschool dance recitals. The kids are cute and small, so the grown-ups clap, but everyone knows the performers have no idea what they're doing.

"Are you three ready to go play games now?" Corin asked, leaning against Leika's side with his fingers laced behind his head.

"I'm ready if you are," Anri said.

Finding games to play was easy. Everywhere they turned, vendors called out to them.

"Hit the dolls and win a prize!"

"Three rings for a bit. Catch a peg and you're a winner. One bit to play!"

"Wheel of fate. Spin the wheel of fate here! What does the future hold for you, young dragon riders?"

Corin led them straight to the bucket ball game. This one cost a little more than the others, but as he promised, it was easier to win. After tossing their weighted balls into brightly colored buckets, they were each rewarded with sticks coated in crystallized honey. Anri managed to make every one of her shots and needed a bag to carry all her candy.

"All right, that was sort of fun," she admitted as they walked away with their prizes.

Corin beamed at her. "There are plenty more games to play. Or we could look at the attractions. There's bound to be a bard here. Or we could look for Madame Maxeem. Last time, someone brought a two-headed pig!"

"Weird!" Will tried to imagine what a two-headed pig would look like.

"I don't care what we do," Rin said. "Did you smell that food, though?" She closed her eyes and took a deep breath through her nose. "Mmm! Sweet bread!"

Corin laughed. "It sounds like Rin's hungry."

"Let's visit some food carts, then," Will said. "I could go for some hot kaffa."

"Nader said the dragonhold cart is making flame steaks too," Corin added, wiggling his eyebrows and rubbing his palms together.

"Thanks," Anri said dryly, "but trying that once in a lifetime is enough for me. Even Trouble won't eat a flame steak."

They laughed and made their way through the crowd with their dragons, wandering from cart to cart and sampling anything that smelled good, which was pretty much everything.

When they couldn't eat any more, they returned to the games to try their luck. Later, they found Madame Maxeem, who amazed them with her juggling and magic tricks. They even found a troupe of actors who put on hilarious skits that made the crowd roar with laughter.

The sky was darkening to a deep blue. In the open courts between the tents and carts, people were igniting bonfires that cast warmth on the surrounding crowds. The scene felt so familiar. Will half expected someone to bring out marshmallows and graham crackers. But, of course, those didn't exist in Avria.

A familiar face flashed in the gap between two carts, then disappeared.

Will froze, then stepped closer, staring hard.

"What is it?" Rin asked.

The others stopped and looked at him.

You saw that boy again. Vortex flashed a memory in his mind. A surly boy's face, seen from a low angle. From a time when Vortex was small enough to be carried in Will's arms.

"Yeah, I think so. I think it was Tavin."

"Who's Tavin?" Corin asked.

Anri and Rin shot each other a concerned look.

"The boy who stole Vortex's egg from me," Will said.

Chapter Twenty-Nine

If Tavin was at the Dragon Games, Will wanted to know what he was up to.

"Come on, guys, let's check it out. I won't be able to sleep wondering if he's slinking around out here."

The others agreed, so they walked around the shufflo cart to the shaded side where Will had seen the familiar face.

Tavin leaned against the wood and canvas of the cart and snacked on a bag of roasted nuts. His eyes traveled over their dragons and lingered for a moment on Vortex. A speculative look came to his eyes, then he twisted his lip up in a smug smirk. "Well, if it isn't the failed cormant trainer. It looks like he became a failed dragon rider too!" He rolled up his bag and stuffed it into his hip pouch, then pushed away from the cart and swaggered toward them.

"What do you mean failed?" Corin asked.

"Isn't it obvious?" Tavin snorted and waved a hand at Vortex.

Although Vortex was a thousand times bigger than he had been the last time they'd met, Tavin still didn't show the slightest hint of respect most Avrians had for dragons.

"This is supposed to be the new white dragon? Ha! I heard he can't make flame or ice or do anything a dragon is supposed to. Can he even fly?" He cackled. "No wonder you were too embarrassed to enter the tournament with him. I would be too! I'm glad I didn't end up taking that weird egg to the Hatching Ground."

Vortex rumbled and looked at Will. Hurt and confusion whirled in his mind.

Will's face heated, and his fists clenched automatically.

To his surprise, it was Corin who rushed forward, ready to fight.

Anri and Rin grabbed his arms just in time, holding him back to keep him from punching Tavin's smug face.

"You don't know anything," Corin spat, straining against the girls. "Vortex is one of the best fliers in the hatching. Even better than Leika. So you can shut your mouth, you filthy egg thief."

Tavin snorted and shook his head. But he looked a little disappointed, too, like he'd been hoping one of them would start a fight.

"What are you even doing here, Tavin?" Will asked. "You think dragons are stupid and useless, but you come to watch the Dragon Games? Seems kinda strange to me."

Tavin folded his arms and lifted his chin. "I didn't come to watch the dragons. My father has something better than a hundred dragons and all their stupid games."

"Oh, come on!" Will waved his hands, dismissing Tavin's outlandish claim. "You expect us to believe you have something better than dragons at the Dragon Games?"

"What could you possibly have that's better than dragons?" Corin asked with a disbelieving laugh.

Tavin watched them all with a pompous smile for a few seconds before answering in a low, secretive voice. "We have a real live swarmer."

For a brief moment, Tavin's words didn't make sense to Will. It was as though he'd spoken gibberish. Then the world seemed to go dark and cold around him. The laughter and music of the crowd around the bonfire muffled in his ears. He could feel his heart thumping in his chest.

Next to him, Corin, Anri and Rin had gone completely still.

Vortex was watching him with wide golden eyes that glistened in the moonlight.

"What did you say?" Will asked, his mouth strangely dry.

"I said we have a swarmer. It's here. Alive! We have it

in a cage." Tavin's eyes glinted and his grin spread as he took in their shocked and dumbfounded expressions.

Anri gasped, taking a step back.

Rin stared.

Corin blinked with a vacant expression, like he wasn't sure what a swarmer was anymore.

After all the legends, the horrible stories, Will understood their reactions. He felt the same. Tavin was calmly telling them he had a monster from the scariest horror movie imaginable locked in a cage somewhere nearby.

"My father caught it when he went up to Fallshore, so we brought it here for the Dragon Games," Tavin went on proudly. "It was stinging hard to travel with, I can tell you. That's why we're late. It wants to eat all the time and keeps trying to dig out of the cage. My father's going to show it to people for a price. Pretty soon, nobody's going to care about your stupid dragons. They'll all be talking about our swarmer!"

"You can't be serious!" Will blurted.

Tavin's eyes hardened. "Of course I'm serious. It's real. I've seen it!" He jabbed his chest with his thumb.

"It's got to be just a silky, right?" Corin asked Will, his voice laced with fear. "Like the dragonlords were saying. It can't be a real swarmer. It's fake. They just want to trick people out of their money."

A cold sweat broke out on Will's brow. "Yeah . . . that's got to be it."

Tavin snorted and scowled at them. Then he shrugged. "Fine! You don't want to believe me? Come on. I'll show you how real it is." He turned to lead the way behind the row of shufflo carts.

Will glanced at his friends, wondering what they would want to do.

I want to see, Vortex said. *Even if it isn't a swarmer, there is something. Tavin doesn't feel like he's lying.*

"Are you coming?" Tavin hollered over his shoulder. "Or are you a bunch of scared cormant chicks?"

Corin shrugged, then he and Leika followed Tavin.

Anri followed too, stroking Trouble's furry head with Jade close to her side.

"Ember and I want to see," Rin said, shuddering. "If it isn't real, at least we can tell the dragonlords there's nothing to worry about."

"Yeah," Will agreed. "That's a good point." So he and Vortex followed too.

Tavin led them beyond the row of shufflo carts and behind bright red and yellow tents. The gap between the tent paneling and the mountain wall made a convenient path that kept them well hidden, even though they had to navigate over ropes and tent stakes and around bales of hay and boxes of pulleys and traction wheels.

They eventually came to a large, blue and yellow tent with golden streamers fluttering from the peaks. Nearby, a group of men was constructing another tent, pulling supplies from a cart, laying long poles and blue dyed canvas in the clearing.

"Swarms!" Tavin hissed. "Why do they have to work so slow? I thought they'd be done by now. We can get in on the other side so they don't see us."

Rin frowned at him. "Are you saying we're not allowed in there?"

Will fought not to roll his eyes. Did Rin think they'd been sneaking in the shadows for the fun of it?

Tavin shot her a severe look. "Do you think my father would let you in to see the swarmer just because you're dragon riders?"

"N-no! It's just—"

"Come on, before someone sees us."

Tavin led them around the corner, where he lifted a loose corner of the canvas. They all slinked silently through the opening.

A foul odor, like a cat had peed on a pile of rotten meat, assaulted their noses. But in the dim light, it was difficult to see anything. Piles of ropes, tent poles, and stacked boxes lined the walls. A thick vertical beam held the center of the tent up. Shadows of the streamers fluttered over the canvas in the light of the bonfire.

A giant iron cage sat in the darkness on the far end of the tent, big enough to house a full-grown shufflo, with bars thick enough to hold back a grizzly bear.

As his eyes adjusted to the darkness, Will saw that the

straw bedding inside the cage looked trampled and wet. A large dark form lay within, motionless and silent.

A rush of relief washed over him, and he let out a relieved breath. Whatever it was, it looked dead. That had to be why it smelled so bad.

"That's it?" he asked.

Tavin nodded and folded his arms.

The dragons huddled back near the tent wall, sniffing the air and making strange low growls, wings halfway unfurled. Vortex's mind flashed back and forth between anxiety and a fierce desire to fight.

Trouble scurried up Anri's shoulder. Her tail bristled like a bottlebrush, and she flattened her ears against her head.

Anri, Rin, and Corin stared at the motionless mound in the cage, faces pale with horror.

Will wondered if that was how all Avrians would react to anything someone said was a swarmer. Would everyone be fooled by a shapeless, smelly lump hidden in the shadows?

Well, Tavin wouldn't fool him so easily. "You've got to be kidding me. You really expect me to believe that gross, smelly lump is a swarmer? What is it really? A chunk of a dead whale? That's what it smells like!"

Rin gasped.

Tavin just stared at him, shocked.

"I've heard about people like your dad. They make big

claims to get people's money, but don't have what they promised. But this is ridiculous. Nobody's going to believe that thing is a swarmer!"

"It is a swarmer!" Tavin said. "It's just asleep!"

Will pulled the corner of his mouth back in a disbelieving smirk. "Yeah, right. That might work on the goons who follow you around like puppies, but it won't work on us. Right, guys?"

Corin gave him a halfhearted smile.

Rin gulped.

Anri stared at the cage with narrow eyes while she tried to calm Trouble down. The kisnit was chittering frantically as she scurried around, scratching Anri's shoulders with her tiny claws.

That thing smells wrong, Vortex said. *It shouldn't be here.* A deep growl rumbled in his chest, and he stepped forward, putting his head between Will and the shadowy cage.

Tavin let out a frustrated growl of his own. "You still don't believe me? Fine! I'll just have to wake it up!"

He went to the support beam and unhooked a ring of long iron keys. Then he walked up to the cage and jammed a key into the lock.

"What are you doing?" Rin squealed.

"Stinging swarms, Tavin, are you insane?" Anri yelled. "Don't let it out!"

Tavin turned the key.

The heavy lock gave a loud, ominous clunk as the catch released.

Rin and Corin jumped back at the sound.

"Don't be stupid," Tavin snorted. "Of course I'm not letting it out. The swarmer is shackled and chained. How do you think we clean the cage and feed it?"

"It doesn't smell like you clean the cage at all," Will muttered. Still, he stepped forward to see what would happen. Tavin seemed awfully sure of this thing. Whatever was in the cage had to be something real or why would he be showing it to them?

The door creaked open, and for the first time, Tavin didn't look at all cocky or confident. He hesitated.

Will took another step forward. Vortex moved forward with him, keeping himself between Will and the looming shape in the dark cage.

Anri sucked in a breath, like she was about to caution them, but stopped herself.

Tavin crouched and took a hesitant step forward, grabbed the link of a thick chain, and rattled it. "Wake up!" he yelled, then jumped back.

The mound didn't move.

Tavin crawled forward again, grabbed the chain with both hands, and tugged on it.

The smelly mound shifted as he pulled on it. A tattered, greasy insect wing moved into the light and shivered.

A thrill of terror tightened Will's throat at the sight. "Tavin, I think—" He never got to finish.

The creature burst to life, knocking Tavin back and straining against its shackles.

The corroded chains held for a moment as the creature flung itself toward the open door, then snapped.

A spiky black leg stabbed Tavin's thigh, and the boy screamed.

All four dragons roared in fear-fueled rage.

Before Will could do anything but blink in surprise, a streak of pale yellow shot across his vision.

Barely as big as the swarmer herself, Leika jumped between the monster and Corin, zapping it with a jolt of bright electricity.

The swarmer jerked in her direction at the shock, spread its spider-like front legs, and snatched the yellow dragon.

"Leika!" Corin cried.

Instantly, Ember and Vortex jumped into the fight.

A plume of flame shot from Ember's mouth, striking the swarmer's side.

The swarmer squealed and chittered.

Vortex bit down on the arms that clasped Leika. Using his claws, he scratched and pulled until they loosened their hold and the yellow dragon dropped to the ground.

The swarmer spun around, shaking off Vortex and swinging its long, barbed tail around.

The side of its tail struck Ember, knocking him into the support beam. He fell in a crumpled heap on the floor. Rin cried out, racing to his side.

Scratched and bleeding, Leika was on her feet again. She shrieked and spread her wings, trying to look imposing, while Vortex and Jade flanked her sides.

Leika zapped it with another burst of electricity. Although a weak jolt, it struck one of the swarmer's big insect eyes, searing it into a charred lump.

The swarmer shrieked and lifted its segmented tail, poised to strike.

Vortex roared a warning.

Jade leaped forward and knocked Leika aside, just as the swarmer's venomous tail darted forward.

The stinger buried itself in the green dragon's belly.

Jade squealed in pain.

Anri screamed and picked up a loose rock to throw at the swarmer.

Will scrambled around on the ground, looking for something, anything, that he could use as a weapon against this horrible creature.

His hands found a long shaft of wood that ended in a metal spike—the bottom segment of a tent pole.

Hoping he could use it as a makeshift lance, Will's fingers closed around the pole, and he whipped it around, aiming the metal spike at the hideous monster.

Anri had found a length of rope attached to a metal

pulley and was swinging it around, striking the swarmer with the heavy wheel. Tears streaked her face, but her expression was nothing but cold hatred.

The swarmer turned toward her, catching the rope under one of its legs, seemingly by accident. Then, to Will's horror, it snatched her up like a spider catching its prey.

Anri screamed as she struggled in its grasp.

"Leika, zap it again!" Corin yelled from the far side of the swarmer. He'd also found a tent pole and was wielding it like a weapon.

Leika sent a shock at the swarmer, singeing one of its legs.

The swarmer flinched and turned toward its attacker.

Will took the opening to rush forward and stab his makeshift lance at the creature's body. At the same time, Vortex jumped on the swarmer, clawing and biting at its legs in a frenzy.

Will's lance deflected off the hard exoskeleton, leaving barely a scratch. But Vortex managed to get one of the narrow leg joints between his teeth and bit down hard, severing the leg.

Anri and Vortex dropped to the ground.

A crowd of people were shouting outside the tent, but it barely registered in Will's mind. He only vaguely wondered why it was taking so long for anyone to come help them. They had to have been fighting this swarmer for hours by now. But he didn't have much time to worry about that.

The swarmer was coming for him.

Will didn't wait for it to grab him like it had Leika and Anri. He dashed forward and stabbed the tent pole into its charred, oozing eye.

The swarmer recoiled with a squeal, yanking the pole out of Will's hands and lashing its curved stinger forward, striking the ground next to Will. With only one good eye, it didn't seem to be able to aim.

Will stumbled back and scrambled for another weapon.

Vortex leaped over Jade's fallen form to fight by his side.

"No! Vortex, run! Get away, or it'll kill you!"

His dragon's only answer was a wordless flood of rage and determination. Nothing would make him leave Will's side.

The swarmer struck again. Will tried to jump out of the way, but he couldn't move fast enough. The venomous barb scratched his leg, ripping his trousers before burying itself in the ground.

Searing pain engulfed his leg. Someone started scream-ing. At first, Will thought it was Anri or Corin, but then he ran out of breath and realized it was him.

Vortex hissed and bared his teeth. With a terrifying expression on his face, he launched himself at the swarmer once more. He clawed at its remaining good eye, tore at its tattered wings, ripped at its mandibles and legs. The white dragon's rage blazed, but he was still young and inexperienced. And the swarmer was fighting for its life.

Will watched in horror as the monster threw his dragon to the ground, pinning him down with its remaining spiky legs.

Vortex squealed and writhed in its grasp.

Will tried to get to his feet. He had to help his dragon. But the burning in his leg consumed him. The world spun, and his stomach churned.

The swarmer lifted its tail and aimed its barb at Vortex's belly.

There was nothing Will could do to stop it.

Chapter Thirty

The swarmer struck.

Vortex jerked his head to the side, and the stinger narrowly missed his neck.

Through the pain and nausea, Will was vaguely aware that more people were in the tent now, shouting and running about. They looked like blurry ghosts, swimming around the corners of his vision.

Someone grabbed his shoulders and yelled something in his ear, but he couldn't hear them. The only thing he could focus on was his dragon, caught in the clutches of a bloodthirsty swarmer.

"Vortex, fight back!" he yelled.

The swarmer tightened its grip, piercing him with its needle-like legs and Vortex squealed in pain. He scratched and clawed at the slick exoskeleton but couldn't get a grip with the awkward angle.

The dragon's thoughts came like a wordless, panicked scream in Will's mind. Vortex couldn't win, and he knew it.

The swarmer raised its stinger again, dripping with venom.

"You can't give up, Vortex. Please! Breathe steam if you have to, just DO SOMETHING!"

Writhing in pained misery, Vortex opened his jaws and spewed a thick cloud of steam in the swarmer's face.

As the steam came, something snapped in his dragon's mind.

The change echoed through Will's thoughts like a dam breaking, the world shifting, a bridge built between two lands that had never had contact before. Suddenly, something made sense that had only been chaos before. Like realizing the random background noise you'd been hearing for hours was actually music.

Vortex sucked in a lungful of air and spewed a thick stream of white frost, coating the front of the swarmer in a sheet of ice.

The swarmer released him and scuttled back, clawing and scratching the ice off itself.

Vortex rolled to his feet, flapped the loose straw from his wings, and leaped to Will's side with a fierce, protective growl.

The swarmer came for them, but didn't get a chance to strike again.

Standing over Will like a vengeful guardian angel, Vortex blasted the swarmer with ice breath so cold that the air in the tent felt like a blizzard.

The swarmer reeled back, buzzing its tattered wings and flailing its barbed tail blindly.

"Look out! Get down!" someone shouted.

Before Will could see who it was, a barb of deadly ice shot through the air, striking the swarmer between its ruined eyes and blasting its guts over the back of the tent.

Everything was quiet for a moment, then the crowd of people rushed about to help the kids and dragons.

Gripping his leg, which felt like it was on fire, Will looked toward the tent entrance. With his vision still blurred, he managed to make out Perrin standing outside, patting Boreas on the shoulder.

"Vortex!" Will gasped. Tears streamed from his eyes. He wiped them away, but more came. "Are you okay? Are you hurt?"

I'm here, his dragon's thoughts came, weary and laced with pain, but also strangely proud. Vortex gently nudged Will's cheek with his nose. *You're more hurt than I am. Don't worry about me.*

"What about the others? Ember? Anri? Jade was hurt. Where is she?" He struggled to stand, but firm hands held him down.

"Easy, lad. You're staggering like a bard on Christmas night. And bleeding! You didn't get stung, did you?"

Will rubbed his eyes with his sleeve and spotted Jade on the ground with Anri cradling her head. The dragon was panting, and thick foam bubbled at the corners of her mouth.

"Don't worry about the green," the voice said. "The injury is minor, and greens always get ill at their first encounter with poison. She'll recover. You, however, need immediate attention. Did you hit your head?"

Will groaned and shook his head no, then leaned against Vortex's side. His thoughts swam. His face burned. His stomach roiled. Thinking about anything made his head hurt, so he just lay there, vaguely aware of what was happening around him.

People bustled about the tent, removing the injured and warning off crowds of onlookers.

Perrin called for someone to notify Tumi and Dragonlord Brom about what had happened.

Something nudged Will's leg, making him cry out in pain. He heard someone warn Vortex not to lick his wounds.

Eventually, strong arms lifted Will outside, where someone poured water over the cut on his leg. He squirmed and groaned at the burning cold sensation.

Gentle hands examined the wound, and he thought he heard people talking about amputating his leg to save his life.

"No," another voice said. Cold fingers pressed against

his forehead. "If he was stung, the venom would have already spread. Amputating the leg would only add to his suffering, not save his life."

Will's muscles ached. His stomach clenched. His head throbbed. He felt feverish and thirsty and sick all at the same time. He couldn't listen to what anyone said anymore.

I'm still here, Vortex said gently. *I won't leave you.*

IT COULD HAVE BEEN minutes or hours later when Will became aware of his surroundings again. He was lying on his back in what seemed to be complete darkness. The pain in his leg had dulled to a deep ache. His head pounded in time with the beating of his heart. The cool air was pungent with the smell of medicine. And familiar, gentle voices were talking nearby.

"So, it really was a swarmer?" Tumi asked.

"Yes, it was," Perrin said. "They'd clipped its wings so it couldn't fly. It was ill and weak, but clearly still dangerous. Somehow, the chains corroded, so when that boy opened the cage . . ."

"Stinging swarms!" Tumi cursed. "The rumor was true all along. Does that mean the swarmers are returning?"

"What do you think?"

Tumi was quiet for a while. "People will panic if they

think the swarmers are coming back. There could be a breakdown of law and order. The rich will hoard supplies for their fortresses while the poor starve. But if the swarmers catch us by surprise, nobody will be prepared. The results would be even worse. Thousands will die horribly."

"Sound reasoning, brother," Perrin said. "But you've failed to answer the question."

"I don't know! What do you think?" Tumi said with a touch of irritation.

"Those of us in the Frozen Peaks often fly to the northern coast," Perrin answered. "In the springtime, swarmer remains can often be found on the shoreline. Usually rotting pieces of their exoskeletons. I believe that foolish fisherman found one before it died and brought it to Avria. But it wouldn't have made it here otherwise." He took a slow breath and let it out with a sigh. "I see no reason to panic. There's nothing to indicate that swarmers can make it to our shores on their own, let alone in numbers. At least not yet."

"I'm glad you think so," Tumi said, sounding relieved. "If Frozen Peaks assures the public that there's nothing to worry about, maybe we can avoid a panic."

Will grunted and lifted his hand to his forehead. A wad of damp fabric rested over his eyes.

"So, you woke up," the familiar voice of Master Healer

Uther came softly from somewhere nearby. "It looks like you'll pull through this just fine. How do you feel?"

Will lifted the cloth from his eyes, revealing the interior of a large blue and white tent, warmly illuminated by hanging lanterns. The front flaps were pulled wide open, and Tumi and Perrin stood just outside. Master Healer Uther stood over him, wearing a concerned expression. Vortex lay on the ground by his cot, watching him with golden eyes. In the far corner of the tent, Anri slept in a chair with Jade's head cradled in her lap. A bandage was plastered on the green dragon's belly.

Will blinked, clearing the last of the blurriness from his vision, although it did nothing to stop the throbbing in his head. "I feel horrible," he answered. "Like my head is going to split open."

"Well, fortunately, your temperature is back to normal. We're going to keep an eye on you for a while. I think with some time and fluids, you've got a good chance at recovering." Uther poured some water into a mug and offered it to Will.

Will took it and greedily gulped down the water. He offered the empty mug back to Uther, then wiped the moisture from his lips with his sleeve. "How are my friends? What about Jade?" He looked at the sleeping green worriedly. "The swarmer stung her. She was really hurt."

Noticing that Will was awake, Tumi and Perrin entered the tent together.

Tumi offered Will a warm smile. "When Jade recovers, she'll be as good as new," he said. "She'll have a small scar, but the swarmer's venom will only strengthen her own poison. That's how green dragons work, you know. Their bodies absorb toxins and use them as their own." He leaned against Will's cot and folded his arms. "Your other friends will be fine, too, with some rest and recuperation. They're all sleeping now."

Will's throat tightened as his eyes found Jade and Anri again, resting far away from everyone. Did this mean Jade was getting her poison already? Would they not be able to spend time together anymore?

"What we want to know is how you're doing," Perrin said. "We were certain that the cut on your leg was a swarmer sting, but you recovered remarkably well." Though his voice was calm, Perrin's expression was incredulous, like he couldn't believe Will was sitting there listening to them instead of cold in his grave already.

"It is from the swarmer's stinger," Will said. "But it got me after it stung Jade, so maybe it already used up its venom. It was only a scratch, anyway."

"It's amazing how well the four of you stood against it," Tumi said.

"It was extremely foolish for you to confront a live swarmer in the first place," Perrin added.

Will winced in shame and rubbed the back of his neck.

"Perrin," Tumi said, "don't act like we never got into trouble when we were young."

"We never attempted to fight a swarmer," Perrin pointed out.

"Only because there was never a swarmer for us to fight," Tumi retorted. "Tell me you wouldn't have sneaked in to gawk at a swarmer if you'd had the chance."

Perrin considered this, then nodded, conceding the point.

"It was stupid to sneak in like that," Will said, reaching down to stroke Vortex's ears. "If it hadn't been for our drag-ons, we'd all be toast. I didn't believe Tavin really had a swarmer until he woke the thing up. But I should've known he was up to no good. Whatever happened to him?"

"Elder Dimuk's boy fainted when his leg was injured," Tumi said, a slight note of amusement in his voice.

"His leg injury isn't serious," Master Healer Uther said. "His father has a family healer who's making sure the puncture doesn't become infected. Is the boy a friend of yours?"

"Not exactly," Will said.

"There's something else I want to ask you about." Perrin took a seat at the corner of the cot, looking between Will and Vortex with a speculative expression.

"Yeah?"

"When Boreas and I arrived to help, there was a significant amount of ice in the tent already."

"Oh, that!" Will smiled proudly. "Vortex figured out how to make frost breath. Isn't that great?"

Tumi's eyes widened. He knelt in front of Vortex and patted the dragon's neck. "It really was you, then? I couldn't believe it when they told me."

"Something just clicked for him when he was fighting the swarmer. His frost breath was strong enough to slow the swarmer down. He saved my life!" Will looked from Tumi back to Perrin, who was still staring thoughtfully at Vortex. "Does that mean he's a blue?"

"He made frost breath. That would seem to be the most logical conclusion," Perrin said. "You're both welcome in Frozen Peaks Dragonhold, of course."

"Wow . . ." Will raked his fingers through his hair. Of all the colors, he never expected Vortex to be a blue. But his dragon had breathed ice, so it had to be so. "What do you think, buddy? We could live in Frozen Peaks with the other blue dragons. Would you like that?"

It doesn't matter where we go. I'll be happy as long as I'm with you. I'll miss our friends, though.

Will sighed. No matter which dragonhold they went to, they couldn't stay with all their friends. "Me too, but I think going to Frozen Peaks is the best plan. Not just because you can breathe ice, but they also have the biggest library in Avria, and I need to learn as much as I can about dragons if I'm going to be a good rider for you."

Perrin flashed a smile. "From what I see, you're already an excellent rider for Vortex. But you're right. Frozen Peaks offers the best opportunity to learn more about dragons than anywhere else. It's a wise choice."

Chapter Thirty-One

The changing of the seasons on Fire Mountain was difficult to notice without careful attention. Heat radiating from the volcanic rocks kept the air within the borders warm year-round. Frost refused to form on the thorny bushes dotting the nooks and crannies on the hillsides.

But as the days marched on, the sun drifted lower in the southern sky, setting earlier night by night. Cold wind raced up the hills, carrying moisture and occasional rain showers. Heavy fog blanketed the surrounding hills in the mornings, drifting between peaks like eerie rivers of cotton candy.

The young dragons had grown considerably. Though they were still smaller than full-grown adults, they could now carry their riders with ease. The day had finally come for them to travel to their separate dragonholds. The dragonlords from Poison Plains, Lightning Cliffs, and Frozen Peaks arrived the night before to escort them to their new homes.

The young riders spent the better part of the morning packing their heavy saddlebags, donning their riding gear, and saying goodbye to their friends.

As the time drew near, they congregated in the training field and arranged themselves by color. The red dragons hung back with their riders to bid farewell to their friends.

While Will checked his saddle and gear, Rin wandered up to him, carrying what looked like a furry blanket. She gave him a one-armed hug and smiled. "I almost envy you," she said with a tearful laugh. "You get to fly so far away. We only have to fly to the next peak over. Ember and I will come visit you sometime, if you like."

"Thanks, Rin," Will said. "We'll miss you and Ember. And we should definitely visit, but you don't have to come to Frozen Peaks. I know it's way too cold there for red riders."

"Oh, yeah!" Rin shifted the bundle in her arms, as though just remembering it. "I brought this for you. Since it's so cold where you're going." She handed the bundle over.

Will unrolled it. It was a long, wooly shufflo-hide coat. "Wow, Rin! Thanks!"

Rin's cheeks colored, and she scuffed a toe in the sand. "It was Anri's idea. She thought the Frozen Peaks might be a little cold for you. I think she would have given you the parka herself, but she's just not been herself lately."

"Where is Anri?" Will looked over to the greens and spotted Jade sitting on a rock behind the others. Anri was busy tying down her saddle.

Jade is sad, Vortex said. *She feels like she's losing her friends today.*

"I'm going to say goodbye while I have a chance," Will said, tossing the parka over his saddle.

"That's a good idea," Rin said. "Maybe you can cheer her up. She won't listen to me."

Will made his way across the field to the greens. The riders ignored him for the most part, too preoccupied with checking their saddles and bags to bother with him. Jade saw him approaching and stepped back to give him space.

Anri turned, and her eyes met his. "Oh, hello, Will."

"Hey, Anri. Isn't this exciting? We finally get to see our dragonholds."

Anri pressed her lips together. "Honestly, I'm not that excited. I kind of wish it could have stayed the way it was before the Dragon Games."

Will gave her a crooked smile and shrugged. "I know what you mean. But we can still hang out." Then he noticed that Anri wasn't carrying her usual shoulder bag, and Trouble was nowhere to be seen. "Where's Trouble? Did you stuff her in a saddlebag or something?"

Anri's eyes went cold, and she looked away, fiddling with a saddle strap. "I'm not bringing her."

Jade crooned softly and lowered her head to nudge Anri's shoulder.

"What? You never go anywhere without Trouble!"

"Do you really think I could keep her in the Poison Plains?" she snapped. Her voice cracked despite the bitterness in her tone. "She'd die If I brought her there. Just like you and Rin and Corin would."

Will sucked in a breath and ruffled a hand through his hair. "Yeah, that makes sense. I guess I just assumed there'd be a way . . . I'm sorry, Anri."

Anri sniffed and wiped a thumb under her eye, then folded her arms, refusing to meet his eyes. "I gave her to Tumi. He said he'd take care of her for me."

Will chuckled. "Tumi will feed her so much, she'll be round as a ball the next time you see her. I bet he'll let you visit whenever you want to."

Anri gave a strange half laugh, half sob and sniffed again. "He will feed her enough to turn her into a ball of blubber, won't he?"

"You know what? We should all promise to come here and visit together sometime. I don't want to fly off to Frozen Peaks and never see you guys again."

Anri finally looked at him, tears glistening in her eyes, and smiled. "I'd like that."

Will wrapped his arms around his friend and squeezed her tight.

Some of the green riders whistled and jeered, but he didn't pay them any mind.

"Will, if you please!" Dragonlord Perrin called.

Releasing Anri, Will turned to see Perrin examining Vortex's saddle. The dragonlord waved for Will to join him.

"I guess I gotta go. I'll see you around, Anri. I promise."

"Yeah. I'll see you around, Will."

Perrin nodded approvingly as Will approached. "Well done. Vortex's saddle is in top condition and well fitted."

"Thanks!" Will beamed.

"I wanted to ask for one thing, if you don't mind."

"What is it?"

"Vortex," Perrin said, addressing the dragon, "I never got the chance to see your ice-breathing ability when you fought the swarmer. Would you indulge me?"

Vortex fluttered his wings and pranced with eagerness.

Will laughed. "Of course he will! He loves showing off!"

Perrin stepped to the side with a smile, clearing the way.

Vortex took a quick breath and spewed a shower of bone-chilling ice over the ground.

"Fantastic!" Perrin clapped.

The other blue riders cheered.

"That's a great idea," Corin shouted, running out from the group of yellows into the drifting frost. "I'm blistering in this riding jacket. Do it again, Vortex!"

Vortex obliged happily, and soon the other yellow riders ran gleefully into the showering ice, shedding their riding jackets, laughing and whooping in the snow.

Next to Vortex, Tundra opened his jaws and sent a thick, icy stream into the mix. His ice was much colder and denser than what Vortex could produce.

"Wow, that's cold!" Tato howled, catching some of the direct stream. He hopped out of the icy cloud, shaking frost from his hair and rubbing his face with his hands.

"Easy, Tundra," Jayda said with a chuckle. "You don't want to freeze our friends solid, do you?" She turned to Perrin. "So that settles it, right? Vortex is a blue dragon because he can make ice."

"You may be slipping into a syllogistic fallacy with that reasoning," Perrin said with a sideways smile.

Jayda cocked her head, frowning, but didn't ask what he meant.

Perrin bent to scoop up a handful of ice and rubbed it over his brow. "It's rather hot here for blue riders, isn't it?"

"Ha!" Tumi bounded over and playfully punched Perrin in the arm. "You never could handle the heat. Could you, brother?"

"I don't know what you're talking about, Tumi."

"Don't you remember the flame flame-steak challenge

last Christmas?" Tumi waggled his eyebrows with a wicked grin.

Perrin grimaced and folded his arms. "How could I forget? Living here must have cooked your brain if you think scalding your tongue off is fun."

"You really are brothers?" Will asked, looking between them. Even though they had the same dark skin and similar features, their personalities were so different—Tumi with his bold friendliness and carefree manner, and Perrin with his subtle tact and cool intellect. It was hard to believe they'd been raised in the same household.

"We sure are," Tumi said, grabbing Perrin around the shoulder. "We were on the same egg hunting team too. Ruby and Boreas come from the same hatching. Even though Perrin took over as Frozen Peaks dragonlord, he still finds the time to come here and check on me. He just can't give up being the older brother."

Perrin tipped his head to the side with a long-suffering smile. "Don't be ridiculous, Tumi. Boreas and I have perfectly legitimate reasons to come to Fire Mountain. As dragonlord, I must be here for Hatching Day. And now—"

"I know, I know." Tumi laughed and released Perrin. "I'm just yanking you around. I'd better go save Brom. It looks like Lamar is talking his ear off, and he still needs to make his farewell speech."

"I'm sure it will be heartwarming," Perrin said with a nod.

As Tumi left, Perrin inclined his head to Will. "By the way, you should know we haven't given up looking for signs of your lost uncle. My team didn't find anything on the shores in their initial search. But there are many cities and villages in Avria where he might have found refuge. I've asked the bards to send word to us if they hear of any new off-landers."

"Really? Thanks! But I'm mostly worried he never made it to shore at all."

"Understandable," Perrin said. "But I don't think all hope is lost. If your family made it here, it's probable your uncle did as well. The same ocean currents that carried you would have carried him as well." He paused and took a breath. "Speaking of your parents, I have some news."

"About my parents?" Will's stomach lurched, and he laid a hand on Vortex's shoulder for support. "What happened?"

"Don't be alarmed. They're quite all right. At least they were when I left them at the bard hall in Ashfield. They seemed to be well on their way to a happy new life there."

Will gasped and staggered back. "W-what? Did you say . . . they're in Ashfield?"

"Yes, well, Ashfield is on the northern coast, quite close to the Frozen peaks." Perrin stretched his arms behind his back and cast his eyes up to Boreas. "We thought you might like to have them living close by. Also, Vortex told

Boreas you were concerned about them. I can't have one of my new riders distracted with family matters, especially not one with so much to learn still."

Will could hardly believe what he was hearing. "They're out of Madoc's farm? They're really okay?"

"It was hardly any trouble at all. Ashfield Academy had an open teaching position. They were looking for a science teacher and reached out to me for assistance in finding one. Knowing that your father is a man of science, and that they'd like to leave their situation, it seemed to be a good fit. The academy is delighted to have an off-lander scientist with them."

"I thought Madoc would never let them go. They were in so much debt! I was going to win the money at the Dragon Games, but—"

"Their debt was paid in full. The academy was happy to pay it. The amount was hardly as much as the usual bonus they use to tempt skilled teachers to move there. And flying them north wasn't out of our way. Your father is an interesting travel companion, I might add."

Overcome with gratitude and not knowing what to say, Will did the only thing he could think to do. He threw his arms around Dragonlord Perrin in a hug. "Thank you!"

The other blue riders gasped.

Perrin patted him on the back and chuckled. "You're welcome. I think it worked out best for everyone this way."

"Dragon riders," Dragonlord Brom bellowed from the middle of the field.

Everyone quieted down to listen.

"You have all come far in your training since Hatching Day, and I couldn't be prouder of you all."

The kids cheered, and their dragons warbled in approval.

"Today, you fly to your new homes. Some of you will go to Frozen Peaks, some to Lightning Cliffs, others to Poison Plains, and some of you will find your drekhem here in Fire Mountain."

Will looked around to find his friends. Corin was already mounted in his saddle, grinning and patting Leika's neck, clearly eager to be off.

Standing at Jade's side, Anri was listening to the dragonlord's speech with a solemn expression.

Among the red dragons, Rin was watching them all and listening to the speech with a sad sort of smile.

"Wherever the winds take you," Brom continued, "no matter how far you fly, remember that you will always be welcome to visit us here on Fire Mountain. Clear skies, dragon riders. Clear skies!"

Everyone cheered after Brom's speech. "Clear skies, Dragonlord Brom! Clear skies!"

The dragons roared and rustled their wings, sending up eddies of dusty wind.

"It's time," Dragonlord Perrin said, turning to them

with a smile. "Blue riders, mount up!" He vaulted up Boreas's foreleg and into his saddle.

Will climbed onto Vortex's neck, not quite as gracefully as the dragonlord, and clipped his riding straps on.

He could feel the anticipation and excitement building in Vortex. His dragon shifted his weight, swayed his tail, lifted and dropped his wings, ready to jump into the air at any moment.

"Okay, buddy," Will chuckled. "We have to wait for Dragonlord Perrin, you know. Let me get my goggles on."

I'll wait, Vortex said. *I want to go, but I'll wait. I want to see Frozen Peaks Dragonhold. I want to fly over the mountains and visit new places. We'll make new friends and learn new things. We'll grow strong together. This will be fun!* He flapped his wings and bounced, shaking Will and making his goggles end up sitting crooked over his nose and forehead.

"You said it, pal. Just chill for a second, okay? I have to finish getting ready."

Vortex obediently settled down so Will could adjust his goggles and buckle his riding cap under his chin.

Off to their right, the yellow dragons were already in formation.

Mounted on Skydancer, Dragonlady Trinley lifted her arm and took to the air. With a massive rush of wind, the rest of the yellows took off in unison, beating their wings to gain altitude as they made for the dip in the southern peaks.

Riding on Leika's pale-yellow neck, Corin leaned to the side and waved to Will as they vanished over the rise.

Will glanced back at Anri and saw that she was mounted on Jade already. The green riders all paid close attention to Dragonlord Lamar as he gave them last-minute instructions before takeoff.

Anri glanced his direction, and their eyes met for a moment.

Will's mouth pulled back in a slight smile.

Anri nodded once, but he wasn't sure whether the gesture was for him or not. The next moment, she gripped her saddle handles, and together, the green dragons surged upward like a small hurricane, aiming straight for the pass that would lead them to Poison Plains Dragonhold.

When the greens had dropped behind the mountains, Dragonlord Perrin addressed them. "We'll be heading north through Stalva Pass. There's going to be a strong updraft over the eastern face of the peaks. We'll catch the warmer air and stay at a high elevation. Follow Boreas in a diamond formation and have your dragon alert us if there's any trouble. We'll guide you to the landing platform when we arrive. Space yourselves when we land. There's plenty of room for everyone, so you don't need to crowd together in the middle. Does anyone have questions?"

Even though Will was confused about the landing

platform—why would they all try to crowd together?—he was sure he'd figure it out when they got there. Beck and Jayda exchanged a puzzled look, too, but nobody bothered asking about it.

Satisfied, Perrin nodded and lowered his goggles over his eyes. "Very well. Let's be on our way, then."

Boreas faced the northern peaks and shook out his wings.

Vortex and the young blues scurried into position for takeoff.

Boreas reared back and launched into the air with a sweep of his massive wings.

The young blues leaped and flapped frantically, taking to the sky and straining to keep up with the larger blue. Vortex launched himself so fast Will had to clutch his saddle for support as the ground plummeted beneath them.

They circled the training field once, gaining altitude and settling into a rough diamond formation.

Far below them, the young red dragons gathered to watch them go. Ember and Rin sat out front. Ember lifted his wings in salute and bugled a happy farewell.

Vortex tipped his wings, and Will waved at them. Then they soared over the northern peaks, leaving Fire Mountain Dragonhold behind.

Distant snow-capped peaks drifted into view, and Will felt his heart swell at the sight. Leaving Fire Mountain

Dragonhold would be a turning point for him and Vortex. Things would never be the same after that day. But he knew they were moving on to greater adventures and, hopefully, a place in Avria that they could finally call home.